DISC
INSIDE.

The circumstances of the unheralded *first* attempted **Lidenbrock Expedition** to the **Center of the Earth!**

The **secret parentage** of the bride of the **Beast God!**

The **apocalyptic origins** and **final fate** of **Queequeg's fetish** and how it went from pagan idol among the wreckage of the **Pequod** to a dust-gathering paperweight at **221 B Baker Street!**

These and other Metafictional revelations in:

THE ELDRITCH NEW ADVENTURES OF BECKY SHARP

Also by MICAH S. HARRIS

Novels

*The Eldritch New Adventures of Becky Sharp
-2020 Visionary Edition*

Murder in the Miracle Room

*Ravenwood, the Stepson of Mystery:
Return of the Dugpa*

Jim Anthony, Super Detective: The Hunters (with
Joshua Reynolds) 2nd Edition

The Chronicles of Aarastad
*Portrait of a Snow Queen
(The Witches of Winter Book One)*

Graphic Novels

Heaven's War (with Michael Gaydos) 2nd Edition

Audio Books

*Ravenwood, the Stepson of Mystery:
Return of the Dugpa*

Jim Anthony, Super Detective: The Hunters
(with Joshua Reynolds)

2020
VISIONARY
EDITION

The Eldritch New Adventures of Becky Sharp is copyright and trademark 2008 by Micah S. Harris. All rights reserved.

Entire contents of this revised edition copyright 2020 by Micah S. Harris.

Cover, frontispiece and title page illustrations copyright 2008 by Loston Wallace. Illustrations for chapters two and thirteen copyright 2020 by Loston Wallace.

Illustrations for chapters five, nine, and fifteen copyright 2020 by M. Wayne Miller.

Original edition introduction copyright 2008 by Mark Schultz.

Introduction for the new edition copyright 2020 by James Bojaciuk.

Book design and logo by Nathan Pride
Additional editing by James Bojaciuk

A Minor Profit Press ™ Edition

"The *Ape Gigans*" previously appeared, in slightly altered form, in *Tales of the Shadowmen, vol. 3: Danse Macabre*.

"The Encounter on Great Pulteney Street," "What Lurked in the Artists Gallery," "The Testimony of Rebecca Sharp," "Out of the Abyss," and "The Judgement of Sâr Dubnotal" were originally serialized as "Slouching Toward Camulodunum" in *Tales of the Shadowmen, vol. 7: Femmes Fatales* and *Tales of the Shadowmen vol. 8: Agents Provocateurs*.

Third Edition, July 2020

ISBN 978-0-9816770-4-0

"My entire being filled with a sense that I was without rival upon the earth."

The ELDRITCH New Adventures of BECKY SHARP

by
MICAH S. HARRIS

Minor Profit Press™
Winterville, NC

Acknowledgements

I am grateful for the enthusiasm with which this novel, in earlier drafts, was received by Angela Bacon Reid and Matthew Baugh, both of whom provided much appreciated editorial input. Additional thanks go to Arthur Congleton who also critiqued portions of the manuscript and provided essential consultation on matters of the British military and historical weaponry.

My thanks to J.M. and Randy Lofficier and Black Coat Press whose *Tales of the Shadowmen* series first allowed me to bring to light Becky Sharp's post-*Vanity Fair* career.

Much appreciation, too, to Mark Schultz for his unflagging support of my writing for three decades now. Meeting him and his wife Denise for the first time, when they lived in a small Allentown, PA home back in 1989, remains a cherished memory of mine. Besides being a superlative illustrator and storyteller, Mark is the kind of true gentleman they just don't seem to turn out anymore. I am proud that he is probably the biggest fan of my version of Becky Sharp...

...rivaled only by 18thWall Productions publisher James Bojaciuk. James not only reread Thackeray's epic *Vanity Fair* to prepare for his introductory essay included herein, but also kindly volunteered to give the manuscript a fresh edit for this 2020 Visionary Edition.

Special thanks to M. Wayne Miller for loaning his excellent talents for black and white illustration to render the drawings appearing here for the first time. Wayne is the Chris Van Allsburg of horror, and I'm happy to have him joining us this time around!

Loston Wallace graced this book's original cover, frontispiece, and title page with his alluring renditions of Becky. All are retained here along with two illustrations by Loston debuting in the current publication. These drawings are not only a record of his talent but also of one of the best collaborations and friendships it has been my privilege to enjoy.

Dedication

For my mom and dad, who, when
I was a kid, were either taking
me to the library or bringing the
library home to me!

TABLE OF CONTENTS

Foreword to the 2008 edition by Mark Schultz _____ xv

Introductory Essay for the 2020 edition by James Bojaciuk _____ xvii

THE ELDRITCH NEW ADVENTURES OF BECKY SHARP:
2020 Visionary Edition

Chapter One: 1840 — The League of Zervan Akarana _____ 1

Chapter Two: 1841 — The Doom That Came to Kor _____ 11

Chapter Three: 1843 — The *Ape Gigans* _____ 22

Chapter Four: 1844 — The Legacy of Captain Clegg _____ 47

Chapter Five: 1844 — Bane of the Barbary Corsairs! _____ 63

Chapter Six: 1848 — Shadows Out of Time _____ 79

Chapter Seven: 1893 — Queequeg's Fetish _____ 96

Chapter Eight: 1893-1894 — *Cette Femme-La Qui Sont Etre S'Obeit* ___ 101

Chapter Nine: 1894 — The Hand of the Black Pharaoh _____ 115

Chapter Ten: 1917 — The Encounter on Great Pulteney Street _____ 129

Chapter Eleven: 1917 — What Lurked Within the Artists Gallery ____ 134

Chapter Twelve: 1917 — The Testimony of Rebecca Sharp _____ 146

Chapter Thirteen: 1917 — Out of the Abyss! _____ 153

Chapter Fourteen: 1917 — The Judgement of Sâr Dubnotal _____ 168

Chapter Fifteen: 1925 — S. Latitude 47°9', W. Longitude 126°43' ____ 171

Afterword: *She and Me* by Micah S. Harris _____ 185

"Frontal Development" by Micah S. Harris _____ 188

Biographical Note _____ 190

Foreword

Why Becky Sharp Has Relevance in a Lovecraftian Universe

Personally, I never would have made the connection. I never would have seen the possibilities of placing William Makepeace Thackeray's realist ur-*femme fatale*, the marvelously ruthless Miss Rebecca Sharp of *Vanity Fair*, in a full-blown pulp fantasy adventure.

Can you blame me? Would you have made the connection?

Lucky for us, Micah Harris has this odd sort of vision and *The Eldritch New Adventures of Becky Sharp* continues his fascinating series of "what if" adventures. There's a correct term for this subgenre that involves the lifting of characters and concepts from any number of popular authors' legacies — often in concert with historical personages — to then mash them into improbably plausible alliances and relationships. Micah has told me the term — often, I suspect — but for the life of me I can't remember it.

Maybe that's because this particular subgenre is beyond my personal capacity for invention. My mind doesn't think down those paths. Which is fine by me, because it makes it all the more pleasurable to read Micah's cross-pollinated hijinks: his inventiveness invariably catches me by surprise. Although we both share similar pulpy interests and both inject them liberally into our storytelling, Micah takes his borrowings in directions of which I can't conceive. True surprise in storytelling is rare enough and always welcome.

Micah has tons of brass and I think he takes his biggest risks in this story. Foremost, it's all good clean pulp adventure, but there is something else underlying the rollicking thrills. Micah has placed moral barometer Becky here for good reason: there is a strong current of morality running through this story, much as Micah has examined in his graphic novel of 2003, *Heaven's War*. Here, however, the morality is of a different sort.

Becky may have been a shockingly immoral character to a mid-19th century culture built upon social and religious convention (and I'll admit I don't know enough about Thackeray, a noted humorist, to guess at his true intent), but, by transporting her to a new context, one situated in a frighteningly expanded universe as revealed by 20th century science, her "immorality" becomes more a reflection of a practical will to survive in a hostile environment. In *Vanity Fair*, Becky does what she must to flourish in the English social jungle to which she was born — and she was pretty darn good at it. She certainly wasn't hypocritical about her aspirations. Here, Becky is given proper respect: her skills are tested in the (allegorical?) jungles of an annihilating cosmos.

My hat's off to Micah for putting those skills to the service of a cognoscenti that has graduated from fretting class distinctions to the bigger problems now recognized to confront the human race in a Lovecraftian universe that doesn't recognize moral superiority. Micah throws so much of the wonderfully *outré* at Becky, so much of the last two centuries' speculative fears concerning our diminished status in the grand scheme of things, that I ultimately can't help but sympathize with her peerless survivalist aptitude. (And if that aptitude includes a predatory sexual allure, hey — she works with the tools she's been given, and all the more fun for us readers.)

I know that if I were lost in Micah's construct, searching out Kor in deepest Africa, or stumbling over Skull Island, or trapped inside one of the Great Race of Yith, or moving towards an inner Earth through horrors borrowed from myriad fevered imaginations, I would absolutely want to have someone as pragmatic and skilled as Becky with me.

Dangerous? Yes. In the end, she might very well have us all as hive insects to her queen bee. But with her on the throne, at least we could be assured that the species would survive.

And that's saying something in a Lovecraftian universe.

Read on and see if you don't agree.

Mark Schultz
April 2008

For his skills as an artist and comics storyteller, MARK SCHULTZ has won five Harveys, two Eisners, an Inkpot, a Spectrum, three Haxturs, and probably four or five other freshly minted trophies while you've been reading this sentence. He has illustrated Robert E. Howard's *Conan the Barbarian*, chronicled the adventures of *Superman*, and currently spends much of his time in the days of King Arthur, giving *Prince Valiant* his marching orders as the writer (first with artist Gary Gianni and now Tom Yeates) of Hal Foster's classic of the American Comic Strip — a legacy which couldn't be in better hands!

Watch for Mark's upcoming graphic novel in which he returns at last to the comic book medium and his classic science-fiction epic *Xenozoic Tales*!

Resembling the Slitherings of a Mermaid
An Introduction for the Special Edition of *The Eldritch New Adventures of Becky Sharp*
by JAMES BOJACIUK

"Ah! *Vanitas Vanitatum*! Which of us is happy in this world? Which of us has his desire? or having it, is satisfied?—Come, children, let us shut up the box and the puppets, for our play is played out."
~William Makepeace Thackeray's *Vanity Fair* (ch. LXVII)

"*Vanity Fair* is a difficult novel." Six words packing an inexpressible amount of understatement. Yes, it's long—300 thousand words compared to an ordinary novel's 50-150. Of course, it's bedecked with characters. Naturally, it requires a familiarity with history that many modern readers are unprepared to handle. But it goes deeper. Most readily available editions excise the illustrations. These are not the kind of illustrations which only help set the mood and aid the imagination (as with Sidney Paget's or Florence Briscoe's work), but are essential to the novel as flesh to the bones. Who murdered Joss Sedley? Only a reader armed with art can say. Yet it goes still further. The novel is written in a sardonic, criminal cant which throws further walls between the narrator and author, the narrator's audience and the author's audience. It does not say what it means, and surely the author would strangle his narrator if only he could get his hands around his neck.

To celebrate this special edition of *The Eldritch New Adventures of Becky Sharp*, let's look under the hood of Harris' novel to find what parts—to stretch a metaphor—he's borrowed from Thackeray's *Vanity Fair*. There are some wonderful connections that might otherwise be missed.

Vanity Fair is no longer a novel we're familiar with. *Oliver Twist*, *Alice's Adventures in Wonderland*, and *Pride & Prejudice* have been kept alive through decades of adaptations—and even if we miss Dickens' commentary, suppose Alice met Tweedledee and Tweedledum in Wonderland, and convince ourselves that Jane Austen wrote serious romances about serious people, we are at least familiar with the outlines of the plots. Oliver falls into the dangers of the poor. Alice falls into Wonderland. Elizabeth falls in love, despite her best efforts. There is no such luck for *Vanity Fair*: left with too much material for even a miniseries to adapt, and a confusing narrator, even the more faithful adaptions have left a great deal of material on the shelf.

The title of the novel is no passing fancy. On the very first page, we find ourselves in John Bunyan's own Vanity Fair, straight from *The Pilgrim's Progress*. Our narrator, the stage manager, emerges. Dismissing morality, he offers us a puppet show put on by children. He is far from a reliable narrator, switching between jaded portraits of those involved to implication and lies. He pretends to be our friend, though he is anything but. We are, at least, distantly familiar with the remainder of the context: Becky Sharp falls to a low social position and carves her way to the top of society, by charm, manipulation or murder.

This may feel unconnected to *The Eldritch New Adventures of Becky Sharp* in every way except for Becky herself. Surely we lack an unreliable narrator. Surely we lack puppets. Surely we lack the cosmic significance implied by *Vanity Fair* being but a show put on *in* Vanity Fair.

Vanity Fair's narrator is worse than unreliable. Unlike *The Cabinet of Dr. Caligari*'s Francis, he does not even do us the courtesy of believing his own press. He lies, he knows it, and he treasures it—as it is his own petty power over the audience. He will paint over pure actions with black, and make black actions blacker. Even the pure-at-heart will be made into monsters—or simply made ineffectual. And yet, for all of the power he seems to have over the reader, and for all the effort he extends toward dominating the text, he is ultimately rendered more powerless then his subjects.

These are aspects Becky assumes in this novel. At moments of importance or uncertainty, the seeming absolutes of third person narration wash away. We are left with the perspective of a known liar. She manipulates us, as she has manipulated everyone else, and she glories in her backstabbing and crimes. She and the narrator of *Vanity Fair* are one and the same, so far as it matters. She will justify her murders, rapes, and horrible abuses to herself, hoping to convince the reader, and attempt to pass on her bigotries as well. She should not be heeded, even if hers is the only voice on the page. Even when third person resumes, we are left at the mercies of her perspective and lies—we cannot get far enough away from her to get away from her perspective. There seems to be no escape, as these narrators indulge in every horrible fancy. But how can we deal with such a vile narrator?

It's not a matter of endurance. Instead, the narrator is the key which turns both novels' lock. Without them, we would see immortality play out without comment or relief. Things would be as black as they appear. They would be acts of evil, free of context, in a dead universe. But this is not what Thackeray's stage manager leaves us with. Though he is immoral himself—though he is a diabolist himself—though he builds a prison of despair around himself and us, this narrator is also the key that frees us from his prison. Goodness and light are nearer when our narrators speak, than when they remain silent.

This was quite Thackeray's intent. As he wrote to George Henry Lewes,

> What is the Gospel and life of our Lord (excuse me for mentioning it) but a tremendous Protest against pride and self-righteousness? God forgive us all, I pray, and deliver us from evil.
> I am quite aware of the dismal roguery wh. goes all through the Vanity Fair story–and God forbid that the world should be like it altogether: though I fear it is more like it than we like to own. But my object is to make every body engaged, engaged in the pursuit of Vanity and I must carry my story through in this dreary minor key, with only occasional hints here & there of better things—of better things wh. it does not become me to preach.

To shed further light on his intent and goals, it is worth turning to a master of this form, Flannery O'Connor. Their approach to fiction, and using their faith in their fiction, was nearly identical. Where Thackeray is brief in explaining this, O'Connor is expansive. She allows us to see into Thackeray's process, and just what he means by creating characters as deplorable as these. In O'Connor's hands, Goodness—and particularly Grace—were proclaimed by everyone from con men to serial killers. They could not help it, even when they set to make the universe a dead and ugly place. As Flannery O'Connor wrote (*A Habit of Being*),

> I am mighty tired of reading reviews that call [*A Good Man is Hard to Find*] brutal and sarcastic. The stories are hard but they are hard because there is nothing harder or less sentimental than Christian realism. I believe that there are many rough beasts now slouching toward Bethlehem to be born and that I have reported the progress of a few of them, and when I see these stories described as horror stories I am always amused because the reviewer always had hold of the wrong horror. (90)

> …My "message" (if you want to call it that) is a highly moral one. Now whether it's "moralistic" or not I don't know. In any case, I believe that the writer's moral sense must coincide with his dramatic sense and this means that the moral judgment has to be implicit in the act of vision. Let me make no bones about it: I write from the standpoint of Christian orthodoxy. Nothing is more repulsive to me than the idea of myself setting up a little universe of my own choosing and propounding a little immoralistic message. I write with a solid belief in *all* the Christian dogmas. I find this in no way limits my freedom as a writer and that it increases rather than decreases my vision. It is popular to believe that in order to see clearly one must believe nothing. This may work well enough if you are observing cells under a microscope. It will not work if you are writing fiction. For the fiction writer, to believe nothing is to see nothing. I don't write to bring anybody a message, as you know yourself that this is not the purpose of the novelist; but the message I find in the life I see is a moral message. (147)

Our narrators are, like O'Connor's characters, agents of a power they do not recognize. They may destroy those around them, they may lie to us, *but we see their lies clearly*. Because we see through their bigotries, their prejudices, their hatreds, and their attempted justifications of terrible acts, we are not at their mercy. We are better equipped to deal with such things in our own lives. Thanks to these narrators, we can "get a hold of" the right horrors, and expunge them from ourselves. All things, whether the narrators like it or not, work together for good.

Let us turn from the puppet master to the puppets. As we've seen, *Vanity Fair* is presented as a puppet show put on in Bunyan's own Fair. Children command the marionettes, as our stage manager narrates their story. In *The Eldritch New Adventures of Becky Sharp*, save for Padre Perditio's effigy, there is nothing puppet like. But consider what another character, the Magus, said, "Another mind controlled her." Whether we are on a string, or our mind is superseded by another, we are but puppets.

However, we discover the Great Race of Yith inhabit the bodies of humans—and can inhabit the bodies of all but a few. As with Thackeray, all humanity are puppets for another force. Whether the immoralists of Vanity Fair or the immoralists of beings outside time, we find ourselves at the mercies of a culture bent only on using us. The stage manager uses us for his audience's entertainment; the Yith inhabit us for their entertainment. Harris seems to have done away with puppets and their masters, but we but we have only traded one immoralist for another, and humanity remains puppets inside their box.

The narrators may continue between novels. The puppets may continue between novels. But surely, you may insist, the cosmic is all Harris. But it is one last inherited angle. All four authors concerned—Bunyan, Thackeray, Lovecraft, and Harris—work from a cosmic vision. Bunyan and Thackeray from the same protestant English viewpoint (though one focused on the glories, the other on the horrors). Lovecraft with his cold universe, inhabited by elder gods. And Harris, who has tied these cosmic threads together. Thackeray's cosmic vision, however, is given the most weight in this novel.

We have seen hints of it among the narrators, and among the puppets, but here it comes to its full flush. It may seem, however, that this angle only exists in Thackeray's use of the Fair itself, but we find that there is a specifically eldritch portrait of Becky Sharp. Indeed, Harris has only literalized one of Thackeray's metaphors for Becky. From her first description, the text compares Becky to a serpent or sea creature (and once to Napoleon upon the shore). She is something deadly, and associated with water, scales, and conquering. It is explored and amplified until these associations and metaphors climax in her incarnation as a mermaid.

> I defy any one to say that our Becky, who has certainly some vices, has not been presented to the public in a perfectly genteel and inoffensive manner. In describing this Siren, singing and smiling, coaxing and cajoling, the author, with modest pride, asks his readers all round, has he once forgotten the laws of politeness, and showed the monster's hideous tail above water? No! Those who like may peep down under waves that are pretty transparent and see it writhing and twirling, diabolically hideous and slimy, flapping amongst bones, or curling round corpses; but above the waterline, I ask, has not everything been proper, agreeable, and decorous, and has any the most squeamish immoralist in Vanity Fair a right to cry fie? When, however, the Siren disappears and dives below, down among the dead men, the water of course grows turbid over her, and it is labour lost to look into it ever so curiously. They look pretty enough when they sit upon a rock, twanging their harps and combing

their hair, and sing, and beckon to you to come and hold the looking-glass; but when they sink into their native element, depend on it, those mermaids are about no good, and we had best not examine the fiendish marine cannibals, revelling and feasting on their wretched pickled victims. And so, when Becky is out of the way, be sure that she is not particularly well employed, and that the less that is said about her doings is in fact the better. (Chapter LXIV)

Lovecraft could do no better. Indeed, one could argue he and Thackeray both describe the same monster. There is a pleasing symmetry between the description above and the advent of Cthulhu from "The Call of Cthulhu."

Steam had not been suffered to go down entirely, despite the departure of all hands for the shore; and it was the work of only a few moments of feverish rushing up and down between wheel and engines to get the Alert under way. Slowly, amidst the distorted horrors of that indescribable scene, she began to churn the lethal waters; whilst on the masonry of that charnel shore that was not of earth the titan Thing from the stars slavered and gibbered like Polypheme cursing the fleeing ship of Odysseus. Then, bolder than the storied Cyclops, great Cthulhu slid greasily into the water and began to pursue with vast wave-raising strokes of cosmic potency. Briden looked back and went mad, laughing shrilly as he kept on laughing at intervals till death found him one night in the cabin whilst Johansen was wandering deliriously.

But Johansen had not given out yet. Knowing that the Thing could surely overtake the Alert until steam was fully up, he resolved on a desperate chance; and, setting the engine for full speed, ran lightning-like on deck and reversed the wheel. There was a mighty eddying and foaming in the noisome brine, and as the steam mounted higher and higher the brave Norwegian drove his vessel head on against the pursuing jelly which rose above the unclean froth like the stern of a daemon galleon. The awful squid-head with writhing feelers came nearly up to the bowsprit of the sturdy yacht, but Johansen drove on relentlessly. There was a bursting as of an exploding bladder, a slushy nastiness as of a cloven sunfish, a stench as of a thousand opened graves, and a sound that the chronicler would not put on paper. For an instant the ship was befouled by an acrid and blinding green cloud, and then there was only a venomous seething astern; where—God in heaven!—the scattered plasticity of that nameless sky-spawn was nebulously recombining in its hateful original form, whilst its distance widened every second as the Alert gained impetus from its mounting steam.

The two descriptions are remarkably symmetrical. The classical references, the horror hidden below the water-line, the resistance of print to feature these horrors, and the sea-born nature of the monster come together as one. It is no wonder that Harris sets Becky and Cthulhu against each other—their creators have, unintentionally, marked them as one and the same. It's only natural these two manifestations of the negative cosmic vision should face each other.

I now turn you over to this combat, to these puppets, to your narrator, and to *The Eldritch New Adventures of Becky Sharp*.

> "And with this, and a profound bow to his audience, the Manager retires, and the curtain rises."
> ~*Vanity Fair* ("Before the Curtain")

James Bojaciuk is CEO Duobus of 18thWall Productions. His novel, *The Vampire Mutations*, will appear later this year as part of Obverse Books' *The New Adventures of Iris Wildthyme*. Always too ready to write Sherlock Holmes stories, he is responsible for "Doppelgangers (and Other Artistic Piffle)" (#1 Best Steampunk Short Story, Preditors & Editors Readers' Poll 2017).

He has had reviews and articles published in *Occult Detective Quarterly* (now *Occult Detective Magazine*), *Sargasso: The Journal of William Hope Hodgson*, *Greydogtales*, among others. Other academic work about the intersection between Victorian literature and science fiction has been commissioned by George Washington University.

The title of this article is derived from Harold Bloom's discussion of Becky in *The Victorian Novel*.

Chapter One: 1840 —
The League of Zervan Akarana

Becky Sharp knew trouble, and she knew men and the kind of trouble men had to offer. But what she saw in these men's eyes was different, unnerving. It was not the usual type of desire she inspired. This was calculating, scheming — in short, what she saw in her own eyes when she looked into her vanity glass.

These days, however, Becky had little to be vain about. Still, she took care to lift the tattered hem of her skirt whenever she had to step over where the horses had relieved themselves in the streets. She had, after all, been down before, and life had taught her how suddenly and unexpectedly fortunes could turn.

The men had followed her from the tavern and were now trailing her down the street of one of the disreputable sections of Bath. Well, that was their mistake. A couple of panderers with whom she consorted were chatting loudly on the corner which she and the men were approaching. Withdrawing one hand from her muff as though to adjust her frayed shawl, she flashed the signal for "danger." The panderers caught it, stopped their talking and attentively looked up at the men following her. They tipped their hats to them, pretended to return to their discussion, and, when the men following Becky were several yards ahead, fell into step behind them.

Becky turned into an alley way that dead ended on an ancient wall covered with ivy. The men followed. When she turned to face them, she saw the panderers just entering the mouth of the alley behind her pursuers. Becky smiled.

Blades flashed in the hands of the panderers. "'ere, now! Oy!" one of them shouted out, and the men who had followed Becky turned to find they, too, had been stalked.

"You want a bit of that on our street — you'll pay for it. One way or another. And you've picked the other." The spokesman of the panderers spat in his attempt at bravado.

The men trailing Becky remained calm, and now that she had time to study them outside the dark, smoky tavern, she was struck with their height and how sturdy they were — muscular arms and thick necks and shoulders. The panderers apparently made a fresh appraisal of their potential adversaries as well and seemed hesitant now to close the distance needed to press the advantage their knives would give them.

"Help me!" Becky implored her suddenly reluctant rescuers.

Shamed, one of the panderers charged. The man he'd picked to attack lashed out a long, muscular arm, and the panderer slammed face first into a large, hard, open palm. Immediately, he felt fingers and thumb hook into his eyes and nose. He slashed with his knife at the extended arm. But he had hesitated in surprise and pain, so his captor had plenty of time to grab his wrist and stop the knife in mid-arc.

Then the man twisted the panderer around, held him tightly against his oak-like torso, and dislocated the arm of his failed adversary: the arm of the hand that held the knife. The weapon dropped to the alley's floor.

"Go away," the man hissed into the panderer's ear. "Next time, it's your neck."

He shoved him half-way back up the alley and, seeing his partner had already fled, the panderer ran.

The men turned toward Becky.

"Who are you? What do you want?" she asked, voice slightly trembling. Almost involuntarily, she cast her gaze down to the place where the dropped knife lay.

Following her line of vision, the man who had disarmed the panderer firmly placed the sole of a boot on the blade. "No, no. No false hopes, Becky Sharp. We are soldiers in Her Majesty's service. And you are under arrest."

"Impossible. I've been found innocent by a court of law of any wrong doing in the matter of Joss Sedly's death," Becky protested coolly. "Whoever you are, you have no right —"

"Your late lover was in possession of sensitive intelligence involving rebels in the Punjab. You sold that information, Rebecca Sharp, and put many of Her Majesty's agents' lives at risk."

One of Becky's hands emerged from her muff and moved up to clasp tighter her frayed shawl around her throat. "I was hungry," she said meekly, eyes wide.

"And apparently willing that the wives and children of those agents go without husband or father to provide for them and thus go hungry in your stead. Fortunately, we intercepted the information in transit — which led us back to you. Now, come."

Becky's affected meekness faded, and, chin in the air, she joined the men who parted for her to come between them. "Raise your hands above your head," the spokesman said.

"What?"

He grabbed a wrist in each hand, pulled Becky's arms up and held them there. Then he nodded at his comrade, who immediately began patting down her body.

Becky started, affronted at the unwelcome familiarity. Her eyes shone with outrage at the soldier who held her wrists fast as she tried to writhe free from him and his groping partner.

"What do you think you are doing?" she hissed icily. "Get off!"

"Suddenly so demure and bashful?" the spokesman asked with a crooked grin. "Perhaps you would not protest so if we were to pay your accustomed fee?"

Then the search of her person was over, both soldiers released her, and the one who had poked and prodded her produced a small icon he had taken from her pocket. He held it up for his fellow to see.

He immediately snatched it away and observed it closely: the figure was that of a naked man's body with a lion's head. From its back sprouted four wings. Wrapped around the legs and torso were six coils of a great serpent whose head surmounted the lion's. In each hand, the creature held large, ancient keys. In its left, it also held a staff a traveler might employ.

The soldier held it to her face accusingly. "Where did you get this? Did you steal it? Or was it given in payment for services rendered?"

"You know it doesn't matter," his fellow soldier spoke for the first time. "She has been *touched* —"

"Many times and everywhere, I'm sure!"

"I mean by one of *them*. Look, it's out of our hands now. We dare not conceal our discovery. *They* have ways of knowing things. We'll be held accountable."

Becky listened to this talk, unsure of how to take it all. Did the discovery of her talisman signify a change of fortunes for the better — did it indeed bring the luck the one who had bestowed it on her had promised? She sensed that it was better not to speak, lest she give away her ignorance of what significance this figure had for the men.

The men had ceased their disagreement. The one who had addressed her pocketed the icon, while the man who had searched her attempted to take her arm. She drew away.

"You do not put your hand on me again, sir," she said.

"As you wish — milady," the leader of the two said caustically.

Becky was brought to a small holding cell in which, once she was secured, the arresting soldiers left her without comment. Less than an hour later, a guardsman appeared, ordered the door unlocked and told her to come with him.

Becky followed him down a back staircase into a basement. She noticed that the door to which she was led contained a small, barred window through which food on a tray could be passed. She assumed, then, that she was being transferred from the holding cell to a more permanent one.

The guardsman unlocked the door, pulled it back, and beckoned silently for her to enter. She did, and he shut the door and locked it behind her. She heard his footsteps echoing as he walked away. But her eyes were focused on the silhouettes of two men before her in the dim cell. One was seated; the other stood a small distance behind him.

She backed against the door. Had she been brought here and left defenseless, with total disregard for what these other prisoners might do to her?

"There, there," the seated man said. "No need to be afraid, I assure you."

"That's exactly what I would expect a man who intended to harm me to say," she said. But now she had caught the aroma of freshly cooked food.

The seated man lit a candelabra, revealing a table prepared for dinner. On a clean plate was set a roasted chicken breast with sparkling silver beside it. "Are you hungry, my dear?" he asked.

"Ravenous," Becky was compelled to admit in a small voice, though she did not move. She had eaten nothing since the day before: it was the off-season for Bath, and customers with whom she might ply her trade were few. She had managed to forget how hungry she was, until this fresh aroma reminded her — poignantly.

Now the man was pouring wine in goblets gleaming by the candelabra. "Come. Do not fear. Look. I'll pour and drink from the same bottle. You have no need to fear being drugged."

While his companion remained in shadow, the seated man looked safe enough. Almost comical, in fact. He wore a powdered wig, unmindful or uncaring that it sat crookedly on his head. He was of average height, thin build, his cheeks sunken, his face skull-like. His true hairline receded, making for a high forehead.

Becky saw that the wine had no effect on him. Her eyes returned to where they had been all but fixated before: on the succulent chicken breast. She descended upon it. Casually forsaking any attempt at decorum, she snatched the chicken up in her hands and began devouring it.

Her dinner companion laughed. "Very good. We do not stand on ceremony here. Eat! Eat and drink!"

"My young friend here," he nodded toward the standing man, "is Benjamin Disraeli. You've heard of him, perhaps?"

Busy chewing on the tender breast meat, Becky shook her head "no."

"No, no. Of course not. Disraeli has been dismal . . . to this point in his political career, anyway. But that is soon to change. I am the Magus," he said. "Lately of the continent you call Australia."

"I assume you were in a penal colony there? Given your current 'lodgings,'" Becky said, rolling her eyes to indicate the cell around them, as she daintily licked her fingertips.

"Not at all. I am one of the Great Race of Yith."

"'Yith?' Is that aborigines? But . . . you're white."

The Magus smiled. "At the moment. And my race has not been remotely aboriginal for . . . ages. The records of our place of origin were destroyed long ago. As for these 'lodgings,' as you put it . . . our current environment is necessary for us to conduct our business."

Becky stopped licking her fingers and looked at him straight on. "What business would that be?"

The Magus produced the tiny figurine that had been taken from her person. "Let us begin with Zervan Akarana." Becky looked at the winged, lion-headed man, entwined by a serpent. "The ancient god of boundless time," the Magus crooned. "I see by your face that the name is unfamiliar. Perhaps you know him as 'Aion,' as he was redubbed by the Roman cult of Mithra who brought his worship to your own isle of Britain. Now, shall I tell you how you came into possession of this particular icon?"

"*You* tell *me*?" an incredulous Becky asked.

The Magus smiled. "First of all, I want to take you back to an episode at the young ladies academy where you once taught French in exchange for room and board. On one Walpurgis Night, you led one of your students in a séance — unknown to the head mistress who would have surely disapproved. This particular student was from the West Indies."

Becky's jaw had gone slack as this "Magus" casually recounted her past, an event she had not thought of herself for decades. "Miss Swartz," she said in a small voice. "But how can you know —?"

"Because she was black and you were little more than a street waif yourself, you both were often ostracized from the company of the other, well-heeled young ladies," the Magus continued. "Miss Swartz, you'll remember, feared the 'Obi,' the spirits of her native West Indian lore, would be summoned by your proposed séance. But she wished your favor so much that she went through with your occult exercise. On this innocent girl, you hoped to inflict something of the measure of your own undeserved suffering at the hands of others. Thus, it gave you pleasure to frighten her. Pleased you, that is, until Miss Swartz began to convulse.

"She began to speak in a language you did not know — that no one of this earth knew — which you dismissed as the gibberish of a hysterical girl. *Until* she addressed you in flawless French, though her efforts in your class had been halting at best. Do you remember what she said to you, Becky Sharp? Among other things? She said —"

"*Je vous vois*," Becky completed the sentence as though in a trance herself, remembering afresh just how unnerving Miss Swartz's tone and gaze were when she spoke those simple three words. Even decades later, it made her flesh creep.

"*Oui!*" the Magus said with a smile. "You were frightened then, were you not, Becky Sharp? You knew you would be summarily put out on the street if it were known you had caused the nervous breakdown of this heiress. To your relief, she became calmer, if somewhat detached. From then on, she watched you like a hawk. That unnerved you. But you dared not confront her with this, for fear you would cause her to speak of the séance and perhaps be overheard.

"Some time later, Miss Swartz began to experience strange nightmares of what she claimed were the Obi. It was around this time that she returned to her old, eager-to-be-friends persona, and you returned to despising her."

"You are wrong, sir," Becky said, trying to gain some sense of the control that she seemed to be losing more and more of since being taken from that Bath alley. "That episode had nothing to do with my obtaining this icon. I had it much later, years later, of a —"

"Of a lover. I know. And the episode I just related has everything to do with it. Becky Sharp, you are, at this moment, conversing with an extraterrestrial consciousness from your planet's far distant past. Just as you did when you spoke with Miss Swartz between her seizure and the emergence of her nightmares. Another mind controlled her. Further, that alien consciousness you engaged during your séance was seeking, not the body of Miss Swartz, but yours, Becky Sharp.

"We Yithians, you see, are able to cast our minds across time and exchange them with chosen human vessels. From our perspective in the past, your planet's future history exists in a haze of parallel, probable realities. We explore them all. One of our race — Yathoth — while inhabiting a host during one of your possible 19th centuries, read a novel that details your exploits up to just a few years ago: *Vanity Fair* will be its title."

"A novel? About me? You can't be serious."

"I assure you, I am. Your adventures offered a perspective on British domesticity surrounding the Napoleonic Wars that promised to be most exciting — as opposed to the more detached point of view of the scholarly type we traditionally favor for possession.

"Using the novel's clues to locate you, Yathoth sent his mind forward to the days preceding the onset of your adventures. After displacing your own mind, Yathoth planned to play out your role as the author detailed. Your little séance seemed apropos for the switch. But imagine Yathoth's surprise when your brain proved impenetrable.

"At first, Yathoth was greatly disappointed, but he was also intrigued. He observed you in the person of Miss Swartz for several days. You drew forth passions in him, Becky Sharp, the expression of which the body of Miss Swartz would not facilitate. So Yathoth departed Miss Swartz's body, and you met him again, unknowingly, much later, as your lover, Lord Steyne."

"It was Steyne who gave me that icon ... that ..."

"Zervan Akarana? 'Boundless Time?' Yes. Do you grasp its significance now? Steyne had learned that you were not alone in your mind's resistance to Yithian possession. Others shared your peculiar brain chemistry which, unfortunately, cannot be replicated in our laboratories. These others, admittedly, tend to be few and far between, scattered throughout human history. Still, they, as you, can be useful."

"How so?" Becky played along, her mind awhirl. This "Magus" was mad. And whoever that other person — this Disraeli — was, he was *not* a legitimate politician. The only explanation was her captors had placed her in the holding cell for the insane.

"Our race is not to become involved with those races we inhabit and observe," the Magus answered. "Our travels through time are intended as a purely intellectual exercise. If we meddle, we will be withdrawn back into our own distant age and not allowed to return. We are constantly monitored, but have found a means to counteract this. Though not for long, lest we become conspicuous by our absence from the psychic chart. This room," he gestured about them, "has its walls padded with felt soaked in mercury, which does not allow our monitors' scans to pass through. From time to time, when I desire mobility and still wish to conceal my thoughts and actions, I venture about with a felt hat treated by the same mercurial salts."

Becky shifted uncomfortably in her chair. She remembered Steyne insisting on keeping his felt hat on when they made love. She had attributed it to some kink of his. But now —

"Yathoth broke the code of the Great Race when the two of you became involved," the Magus continued. "But, alas, as I said, our psychic forays are monitored. Yathoth's enthusiasm for you made him sloppy, and his actions were called into account.

"He is now quarantined in the remote past. But not before he could get *this* to you," the Magus held up again the figure of Zervan Akarana, "so others of our secret society within the Great Race could recognize you, if need be."

"What do you want with me, then?" Becky asked.

"As I told you, your brain chemistry is almost unique. Your mind cannot be possessed by my people, nor can your thoughts be read by them. Unless a Yithian is purposely attempting to probe your mind — and Yathoth's interest in you was an aberrant one for my kind — you are effectively invisible to us. Another such potential agent, equal to your capabilities and capacity for amorality, will not be born within the perimeters of the relevant time period until it is too late to do anything. And *then* it will be too late for all.

"Remember, from the Yithian perspective, your human history exists in a state of probabilities. Parallel realities. Some in which even the fiction of *Vanity Fair* is true. But there are certain junctures, catastrophic junctures, in which all may collapse into one . . . doom. Such a juncture is approaching just after the first quarter of the twentieth century."

"Then how can I be of any use, since I am nearing middle age in the first half of the nineteenth? Surely you cannot expect me to survive?"

The Magus smiled and returned the image of Zervan Akarana to her. "We do, actually. Mister Disraeli here is a liaison between my people, the Great Race, and the Meonia, an ancient order charged with overseeing the destiny of Britain. You see, there are those within the British government — as young Disraeli here is being groomed to be one day — who maintain higher allegiances to those whose purposes supersede that of the temporal powers they also serve."

Then Disraeli spoke for the first time, addressing Becky. "I have come to understand, Miss Sharp, that the world is governed by very different personages from what is imagined by those who are not behind the scenes. But, I assure you, *we* are on the side of the angels."

"Isn't Lucifer supposed to be an angel?" Becky asked in a tone that managed to be both guileless and caustic at once.

Disraeli slightly cocked his head to the side. "A *fallen* one, yes. But it is not with the Devil that the Meonia — and you, if you become our agent — are allied. Refuse us, however, and you *will* meet with Lucifer, I promise, much sooner than you have ever expected."

"I am slated for execution, then?" Becky asked, her voice suddenly small. "Is that what you are saying?"

"You became a traitor to your country when you passed on those military secrets; you willingly aligned yourself with Her Majesty's enemies."

Becky's face paled. "Why should I believe you? Both of you . . . you're mad men! And you're prisoners yourself! What possible clout could you have with the government?"

"Soon, you will find, Becky Sharp," the Magus said calmly, "that while Kings and Queens have their own schemes, their plans, on occasion, will serve to carry along our own."

"'Yours?' You mean the otherworldly Great Race and this fantastical 'Meonia' who 'truly' govern the British Isles?" Becky asked. "What you're saying is impossible!"

"Another of our agents, when confronted with this reality, determined thereafter to believe three impossible things before breakfast each day. I suggest you try hard to wrap your mind around this *one*," the Magus said. "An opportunity is about to be presented to you, one which those who make it will not understand why. But they will obey. And if you accept, then you have your freedom and your life. But say nothing of our meeting: make no mention of either the Great Race or the Meonia.

"Miss Sharp, you haven't finished your meal. You'd best be about it. Our interview is done and you will be returned to your cell forthwith. Eat! Eat!"

Becky, however, had lost her appetite.

As the Magus had said, she was soon escorted back to where she'd been held before. At sunrise, the two men who had arrested her rejoined their captive.

"Good morning, Miss Sharp," the spokesman of the two, whose name was Campbell, said. "A fine one to die, isn't it?"

Death? She was going to pay the ultimate debt, then? But, of course: had she really come to expect the promised option to materialize? Those men were insane! Very well then; she could not rely on succor from powerful agencies within the government. She would have to resort to basic — but definite — rights:

"Am I to be executed without a trial, then?" she asked.

"Yes. You are to be hung until dead. Your tongue will protrude, your eyes will bulge, and you will have soiled your petticoats. All very undignified."

"Such pretty talk. Why do you take the pains to torture me with anticipation?" Becky asked.

"So that you might consider seriously the opportunity I am about to offer. You are, if nothing else, a survivor, Miss Sharp."

"Opportunity? *What* opportunity?"

"You may, or may not, have read the sensitive intelligence you passed on. We only have your word as to the matter, and we can't trust you. That information is still sensitive and shall remain so for the foreseeable future. We cannot let you go and risk our operatives' lives. We could kill you, imprison you indefinitely, or 'bring you into the fold' as it were, of the Special Military Unit. But then you're in for life."

"I live, then. With at least a modicum of freedom. Very well, I accept. What happens now?"

"Why, we three head for Africa. To the land of Kor. There are credible rumors of a natural resource there of extraordinary value to Her Majesty. If it can be harnessed, then her reign — and the supremacy of the British Empire — will be secured throughout our century and the one following. Indeed, into the next millennium."

"And, for some reason," Becky said, "this requires a woman's stealth instead of a man's blustering frontal attack. Is this resource located in the realm of some fierce tribal chieftain you wish me to seduce, then slit his throat while he sleeps?"

"Not at all. In fact, the Amahagger people inhabiting the environs of Kor are a *matriarchal* society. Among them are many who desire to topple the current cruel queen. We intend to see that they succeed, and then set you up as their new sovereign — a puppet ruler, sympathetic to Her Majesty's interests."

"And if all fails, and I draw the wrath of this terrible queen?"

"Well. Among the qualities which recommend you for this mission — your sex, your sense of preservation — there is also that of your expendability."

"I see. But why do these Amahaggers not rebel on their own and set up a ruler of *their* choosing?"

"They are terrified of their queen, 'She-Who-Must-Be-Obeyed.' And of the ghost city of Kor which stands between them and her source of power. It is thrice cursed, and no one dare pass through it lest its doom falls upon him.

Chapter Two: 1841 —
The Doom That Came to Kor

**From Becky Sharp's Journal:
March 18, 1841**

The revolution has failed before it began.

I write these words in a sepulcher, one of an infinite number of caves near Kor. It has been adapted into a holding cell for me. I leave this record with no hope that any one may read it, but to occupy my mind as I await the inevitable.

We departed for Africa three months ago. While the journey by ship was uneventful, the trek into the interior was miserable. Perspiration drenched me, mosquitoes worried me, and my progress over the rough terrain was rendered more awkward than necessary, swathed as I was in a ridiculous dress that reached to my ankles and encumbered my legs. It was mere foolishness that my colleagues Campbell and Black insisted on propriety here in the wilds, when I might have eased my plight by borrowing a spare pair of their trousers.

We finally reached the settlement of the natives that live under the rule of "She-Who-Must-Be-Obeyed," and they were much impressed when I removed my helmet and they saw my reddish blond hair. They took it as a portent that their deliverer had arrived. But those who met us bade me quickly cover my head, lest reports of my fair hair draw the attention of their queen.

Captain Campbell spoke in Arabic to the natives, these "Amahaggers." A map was prepared to lead us to the lost city of Kor and then unto the cliff beyond it, where we would find the caverns containing the coveted source of power.

The following morning, before sunrise, we set off. We arrived at Kor by noon. The sight of the city was ominous, and to our minds, weakened by exhaustion, the Amahaggers' fear of it seemed most sensible. We determined we would pass through and not spend the night there.

The dead city, with its majestic temple and ornate buildings, was a veritable eighth wonder of the ancient world. Still, we were willing to leave it to others to explore and exited Kor with much relief as the sun set. Before us, now, loomed the cliff we must needs ascend in the morning.

Though difficult, the climb was uneventful. We found the natural tunnel which, Captain Campbell remarked, appeared to have been formed by an explosion of lava. Journeying through the cavern, we came to a great rift, but our way had been prepared: a bridge of loosely connected slats swung over the abyss which we needed to cross.

I hesitated there at the threshold of destiny, even after having come all this way. My colleagues were having none of it, and positioned me between them, so turning and fleeing was not an option. The bridge rattled and swung, but the slats were firm, and, after exceedingly long minutes, we were on the other side.

There, in a small grotto which opened into another, much larger cavern, we discovered a man's skull possessing but a single tooth. Intriguing to be sure, yet Captain Campbell insisted we not tarry pondering its presence here but proceed into the huge cavern. Here was said to issue that which would render the reign of Victoria nigh everlasting.

At first we saw nothing but rock, though it glowed faintly with rosy light emanating from the center of the cave's floor. The effect was soothing, sensuous even, and when the ground below us began to rumble, neither I, nor the men with me, offered to flee. Instead, a feeling of ecstasy intensified, and we had no doubt that all would be well.

At that point, before us, a column of ruby red flame erupted from the center of the floor and touched the cavern roof, which was a good thirty feet above. Our countenance was made ruddy, and the sense of bliss mounted. I found myself wondering what effect this phenomenon might have on the act of love....

It was then that I noticed the two men were making their way toward me. Dubious of their intentions, I still hesitated to move for fear of losing the ruby rapture that took me. Then their hands locked upon me. I struggled, but I was helpless before their desire. And then, I realized —

They were dragging me to that pillar of flame! And even as the realization of their intention broke upon me, it was too late, and I was thrust into the light...

Where I expected searing pain, the fire bathed me in a sensuous warmth, held me transfixed in bliss, as my clothing, touched by flame, withered away and I stood naked. Though handsome yet in early middle-age, in that light I felt my youthful beauty flush through me afresh. To judge by the expressions of the men, I was indeed a goddess incarnate. My entire being filled with a sense that I was without rival upon the earth —

Ah, it was not so, as we were all soon to learn.

The pillar of light suddenly withdrew into the floor of the cavern and into whatever depths from which it had issued. The men continued to gaze at me, worshipfully, and when I demanded the shirt of one of them to cover myself, they responded meekly — if reluctantly.

"You planned to throw me into the flame all along; you could not have known

Chapter Two: 1841 — The Doom That Came to Kor

if I would survive it or not!"

"That," smiled Captain Campbell as the residual effects of the flame receded and he regained his full presence of mind, "was a risk we were willing for you to take."

"Yes. 'Expendable' was how I believe you described me."

"Fie! Let us be friends, Rebecca. It was not our wish that you perish, for then this adventure would all be for nothing. Your youthful beauty is returned, and, I daresay, superseded. What more could any woman desire? And, if the rumors of the flame of Kor are true, your mortal substance is nigh eternally young. For you, the kingdom of Heaven is come — as well as for Her Majesty and those to whom she would give it."

Ah — but to sit on the right or the left hand of divinity would not be for the Queen of England to grant. When we returned to make the appointed *rendez-vous* with the rebellious faction, we were intercepted instead by the men of "She-Who-Must-Be-Obeyed." Campbell and Black fired but could not re-powder their muskets quickly enough, and the natives swarmed over us. "She-Who-Must-Be-Obeyed" had anticipated the revolt, and, as one of the Arab speaking natives told Captain Campbell, our collaborators were already in the torturous process of a slow death.

"We are to understand," Campbell informed Private Black and myself, "that we can expect no less."

Upon entering the caves of Kor where "She" held court, I was separated from the men. My pack in which I carried my effects was rifled through before it was thrown in my cell with me. I retained pencil and paper inside it, and with that I have recorded my final adventure. It seems terrible to be so freshly filled with the essence of life only to lose it all, but I have no doubt that this "She" will not spare me.

There are footsteps in the passageway outside. My time has come.

Escorted by muscular mutes, Becky Sharp was led into the personal chamber of their mistress. Sitting at the Queen's side, reclining on her bosom, was none other than Captain Campbell. The woman beside him was astonishingly beautiful: finely sculpted features, alabaster flesh and dark tresses that fell to her waist. Her delicate hands and long graceful fingers stroked Campbell's bare chest — Becky still wore his shirt. He seemed the willing slave of Ayesha — for that was the name of "She-Who-Must-Be-Obeyed."

Ayesha then spoke in her Arabic tongue, and Campbell translated:

"Rebecca Sharp, I know that you have partaken of the flame of Kor. My vision traverses great spaces, and I saw from afar you three enter my land. When your fellow conspirators spoke of your plan under torture, I allowed you to continue on so that you might serve my purpose."

"Why should I serve you?" Becky asked, looking the queen in the eye.

Campbell posed the question in Arabic. Ayesha smiled, answered, and as he translated, Campbell smiled as well. "Because, from what I have heard of you, Rebecca Sharp, you always serve your own best interests."

Ayesha continued: "What think you of the force that flows through you now? Extension of days is given to you, and I myself have lived over two thousand years. But what is length of days if this world you must inhabit is made desolate? If the doom of Kor becomes that of all?"

Becky, careful to keep her eyes level with Ayesha's, asked soberly, "How can that be?"

"I am Arabian by birth," Ayesha spoke through her interpreter. " 'An Arab of the Arabs,' a descendent of Yarab, not Ishmael, who inhabited the land long before Abraham's seed. In the ancient city Ozal I was born. But older than Ozal — older than Yarab himself — is the Thousand Pillared City of Irem, which bears the same mark of doom as Kor.

"Irem died in one day, when things older than men rose up and blighted its proud, beautiful gardens. The only clue to its destruction was inscribed in one of Irem's fallen pillars: 'That is not dead which may eternal lie . . . and in strange aeons even death may die.' It was not so written in the ruins of Kor when I came — yet the cause of this city's desolation was clear to me, for I had also seen Irem. Though the last priest of Kor left an inscription that his great city fell after twenty-five years of pestilence, 'twas only to conceal the disgrace that some greater power shamed his own god.

"For Irem, there was no hope when what stirred beneath the desert sands rose up, but for Kor there was a power in the mountain nearby that might have repelled its destroyer. Alas! It was only after the city's passing that the mountain side opened up the pathway to the pillar of fire. And so Kor was purged, hundreds of years after it fell, of the Abomination pleased to dwell in the ruins it had made. For then he came, he who dwelt by the flame — a seer and a holy man named Noot — who channeled the power of that hallowed light into the wreck of Kor and sent its destroyer beyond the veil of atoms."

"Was that his skull in the grotto?" Becky asked.

"Yes."

"Then he did not partake of the flame as we have."

Chapter Two: 1841 — The Doom That Came to Kor

"Aye, and was loath that I should, when I came to him," said Ayesha. "Only his death allowed my immersion. In this Noot was much mistaken. For such horrors as the Doom that Came to Kor appear throughout the world, and *those* Great Old Ones will not conveniently appear near the Fire of Life.

"But had Noot bathed in the flame, then he like I — and you, now, Becky Sharp — would have that force within him, and he could carry it and strike where he would. In you it is presently but a seed, and neither had I the ability to wield it at first, but in years to come you shall. Watch! I will show you!"

Ayesha barked something at the mute who guarded her door. He nodded his consent, stepped out, and in a few minutes Private Black was brought into her chamber, held by her men.

His struggles ceased as he laid his eyes on Ayesha. They filled with the same bliss that shone from Captain Campbell's. Ayesha stood, raising her arms and dropping her mantle from her. She nodded, and the mutes released Black and fled the chamber. Black still stood as though the sight of her was the beatific vision, and then Ayesha struck him down from across the room, her force like sheet lightening dropped from the sky.

And Black was dead.

Becky sat down — hard — on a silken pillow pallet behind her. Here was a ruthlessness manifested that stunned even her. Captain Campbell continued to smile up at his beloved, and Ayesha turned and spoke in a matter-of-fact voice, which Campbell then translated:

"At least one white head must be raised on the stakes with the dark ones, to show that ALL who disobey me can expect no mercy. Otherwise, I would encourage future insurrections, and more blood would be shed. Since this man —" she indicated the fallen Black — "— was not as useful as the one who may speak for me, it is only reasonable that he should be the one to die.

"Now, hear me Becky Sharp — another abomination like unto that which destroyed Kor festers in the waters at the bottom of the world. So Noot foresaw. I might venture forth myself to confront it with the power of the flame inside me, but love holds me here, as it ever has, waiting for the man who traverses the centuries to return to Kor.

"The precise season of his arrival is unknown to me, and to have endured two thousand years among the dead and imbecilic and then miss *him* — no, it must *not* all be for nothing! Yet, it *shall* be so, if that thing some have called Tulu comes to power, for then nothing human can abide.

"Therefore, I send you in my stead, Becky Sharp, in whom the power to repel Tulu now resides! I see in your expression you already wonder how I might hold you accountable once you have crossed the borders of my kingdom. I need do no more than I have already, by giving you a youth that will not fade for millennia. Combined with your shrewd mind and the power that resides in you — you may live out your extended life as a queen. Yet, what life will you have, Becky Sharp, if Tulu is allowed to rise up and blast the world beyond human habitation?"

Becky held her lips pressed together, grinding her teeth. It was an old habit she had, a way of venting displeasure when it would not be in her best interests to let the source of irritation know her mind. She did not want this task, but if the entire world were made as Kor —

Eyes projecting a calculated meekness and deference, she asked,

"What would you have me do, oh Queen?"

From Becky Sharp's Journal: March 18, 1841 — later

It seems Captain Campbell and I have been elected by Ayesha to recover a mystical caduceus of sorts whose current whereabouts are unknown. The long-deceased Noot forged it from an ore found in a vein exposed by Kor's caves. Only Noot's secret craft has ever successfully tempered this ore into an instrument of any kind. This metal has an affinity for the eternal flame nearby, is able to absorb its power, contain it, intensify it, and then project it. As Noot carried the charged caduceus into the desolate city to purge it of the ancient thing haunting it, so I must bear it for like purpose.

The headpiece of the staff was carved in the shape of a recurring nightmare which Noot was experiencing. He later prophesied *this* would be the form of the next Great Old One that would come into the world.

According to Ayesha, the caduceus of Noot was taken from him when looters came and found him wandering Kor's ruins with it in hand. They believed it was this magic staff that allowed him to pass unharmed through the city. Noot had not charged the caduceus with the flame of Kor, for he believed there was no longer anything to threaten him there. He was simply using it as a walking stick. So the plunderers beat Noot and took it from him. Nor did they return the caduceus, but carried it off as part of their spoil.

Thus, Captain Campbell and I will set out to recover it after a few days' rest. I do not know how he shall ever be able to tear himself away from Ayesha, but if he doesn't fulfill her command to act as my protector, she has made it clear that she

"He laid eyes on Ayesha. They filled with bliss...and then she struck him down from across the room...."

will be much displeased. Hopefully, he will recall that what she did to Black, she did while in a *good* mood.

From Becky Sharp's Journal: March 31, 1842

Were there ever a needle in a haystack, this wretched caduceus is it, and Africa a continent of straw through which we must apparently sift every last stalk! According to Ayesha, Noot prophesied the next Old One will appear not long after the passing of the first quarter of the next century. At this rate, we should have just cleared the Congo by then.

Can I truly expect Campbell to stick with me through this? I think so. I believe he would gladly walk barefoot over every ant hill in Africa in hope of pleasing Ayesha. The fool! Her heart belongs to another, and I dare say she's not inclined to toss away a torch she's been carrying for a couple of millennia for this lovesick swain.

October 22

At last a lead! We have finally picked up the trail of the band that took Noot's caduceus. The oldest man in a recently Christianized Congo tribe told us of the fate of the looters of Kor: they were set upon by his ancestors long ago. The sight of the caduceus had provoked them into a frenzy, and they sacrificed the plunderers to the headpiece of the staff as though it were a god. The old man's face was terrible as he recalled their chant: "Tulu! Great is Tulu who will come from his sunken city in R'lyeh!"

The natives then made a temple to house the caduceus, and, in worshipping Tulu, reverted back to acts of cannibalism their society had forsworn long ago.

Unfortunately for myself and Campbell, during the intervening years, Noot's caduceus has undergone a change of fortunes. The Congo tribe had originally kept the image of Tulu mounted on the staff, using it to carry their god with them into battle. When they attempted to plunder the hidden African city of Ophir — the source of Solomon's gold — the fight did not go well for them.

For the men of Ophir were stirred into even more of a blood frenzy at the sight of the idol, and sought to seize Tulu's icon. In the struggle, the idol was separated from the pole, and the Congo tribe was fortunate to escape with Tulu himself, while the lost city's inhabitants took the pole which had touched the image for their own talisman.

The tribe's recent conversion to Christianity prompted a sojourner among them, a wanderer from an island far away to the West and South, to flee the Congo with their idol. He had opposed the missionaries and feared the fetish would now be destroyed. For they of his homeland remain wed to the old faith.

From the old man I learned this, along with the absconder's name: Queequeg. It seems he returned to sea to be closer to his higher power in hopes of greeting Tulu's sunken city of R'lyeh on the day when it should rise again.

October 23

Last night after Campbell was asleep, I met again with the old man, who is actually an out-of-work Shaman. He was accompanied by his sole acolyte, a man who looked to be in his early twenties. Like Queequeg, these two remain followers of Tulu, but they dare not openly voice their beliefs.

The old man knows the way to the land of the people who took the staff, and has promised to take me to Ophir if I return to the Congo with the purloined idol. Then, together we will journey to the hidden city and reunite the icon with its sacred staff. He believes we can thus bring the men of Ophir under our sway, and we will raise an army to bring against his own faithless Congo tribe.

Blood will be shed, but I must have the staff Noot made as well as the idol itself: the staff is a necessary intensifying conductor through which the power of Kor's flame must travel from my hands, concentrate in the fetish-headpiece and thence strike Tulu. The staff, made of the same rare ore as the headpiece, is the only substance which can touch said power and not be rent.

Campbell must not know of my new alliance, for I must jettison him before my return here. The presence of a white man with me gives the old man the impression that I am Campbell's woman. Like old Queen Bess, I think it will be to my advantage to appear decidedly unattached. The Shaman — and any other men with whom I may become involved in this adventure — will be more eager to follow my wishes if he thinks that to obey means a chance at my favors.

Tomorrow, Campbell and I leave for what will be no less than a two week journey by foot to the nearest sea port — a journey I suspect Queequeg himself made. We hope to pick up his trail there in the city of Safaqis.

November 2

Bother! En route to the port, Campbell and I were waylaid by a pith-helmeted fool with ridiculous waxed mustachios. His name is Lemuel Beesley, and he is an agent of the Meonia, sent to find word of our success — or lack thereof — in causing a revolt in Kor and securing the flame of life.

Of course, we admitted to being abject failures, losing poor Black's head in the process and barely escaping with our own lives. Understandably, we mentioned nothing of now serving as agents of the very queen we were to overthrow.

So it seems I have been elected to return to England and give an account of our misadventure to Disraeli in person. "Why me and not Campbell?" I asked, for between the two of us, only I have the power to deal with Tulu once the caduceus is recovered.

"On that point, he was most insistent, ma'am," Beesley said, tweaking the tip of each mustachio in a most irritating way. "In the event of a failed insurrection, Captain Campbell is to make contact with a powerful cult said to dwell in Western Africa and seek their aid in overthrowing the current regime in Kor, and I am to deliver you to Meonia headquarters myself, to make certain you remain unspoiled."

Privately, Campbell and I agreed that he should ignore Disraeli's orders. Once Lemuel Beesley and I had departed, he would continue on to the port city on the Barbary Coast and try to pick up on Queequeg's trail before it became any colder. I would satisfy the Meonia that our spectacular failure had botched any further attempt at regaining Ayesha's throne and then seek the earliest opportunity to slip Disraeli's leash.

"Lie low in Safaqis," I said, "and wait for my return."

Chapter Three: 1843 —
The Ape Gigans

"Well, Miss Sharp," Disraeli said dryly as he shuffled the papers of the Kor file on his desk into their proper order, "for an insurgent who has survived a failed *coup d'état* and, consequently, spent the better part of 1842 fleeing for your life across the African wilds" — here he caught his breath — "I must say, you look most . . . refreshed."

Becky sat rigidly upright, hands on her lap, and, maintaining her own cool gaze, said, "Sir, do you mean to hold me responsible for the failure of the Kor Affair? Do I have to remind you that I was but a pawn? That I was to be your puppet queen? And as for my being 'refreshed'. . . well, that is your doing as well."

"Is that accusation in your tone, Miss Sharp?" Disraeli asked stringently.

"Indeed it is, sir! Do you deny your men were under orders to toss me into that column of fire? Was it not your plan that that flame endow me with the same preternatural qualities it had given the queen I was to supplant? And the entire scheme was hatched and enacted without my knowledge or consent! I only knew we were looking for a rare, natural resource in the environs of lost Kor." Here, Becky affected a shiver, tucked her head and brought a clinched handkerchief to her mouth. "I thought I would burn horribly."

"'Frailty thy name is woman,'" Disraeli said caustically, leaning back and steepling his fingers before him.

Becky's hand with the handkerchief dropped into her lap, and she raised her cool gaze to meet Disraeli's again. "You owe me an apology, sir!"

Disraeli laughed. "Your country owes you no more than a hangman's noose, Miss Sharp!"

Becky scowled in silence, for she could not deny it.

"So, what happens now?" she asked Disraeli as he returned her papers to their folder.

"If we can trust your report, that this 'She–Who–Must–Be–Obeyed' possesses a mystical means of surveillance — well, she'll be more vigilant than ever now, shall she not? Even if Campbell is successful in contacting this cultic element in Africa, and they are so inclined to help us, it seems we cannot expect to succeed on that front. Our mission is hopelessly botched; we both stand in the displeasure of my superiors. And our friend the Magus has taken one of his perennial unannounced walkabouts, leaving the two of us to hold the bag. But fear not, Miss Sharp. There is a way we may both disentangle ourselves from this untoward affair."

"Go on," Becky said.

Disraeli patted the folder containing her report. "You mention in your notes that the flame in the caves of Kor issued up from somewhere far deeper in the subterranean realms. The source of the flame, then, lies elsewhere, and if we could find that source, then we need no longer be concerned about our failure to take the throne of this 'She–Who–Must–Be–Obeyed.'"

"That all hangs on a rather enormous 'if,' sir. First, one would have to find appropriate ingress into the Inner Earth . . ."

"Yes, well, it appears 'one' has. The Meonia is secretly backing an expedition to Antarctica to locate a polar entrance into our allegedly hollow world. You will sail with a Yankee captain, one Obed Marsh, upon his *Sumatry Queen*."

"Why a Yank ship? Is the Royal Navy so insufficiently stocked that you might not borrow one of our own?"

"One must give an account of each vessel of Her Majesty's fleet, whereas there is no accounting for Yanks. And Captain Marsh needs the money desperately enough to agree to our irregular demands. It seems a local massacre wiped out the natives of the island of Kokovoko with whom he had established a profitable trade."

"'Kokovoko'? Bosh! I dare say it's not set down on any map."

"True places never are, Miss Sharp. All that is important is that we have a captain who needs us as much as we need for him to hold his tongue. Besides . . . the name of his vessel seemed propitious somehow. And you will need all the luck you can get."

"And why might that be?"

Disraeli paused, slightly tucked his head and narrowed his eyes. To Becky, it seemed as though he were trying to decide if he should explain or not. Then:

"The expedition is to be led by a prodigious German youth named Lidenbrock," he said, "and his assistant, Miss Fatima Talisa."

"He has a female colleague?"

"Yes. A most taciturn young lady in public, but Lidenbrock's looks toward her during our preparatory meetings indicate she has much to say to him in private. Frankly, Miss Sharp, there is something unsavory about the whole business. We of the Meonia sense it, yet none of us attempts to stop it. But we have determined to manipulate the manipulator.

"Your mission, then, is to enter the underworld through the South Pole with the Lidenbrock expedition. Secretly, you will search for the wellspring of the flame of Kor. You will have one other associate in the expedition who shares this intelligence: Mr. Lemuel Beesley.

"You should, of course, seduce Lidenbrock so that you may replace Miss Talisa in his regard. Your agenda may, at times, be at odds with hers. In which case, your interests — by which I mean 'ours' — must prevail.

"I suspect you will have a worthy rival in Miss Talisa, Miss Sharp, one whom you must supplant, perhaps even crush." Whatever had given Disraeli cause to hesitate about telling Becky of the Meonia's misgivings concerning this polar journey seemed no longer an issue. In fact, he seemed pleased with himself for having overcome his faltering. Now he smiled, leaned back, and templed his fingers again. "How I wish I could be there to watch you at work. Keep an account of it all, will you?"

From Becky Sharp's Journal: February 16, 1843

I have met the sphinx Talisa.

And Disraeli was correct: she does have some hold over young Lidenbrock. The looks they exchange are the same that have passed between myself and Joseph Sedley before he met his untimely demise. Lidenbrock fears her.

All the men on the expedition sense he is cowed by a female and regard Lidenbrock with contempt. They do not know what such a woman is capable of. I do. I am such a woman.

Talisa senses this. Indeed, she tries, as much as is possible on a ship in middle of the ocean, to avoid me. Unfortunately, the same limited confines make it difficult to get Lidenbrock alone.

February 17

Something will have to be done about Lemuel Beesley. Tall, muscular, balding, with a pocked complexion and his waxed mustachios, the man is as determined to adhere to me as Talisa does to Lidenbrock. I could not have been out of his sight for five minutes when he found me taking refuge on the quarterdeck.

"Sir, I realize you have been charged by our superior to keep an eye on me. But we are miles out to sea. The scenery here is monotonous enough; must it include your face everywhere I look?"

"But the sight of you is all that makes these endless miles of sea bearable, Miss Sharp," he rejoined with a smile, twisting by turn each tip of his mustache as though snuffing a wick between thumb and forefinger.

"I assure you, you will be as sick of me as I am you once we are shut inside by the frozen climes and no longer have the use of the deck."

"You haven't realized, then."

"Realized what?"

"We're no longer sailing for the South Pole. We haven't been for days."

I was taken aback by this revelation. "Well, where then?"

"I am not a prophet, Miss Sharp. As of the moment, we are veering in a southwestern direction, but as for tomorrow? I suspect we will not know our destination until young Lidenbrock tells us we have arrived. Though, perhaps a face prettier than mine might persuade him otherwise. Until then, I shall trace our course so that you and I might find our way back, should we part ways with the good Professor."

"I suggest, then, that you spend less time following me, and more tossing bread crumbs on the water in our ship's wake. Good day, sir."

Remarkably, he did not follow, nor have I seen him since. He is giving me space so that I might have latitude to approach Lidenbrock and work my feminine wiles. But to do so successfully, I must also circumnavigate Talisa.

February 18

At last I have had the long desired interview with the good Professor Lidenbrock.

Wagering that Talisa would surely not accompany him to the ship's water closet, I caught him as he exited, pretending I was about to enter.

"Oh, Professor, I am mortified that you have found me dealing with nature's . . . necessary business," I said demurely.

Although visibly chagrined, he strove to be chivalrous. "Miss Sharp, do not be embarrassed. Our quarters are close after all."

As he started to pass, I took his elbow and gently drew him back. "Pardon me, Professor, but I need to speak to you alone. And you and Miss Talisa are usually all but joined at the hip."

"I . . . I . . . ," he stuttered.

"I do not mean to exacerbate your humiliation, Professor. But it is clear to me that she is a harsh mistress. Let us cast aside all social niceties, and tell me frankly all your woes."

He immediately drew away. "I must say that if you believe Miss Talisa to be a source of woe to me, you are quite mistaken. I owe all to her."

"Certainly not 'all.'"

"She did not grant me my genius, no, but she gave me focus. 'twas she who introduced me to the notion of a Hollow Earth, the theories of Symme. More than once, when I have been wearied by this endeavor, she has taken my head in her lap and sung of the heart of the Earth as though she has been there already, assuring me that where one would expect, at best, to find all opaque, one discovers a most brilliant, most pellucid world."

Initially, I was taken back at the revelation of this touch of tenderness. But, of course, I understood very well the technique of "punish then stroke." And so I responded thus to his rhapsodizing:

"And you believe her fancies?"

Lidenbrock blinked rapidly, as though incredulous that I could not. "You would have to hear her, I suppose . . ."

"And is it to Miss Talisa's singing that we owe our change of course?"

"What do you mean?"

"You know well what I mean: we are no longer headed for the South Pole. And if we are following only your siren's voice, then I feel I justly fear this vessel's fate!"

"But how did you know? The captain and crew have been paid well for their silence . . ."

"Come, Professor Lidenbrock! To achieve your goal, you have sought sponsorship from certain powerful personages. Did you really think they would be so trusting that they would have let you out to sea without a system of checks in place? Now, explain yourself, or I assure you, this vessel will be turned back to England so quickly your head will reel!"

"Miss Sharp, please. It is not mere fancy that guides us. Miss Talisa and I discovered a journal with a map in the Royal Society's secret archives. That map charts our destination."

"Produce it, then. I want to see it. Now."

"First, I must confer with Miss Talisa —"

"And then you will confer with myself and Mr. Beesley *tout d'suite!* We will meet in the mess hall in one hour. You have this one opportunity to make your case, so bring more than Talisa and her repertoire of sea shanties!"

Our interview had taken a turn I did not foresee: I ended up being most stringent with him, but if it means having all his cards face up on the table, then so be it.

February 18, later

I have spent the balance of the day with Beesley, Lidenbrock, Talisa, and Captain Marsh in closed quarters. Talisa stood against the far wall, apart from the rest of us. Several times I found her eyes riveted upon me. Clearly, she knew I had forced Lidenbrock's hand.

Her expression made it clear that when she retaliated, I could expect no pity. The sphinx Talisa had spoken.

"We were never journeying to the South Pole," Lidenbrock said. "Forgive my deception, but I could not risk another learning of our true destination before we were well underway. I assure you that we have secretly stored attire appropriate to warmer climes. You see, we sail to an island described only in the journal of one Bishop Brom Cromwell, a 16th century missionary to Malaysia.

"When he heard of a forgotten people dwelling in nearby, uncharted waters, he set out to preach to these souls as well. He named their island 'Golgotha.'

"Upon landing, he observed 'ancient serpents that did walk upright as did Satan before the Fall, dragons filling the land, sea, and sky.' Further, among abandoned ruins he discovered a temple built round a bottomless pit from which, he learned from the island's human inhabitants, the isle's creatures had issued."

"There are people there, then?"

"It is unlikely they've survived. In Brom Cromwell's day, they were already dwindling. And they were already in the decadent state of a pagan civilization, as described by the Apostle Paul, which 'worshipped the creature more than the creator.'"

"But why should you regard so seriously this religious fanatic's account of 'dragons'?" I asked.

"Because, Miss Sharp," he answered, "skeletal remains of 'ancient serpents that did walk upright' have been excavated since ancient Greece. Fatima — Miss Talisa — suggested to me that, should one dig even deeper, one might discover living specimens. And, indeed, it is from the depths of the earth that Brom Cromwell says these beasts emerged."

Lidenbrock paused, surveyed our small group, and then announced: "Gentlemen and Miss Sharp, I mean to find this island with its bottomless pit, and from there journey to the center of the Earth!"

(The above entries are all that remains of Becky's entries of the failed Lidenbrock expedition.)

Seething in tropical steam, rivulets running from its twin, upper apertures, like tears streaming from empty sockets, the island mountain's death's head veiled then unveiled, veiled than unveiled, its skeletal visage from within the shifting folds of an ephemeral shroud.

Becky Sharp could hear the unseen breakers crashing against the shore of the approaching isle she observed through the fog. As heavy droplets materialized on the railing under her hands, she wondered how Captain Campbell was faring half a world away, and if she would indeed still find him in Safaqis upon her return.

Her thoughts were cut short by an unfamiliar voice calling her name from the thick mist that enswathed the ship's deck:

"Miss Sharp!"

Becky looked about for the source of the disembodied summoning. Its note was urgent. Who sought her out under cover of the fog?

"Professor Lidenbrock?" she asked, proceeding cautiously.

Then a horrific shape divided the mist and lunged toward her. Becky screamed, narrowly avoiding the slicing of the creature's claw. It caught instead in her sleeve, rending it.

Becky turned and fled, vainly hoping the fog would be enough to shield her from her attacker. But even were she hidden to its yellow, reptilian eyes, the nostrils on either side of its saw-like beak had already taken in her scent. Now the creature spread scaly, leathery wings, lifted, and flew after her.

Becky stumbled and fell. As she attempted to rise, the gargoyle descended upon her, flattening her to the deck. Becky screamed again, covering her head with her arms as the creature's beak just missed clipping off an ear.

And then the voice again: "Miss Sharp, I am much disappointed. I thought you to possess more grit than you are displaying."

"Whoever you are," Becky cried, "Please! Drive this creature away!"

"But I am the creature. I, Talisa."

Becky started, incredulous: this revelation alone was stunning, but she realized now that the voice was inside her head!

"It's too fantastic," she gasped out. Now she could hear the rapid patter of feet, men calling, but the fog! They were drifting into a thick patch, and it would hinder the speed with which they could come to her aid. She had to purchase the necessary time.

"Talisa?! How can that be?"

"The woman you have all seen among you these past weeks was only an illusion. All of my kind, in the world from which I came, possess supreme powers of mesmerism."

"'Your world?' You mean the world below? Then, your plan all along has been to return there. You've mesmerized Lidenbrock — you've mesmerized the entire Meonia to serve your ends!"

"Astute girl. Have you also grasped my plan for you?"

The cries and footfalls of the others seemed yet, in the fog, impossibly far away. In a small, childlike voice, Becky asked, "Why kill me?"

"True, the pressure you exerted on Lidenbrock to tip his hand did not abort my scheme. But your will is formidable, Miss Sharp. I cannot risk your further interference."

"I shan't interfere! I understand now: you only wish to return home."

The creature's screeching laughter drilled through Becky's head so that she winced. "No, no, Miss Sharp. It is not as simple as that. There is to be more, much more, which you would most strenuously oppose should I allow you to live!"

A talon lashed out, ripping away Becky's frock from collar to shoulder. Becky screamed, wild and shrill, as the serrated beak began to cut painfully into her exposed flesh.

A flash suddenly lit the fog and a musket ball struck Talisa's arm. She shrieked, and Becky looked up to see a startled crewman, still holding his musket out and staring wildly.

Now the other men's footsteps were closer, coming from both sides. The monster that was Talisa hissed in rage —

— then, shrieking again from the pain the effort cost her, she grabbed up Becky and leapt over the ship's railing, vanishing immediately into the mist.

Lost in the cloud, borne along on reptilian wings, Becky had no sense of up or down, a sickeningly disorienting experience. The screeching of the creature was terrible to hear, for each labored beat of her right wing exacerbated her pain.

Finally, she was forced to release her hold, and Becky was suddenly plummeting. She twisted and turned her body in the air as she slipped through a parting of the mist into the lunging, tumbling breakers beneath her. A wave immediately lifted her again, as though to toss her back into the sky —

— then thrust her ashore instead. She clawed into the sand, dragging her body forward over rough, scraping shells.

No sooner had she gained dry earth than she saw, just a pace apart, the fallen and unconscious form of her captor. Becky rose cagily, looking about for a stone she could use to smash the gargoyle's skull . . .

Finding one, she crept cautiously forward until she stood over the otherworldly creature. Suddenly, its yellow, reptilian eyes flew open and quickly filled Becky's mind . . .

She fought losing control and felt Talisa's surprise at her strength. In her head, she saw Talisa in her reptilian form, expelled to the surface world by others of her kind through a dormant volcano. Becky gleaned from her mind the surprising fact that Talisa had been a political revolutionary . . .

The creature tightened her psychic grasp, but not before Becky saw Talisa's attempted return through the same opening after much time in exile, only to find the volcano alive again, rivers of incinerating lava blocking her passage . . .

. . . and then Becky's will was gone. There followed only impressions of being shepherded by Talisa, pushing through jungle foliage filled with fluttering, feathered lizards that cawed; of large, rough fronds, licking out, catching; bramble sticking her as she tore through scrim after endless scrim of vines and branches; sweat stinging eyes that always seemed to blink too late to flick the drops from her lashes . . .

Becky came to on her stomach, her face pressed down into soft, rotting vegetation. Her muscles ached and her skin was scratched. She slowly peeled her face from the jungle floor, and rolled onto her back. Just inches from her, Talisa hunched in reptilian form.

She felt again the hateful voice in her mind: "Up, stupid cow! How can I herd you if you do not walk?"

Becky rose to her knees, a queasy sense of violation passing over her. "You took my mind," she said accusingly. "How dare you . . . ?"

"Your will is not so strong, it seems, when I have no need to appear human, and can focus my mesmerism entirely upon you."

"Why did you drop your illusion when you attacked me on the ship?" Becky asked.

"So that your death, should it be seen, would be blamed on one of the aerial beasts of the island. Then that fool shot me. The pain was so intense, I knew I could no longer manage the illusion of humanity among so many. I took you then to discourage their firing after me; I take you with me now because . . ."

Here, the creature's beak parted slightly, a serrated smile, " . . . because I must *eat*, Miss Sharp."

Becky rose shakily, knees atremble. Her eyes darted wildly about: the jungle hemmed her in from every side. She had no idea of how many days they had been traveling, whether Lidenbrock and the others were searching for her or not. And that thing . . . she couldn't outrun its influence, not once it brought all its attention to bear on her again.

She faced her captor, her eyes narrowing. "I am only one," she said coolly. "And, as you said, your wound keeps you from reassuming human form. If you abandon your designs on me, I will help you procure the others for your . . . appetite."

Talisa laughed. "My wound is almost healed. And *they* are to feed my sisters and myself when I return with them — those we do not need to take us back to Europe."

Becky's jaw went slack. "Europe? What do you want with Europe?"

"My dynasty no longer rules the world beneath, so this world shall be our domain and our feeding ground!"

Becky's upper lip curled with revulsion. Before her stood the beginning of a threat more immediate than that of Tulu, which, if less cosmic, was dreadful in its own right. She searched within herself, seeking to draw upon the endowment of

Kor's flame Ayesha had said was now in her, hoping to strike dead the obscenity before her . . .

. . . and found no such power at her disposal. At least, not yet. Well, she needed no mystic potency to deal with Miss Talisa, nor any occult caduceus. Only her hands around the gargoyle's neck. Drawing back her fist, she lunged forward to strike the monster —

— and then, once again, her will was gone.

She came to, standing upright, before an enormous amphitheater in the ruins of an abandoned city. The jungle had long ago, in a fecund green tide, swept up along the buildings of hewn stone. Branches erupted from their sides; plants burst through the fissures of the flagstones upon which she stood.

A horrible screech was emanating from within the amphitheater, and with that screech Becky's full consciousness had returned. She realized it was Talisa, and, whatever that scream meant, it had caused Talisa to lose her hold on her.

She turned and ran.

For half-a-day, she put distance between herself and Talisa without incident. Then the jungle trees parted to create a glade. Becky was halfway across when an upright lizard, eight feet from snout to tail, propelled itself over the glade in a series of hops that ended with its hind talons atop Becky's shoulders, bearing her to the ground.

Becky screamed as its opening jaws rained saliva upon her. Then the air cracked and cracked again. A small hail of musket balls slammed into the lizard, one plowing a trench in the earth by Becky's head. The monster sprang back, releasing her.

"Lidenbrock! Beesley!" she cried out. "I'm here!"

"Stay down, Miss Sharp," Beesley shouted out as flashes of smoke heralded another round of fire. Staying where she was seemed to be a good way to be shot, so bending low, she scampered toward her rescuers. While the Englishman and some sailors moved in on their saurian quarry, Lidenbrock ran to meet her.

"Are you all right, Miss Sharp?" Lidenbrock asked.

Becky grabbed at him desperately. "How long?" she sobbed. "How long since that creature flew away with me?"

"Almost a fortnight. We had given you up as lost. Thank Providence your path crossed ours."

More musket shots. Becky looked back: the twitching giant reptile lay supine on the ground.

"This is such a miracle — to lose you both in one day and then, find you both alive and well!" Lidenbrock was beaming.

"Wait — both of us?" Becky asked, placing her hand on his upper arm.

"My Talisa, Miss Sharp! She vanished from the ship, carried away, she tells us, same as you. We found her about a mile or two on the other side of this glade."

Lidenbrock winced, and looking down, saw that Becky's nails were biting into his bicep. "Miss Sharp . . . my arm . . ."

Becky released him and looked about for her hated adversary. Yes, there she was, just emerging from the trees. The infernal harpy! Whatever made her scream in that temple, it hadn't meant the end of her. And after two weeks, she was healed enough to cast her spell over them all again.

Beesley now approached her. "Miss Sharp! Very glad to see you are unspoiled," he said by way of salutation and then tweaked the tip of each waxed mustachio.

"Is your musket loaded, Mr. Beesley?" she asked.

"Ho! Now that the danger is passed, you still wish to have a shot at that thunder lizard that attacked you, just on general principle, eh? You women are a spiteful lot! Very well, here you go, lass," he said, cocking the long gun and handing it to her. Becky put it to her shoulder and turned it on Talisa, who now stood less than twenty-five feet away from her.

Talisa's eyes widened. Becky fired —

— just as Beesley knocked her to the ground in an attempt to insure the musket ball went wildly off mark.

"That bitch is a monster!" she shouted up into his face. "Do you hear? That thing will be the death of us all!"

"Have you gone daft?!" Beesley asked, wrenching the gun away. "That's Miss Talisa!"

By now, Lidenbrock had reached them, having begun to run when he saw Becky aim the long gun at Talisa.

"Do not do it, Lidenbrock!" she shouted at him. "Don't take her to the pit! Do you hear? You don't know what you'll be setting in motion! Lidenbrock — 'twas she who flew away with me!"

Lidenbrock shook his head in pity. "Poor creature," he said. "This infernal sun has been too much for her. I'll fetch some rope —"

"*No!*" Becky cried desperately. "Beesley! Get off! You can't tie me — you have to listen — *No! No!*" she protested as he turned her over on her stomach, and soon her arms were bound behind her.

Her legs were left free to allow her to walk. During the journey under Talisa's guidance to the abandoned city, Becky continued to vilify her adversary, salting her adjurations with such profanity that even the sailors began to complain. Finally, the grieved company as one consented to her gagging. Becky thus seethed in silence.

Lidenbrock all but swooned at the sight of the ancient amphitheater, Brom Cromwell's temple of the pit. Soon, he was urging them through a large open archway through which a solitary stone pillar was visible. The theater's floor consisted of flagstones. In its center, a 15-foot tall stone idol of a large ape perched vigilantly on a large, round pedestal.

"Why, it is the *Ape Gigans!*" Lidenbrock exclaimed and peered at the figure's base. "There is writing here...."

Lidenbrock's eyes widened and his jaw went slack. "Why, this is nothing less than astounding!" he said. "These are the exact esoteric Pnakotic characters which Arne Saknussemm, the same alchemist who discovered the inner earth, translated from an ancient, Hyperborean manuscript into his sixteenth century grimoire, the *Reglur Ormunnar.*"

"Can you make it out?" Beesley asked.

"I can," Lidenbrock said, "for I have studied the Pnakotic Fragments myself. Just a moment...."

He read over the engraved script silently, his lips moving. Then:

"It says that, long ago, this city's inhabitants, the Blessed People, enjoyed a benign existence, 'not as much as a snake' to threaten them. Game was plentiful. But the god of the dead, Malgoghphoni, 'miserable in his underworld, envied their bliss.'

"'Malgoghphoni opened the Earth, and sent from his domain his progeny: great serpents who walked. They came forth continually. All stood in jeopardy.

"'Then from the same depths rose our salvation. Before man, when the gods fought, Malgoghphoni made eternal prisoners of those...'"

Here Lidenbrock frowned. "Apparently, they identified the ape on this dais as belonging to some demigod class out of their mythology. They appear to have regarded his sudden appearance as the fulfillment of a prophecy. Let me start again:

"'Malgoghphoni made eternal prisoners of those demigods who opposed him. But one...the 'cunning'...this *Ape Gigans*...torn free of his fetters, came now to the Blessed People's aid.

"'The *Ape Gigans* did what men could not do: by his strength, he beat back the serpents and took a great stone, sealing the pit against Malgoghphoni's progeny...'"

Now Becky understood Talisa had screamed in frustration at encountering this unexpected obstruction.

"'In the doing, the *Ape Gigans* severed himself forever from his brothers, captives in darkness below. Never could he return to free them, lest he unleash again

Malgoghphoni's brood upon us.

" 'To console his loneliness, the Blessed People to this day offer him brides of our own virgins in this his temple we built him, and here we also set up his image over the pit.

" 'Thus were our days extended, but because of the increase of Malgoghphoni's progeny, the time will come when we must leave forever the works of our fathers' hands. Great is the *Ape Gigans*, the bane of Malgogphoni's brood. Blessed is he.' "

Lidenbrock looked at the idol. "We will have to blow that thing up, then," he said, and Talisa smiled. "It's the only way in. You men — bring the powder kegs while I take some rubbings of what is written here. I wish to be able to attempt a more extensive translation at leisure, and the opportunity to study the originals is about to irrevocably pass."

"I'll take Miss Sharp back a pace — to that pillar in front of the archway," Beesley said. "That should shield her. You should come along, too, Miss Talisa . . ."

While the other men prepared the powder, Beesley took Becky to the ancient column and began untying her arms preparatory to resecuring her. The moment her hands were free, Becky reached up and snatched her gag away.

"Beesley, listen to me!" she implored. "You mustn't allow them to open that pit! It will be the beginning of the end!"

"Bosh! We can handle these thunder lizards all right, should any pop up," he said, retying her wrists before her. Just above Becky's head, he had noticed an iron ring in the pillar, and so had left a length of rope to tie her to it. "Sorry, lass, but I don't trust another to hold your leash, as I'm the one who has to answer for you to our Meonia masters."

He secured the rope through the iron ring, pulling her hands over her head. Becky groaned and turned her face from Talisa's victorious sneer. Once Beesley rejoined the men, she began pulling against the ring. It held secure. Perhaps, she mused, the *Ape Gigans*'s brides tended to be unwilling.

There were shouts now from the area of the idol. Becky looked from around the pillar to see Lidenbrock, Marsh, Beesley and the sailors sprinting for cover. Toward the dais and its statuary, a flame was slithering and sputtering along a trail of jet . . .

With a 'boom' that left all their ears ringing, as though the idol itself roared with defiance and indignation at its dethronement, the pit erupted in a shower of stone and earth. Pieces of statuary sprayed as far as Becky, flung over and beyond the sheltering pillar.

She was just beginning to peer around it at the resulting rubble when there was another terrible roar, this from far behind her, beyond the abandoned city itself.

"Somewhat of a delayed echo, that," Beesley commented.

"This island possesses unusual acoustics along with everything else," Lidenbrock responded. Talisa stared intently into the smoke still boiling over the pit.

Amazingly, more than half of the pedestal, sans ape, still obstinately plugged the hole. But there was enough to pass through. Talisa's eyes flashed with triumph, and she bolted for the ingress.

"Wait!" Lidenbrock called after her. "We must yet be cautious! Talisa, stop! The ground about may give way . . ." Orpheus reversed, he followed his Eurydice toward the underworld.

She reached the edge, almost toppling over it, but Lidenbrock caught up to her just in time, pulling her back over the lip of the half crater. "Wait, Talisa! We need ropes to begin our descent."

As the others thus prepared, Becky found herself momentarily alone and forgotten. So when she heard trees crashing in the jungle beyond the city ruins and cried out to them, she was ignored.

The men had secured a rope ladder and lowered it into the pit when a roar sounded that was clearly neither echo nor distant.

Bending to squeeze his black, hairy bulk through the large archway, the *Ape Gigans* re-entered his temple.

"It is the *Ape Gigans* himself!" Lidenbrock gasped out.

Rising now to his full height, which fell just short of the amphitheater's great walls, the *Ape Gigans* stretched out his long arms, and then brought his fists back against his enormous chest, drilling them in a rapid-fire staccato. He roared again, eyes riveted on those who stood guiltily among the rubble of his image.

The pillar to which Becky was tied placed her right before the towering hulk, but he had yet to notice her. She yanked furiously at the rope that held her, but to no avail. And so, she at last gave in to her fear and screamed.

The *Ape Gigans* looked down and immediately reached for her.

"No, No, No!" Becky pleaded as she was enveloped in the sweaty, fleshy folds of the great palm, fetid with musk. With his other hand, the *Ape Gigans* snapped the rope free of the pillar.

Becky's wrists, still bound, now dropped before her. She used her bunched fists to strike back and forth at the monstrous hand grasping her, as the leathery skin of the ape's face molded into what Becky recognized as a grotesque parody of a human smile.

This offering was unlike any he had seen before: her clothing enveloped her body, but the skin which was exposed was white, and her long hair shone like flame. He twisted her waist-length locks around a fingertip, tugging Becky's head back so that she thought he would tear it from her shoulders. She screamed again, and the Ape Gigans ceased his pulling.

"Lidenbrock!" she cried out. "Beesley! *Help me!*"

The sailors were already rushing to her aid. Lidenbrock stood at the edge of the pit, suspended on the cusp of two worlds. Talisa, seeing that the giant ape's attention was turned, began to scramble down the rope ladder.

Lidenbrock moved to join her and immediately felt Beesley's musket barrel in his ribs. "Not so fast, professor. Miss Sharp first!"

Meanwhile, the sailors were already loosing their long guns upon the *Ape Gigans*. One ricocheting ball grazed Becky's head. She heard her captor roar in anger, and the last she saw was his long arm lashing out, sending the sailors scattering like tenpins …

Pain returned with Becky's consciousness. Her bound hands touched gingerly at her blood-scabbed scalp. She opened her eyes and found herself upon a large leafy mat in an enormous cave. It was well lit, and she quickly saw why: two large, paired apertures in one of the cave walls above her were flooding the cavern with light.

A deep, rapid stream flowed through the cave. Still a bit dazed, she crawled to it, and, lowering her mouth, drank. The icy cold bit when she splashed it over her face and into her hair with her bound hands.

She suddenly realized that the twin openings above her must be those of the island's mountain topography. But how had she come here? The answer hovered as a shadow at the furthest periphery of her consciousness: she flinched against it. And then it seemed the shadow would not be denied, that it had slipped from her mind and now blocked the sun from the openings above …

Becky looked over her shoulder as though against her will and screamed at the large dark form hovering behind her. The *Ape Gigans*'s hand reached for her, but instead of snatching her up, he first gently brushed with his fingertips her injured head.

She now rose shakily to her feet. The giant anthropoid shifted, and the sunlight struck Becky full on, making each tiny hair along her arms an incandescent wick, her reddish-blond head a conflagration. A look of wonder spread over the *Ape Gigans*'s face.

Becky backed away, but he imposed his hand behind her, grabbing her up again. On some level, he had understood her need for healing rest and thus had spared her his more robust attentions. But now that she was awake, he meant to renew the investigation of his catch in earnest.

He reached for where the dress was already torn over her shoulder, revealing the intriguing pale skin. He caught the loose fabric, pulling down and popping free the buttons that held the back of her frock together. Part of the chemise beneath ripped away as well, revealing the shapely protuberances of her shoulder blades. Becky flinched as the *Ape Gigans* stroked her, tactilely savoring both her softness and the distinct, unfamiliar textures of the shredded outer and under garments.

The loosened dress slid off Becky's shoulders and to her bosom, where her bound hands desperately caught it. She was soon compelled to let drop the clutched frock to box the returning, worrying thumb and fingers.

Now only in a torn chemise and boots, Becky fought more frantically against the ape's plucking, which nevertheless soon reduced her undergarment to hanging tatters. The abundance of unfamiliar white skin in the ape's palm dazzled in the bright sun, a wonder from outside the Ape Gigans's existence, as though he suddenly held a handful of snow.

Becky continued to fight him off with her bound fists. Then the ape caught the dangling length of rope from between her wrists and ripped her bonds loose. Becky yelped at the rope burn. Still, caressing her stinging wrists, she muttered, "That much was useful, at least."

Now the *Ape Gigans* focused on the flaming hair, curling the reddish-blond strands about his fingers. This time, however, he took care not to tug as hard as he had before.

"He remembers," a breathy Becky spoke to herself as he let her long hair gently unwind.

She realized her fascinated captor would never willingly free her. And she suspected his former brides had angered him by attempting to escape — hence this prehistoric Bluebeard's perennial need for a new one. One bid for freedom was all she would have.

The *Ape Gigans* plucked and gathered fruits which, for Becky, were the size of melons. She ate, and this necessitated visits to a tall, thick bush by the cavern stream. When he followed her warily, she would squat behind the bush, shooing him while rattling its branches. Once he connected that rustle with certain odors, the ape seemed to grasp her desire for privacy. He would turn away until the rustling stopped. Having established this pattern, Becky slowly began increasing the time she rattled the bush and was thus out of his sight.

When the *Ape Gigans* ventured out, he was always careful to place her on a high outcropping for safekeeping. From this vantage spot, through one of the high, twin apertures, Becky could look out over the island.

And it was from here that she saw the distant wisp of smoke like that from a camp fire. Her heart leaped. Did this represent a party searching for her? She knew she could not afford to lose the chance that it was. She must risk all and hatch her scheme as soon as the *Ape Gigans* returned.

After much pacing about, she heard her captor lumbering home. She quickly composed herself lest he smell her desperation. He entered, carrying more melons which he let roll to the cavern floor. Then he collected Becky. As usual, he poked, stroked and pulled at her person. She now wore a tiny loincloth and another rag that barely contained her ample breasts, both articles of clothing fashioned from her chemise's remains. For days, she had been unraveling into string the discarded outer frock and the rope that had bound her.

Upon her release, Becky went through the motions of eating as the *Ape Gigans* peeled and ate the melons as though they were oranges. While he concentrated on slaking his thirst and hunger, Becky produced her latest little bundle of string from where she had hidden it in her grass mat.

Tucking the thread into her bosom, she moved toward the bush. The ape sucked the sticky juice from his fingers and watched her. Once concealed behind the bush, she quickly added the most recent bit of thread to a long single strand, already tied there, whose length she had been increasing every trip to the privy.

The *Ape Gigans* sensed something more was going on than simply answering nature's call. He moved toward the bush. Becky quickly pulled the string, rattling the branches. The ape hesitated, then, by force of habit, looked away.

Using the thread to continue tugging on the bush, Becky kicked off her boots and slowly waded into the stream. She didn't even feel the sting of the cold as the water rose over her thighs, her fast-beating heart had so suffused her body with warmth. Now she let the quick current carry her along, unfurling the string behind her, all the time still tugging it.

The speed of the stream increased and shot her out of the cave and into the sunlight — just as an angered roar sounded behind her. Suddenly, she was yanked back like a fish on a line. She released the string and swam hard, afraid to look back, trying not to think of what would happen should the *Ape Gigans* recapture her —

But the stream was carrying her along now even faster, and Becky realized she had entered a rapids. She went limp, bumping off of large stones, shielding her head for fear of being knocked unconscious. The ground beside her shook with the ponderous *thud, thud, thud* of the *Ape Gigans*'s bulk going up and down as he ran on his behemoth's hands and feet, now coming alongside her. Becky frantically ducked underwater, but upon resurfacing, saw he still kept pace with her.

She ducked beneath again, and when she burst to the surface saw a new reason for fright: a waterfall. The inexorable rush of the stream left her no choice. She looked desperately now to the ape along the bank — just as the rapids took her over. Simultaneously plunged underwater and falling, she could still hear her captor's roar of frustration and failure. She struck the river below, plummeting to the bed, then writhing back to the top in a rhythmic, sinuous flow of her supple body.

Becky broke the surface, gasping in sharp, painful draws of breath as she splashed frantically and peeled away the hair plastered over her face. Her starting eyes looked about for the giant ape. No sign yet. And the swift flow of the river was taking her further away every second. She was bruised, but no bones were broken or out of joint.

She had no idea where she was now in relation to whomever had started that campfire. But if she set one of her own — might they come to her? Would she also draw the *Ape Gigans*'s attention — or any of the other island creatures? As she came ashore far down river, she decided that risk was better than blundering blindly through the danger laden jungle.

Becky had learned how to start a fire in the wilderness from Captain Campbell during their time together in Africa. As always, the process of striking stone to twigs was frustrating and she nicked and scraped her fingers more than once, provoking bursts of swearing. But she finally succeeded, sending and maintaining a plume of white smoke above the tree tops. She tried to stay awake, but her ordeal had exhausted her, and she fell asleep by the fire.

A crashing of jungle foliage moving in her direction roused her, along with shouting: "Miss Sharp! Miss Sharp! Are you there?"

It was Beesley's voice. With the men approaching, she suddenly felt keenly the state of undress in which the *Ape Gigans*'s hands had left her, and scampered for shelter behind some large fronds.

"I'm here!" she shouted and a few moments later, Lidenbrock, Beesley, Captain Marsh and the sailors who had survived the jungle were grouping around her fire. "Gentlemen," she said from where she remained concealed, "I fear my ordeal has left me nearly *au naturel*. Will one of you be so kind as to toss me your shirt?"

Lidenbrock immediately removed his, and, averting his gaze, handed it to Becky.

"Thank you, Professor," she said. "You are most solicitous."

Here, Lidenbrock's face burned, and he was glad to be turned away. "Alas, Miss Sharp, to my shame, I must admit Mr. Beesley had to persuade me to pursue you and not follow Fatima — Miss Talisa — into the pit."

"I do not think poorly of you, Professor," Becky said. "I'm certain you were not completely yourself." Becky now emerged wearing the shirt, which reached only as far as her knees. Still, she could hardly begrudge her gallants a display of leg after their efforts on her behalf — especially if it added to her powers of persuasion.

Marsh and Beesley looked on appreciatively while Lidenbrock blushed and said, "Once you are safe, I intend to descend after her."

"Listen to me, Professor," Becky said, placing her hand on his arm. "You must not! We must reseal that opening in the Earth, else that pit shall be the threshold of doom for many."

"And desert my Fatima? Miss Sharp, how can you suggest such a thing?"

Here Beesley drew her aside. "Are you forgetting your mission in all this?" he asked, voice low. "You have certain obligations it is my duty to see you fulfill —"

"Disraeli sensed there was something insidious about this expedition," she whispered. "I have confirmed that."

"And what proofs do you have to offer? Because he will require them, as do I."

Becky started to speak, but caught her tongue. She dare not bring more unsubstantiated, fantastical railings against Talisa, lest she be bound and gagged again.

"If you do not seal the pit upon our return," she said instead, "I promise you, you will soon have all the proof you need. But it will come too late."

"Then, Cassandra, I will acknowledge you a prophetess. But now let us get moving."

The group began its march through the heated stillness and into the lengthening jungle shadows.

They walked through the night non-stop, arriving back at the ruined amphitheater with the dawn. There, they paused for food and rest, though it wasn't long before Lidenbrock was urging them to begin their descent. Beesley, however, argued they return to the ship first and see that Miss Sharp be outfitted properly for the journey below.

"Surely Miss Sharp, after her recent ordeal, has no desire to risk more peril," Lidenbrock snapped. "Now, I have seen to her safe return, Beesley! Just as you required. But I will put off seeking Fatima no longer, even if I must do it alone!"

Beesley started to retort, but the angry twist of his mouth froze on his face. His eyes widened at something happening behind Lidenbrock. Marsh and his men immediately began cocking their long guns, and Lidenbrock turned to see what was the source of their agitation.

Slipping through the pit's opening, like a grub from under a moved stone, came a winged, human-sized reptile, one of Talisa's true people. The narrow egress slowed its progress, and before it could clear itself, it was so shot through that instead of taking flight, it fell dead to the ground.

"Miss Sharp was right," Beesley announced. "Fetch powder — we'll seal this hell-hole immediately!"

Lidenbrock opened his mouth to protest when Captain Marsh pointed at the hole and shouted: "Look!"

Guns were immediately trained upon the pit.

"No!" Beesley shouted. "That's a woman's hand!"

Lidenbrock sprinted for the pit. "Do not shoot, you fools!" he cried. Reaching the hand, he took it, pulling its owner up and free of the crevice.

"You are not my Fatima," Lidenbrock began, his tone one of surprise, but not complete disappointment.

For the possessor of this hand was a winsome blonde, her peach-flushed flesh the effulgence of the morning sun.

Smitten, the men lowered their guns and stared instead in a stupor of delight. Even Lidenbrock did not shift his gaze but willingly drank in the feminine radiance.

Becky gasped, "*Another* one!"

A second beauty with hanging reddish locks rose from the hole.

"And another!" Becky exclaimed. "And *another* . . ."

Soon, a display that would rival the *crème* of the finest seraglios sashayed about the pit's opening. Beesley and the others dropped their long guns to the ground and moved to join Lidenbrock, who remained planted to the spot.

Becky snatched up a rifle and fired a musket ball in the direction of the "women," striking instead the pate of one of the sailors.

"*Merde!* I missed!" Becky exclaimed as the man fell. She didn't know how to reload, but several pairs of long guns were at her feet. All of the men — including Lidenbrock — were already running back for her, and before she could fire again, they had tackled her, then pulled her roughly to her feet.

Becky looked back at the women. To her horror, she saw Talisa had come up from the pit to join them. Lidenbrock, his expression bliss, took a step toward her, but she nodded him back. All the women nodded, a silent communication to the men . . .

One sailor grabbed Becky and drew her taut. Beesley brought his open palm hard against her face, then the back of his hand across her mouth. She saw with satisfaction that the skin of his knuckles was blood-scraped from her teeth.

He looked back, as did all the men, at Talisa and her sister-things, who tittered and nodded again.

Now Becky was pummeled by all: blows to her stomach, to her ribs, blows placed to her kidneys. Sagging ground-ward, she was hefted up for more punishment, the unnatural tittering urging it on —

— With a roar, a rapacious storm of black fur, claws and fangs descended upon Becky's molesters, tossing them carelessly.

The *Ape Gigans* plucked up Lidenbrock and flung him far afield. He careened over the flagstones on his stomach, his head striking the sacrificial pillar so that he blacked out.

The man holding Becky to be beaten dropped her to the ground to flee, but was halted when the titan's paw snatched him up by the neck and quickly wrung it so that the body tore free of the head. Becky saw Beesley sliding down the amphitheater's wall, his skull open, his exposed brain leaving a trail like a giant slug.

The mangled corpses of the sailors who had not successfully fled now littered the amphitheater floor. The same deadly paws that had put them there gently picked Becky from the ground and brought her close to burning amber eyes. On her back in the *Ape Gigans*'s palm, Becky weakly turned her head and nodded toward the women. Then she wondered — would he be susceptible to their charms as well?

The *Ape Gigans*'s upper lip curled, exposing fangs, his eyes narrowing. Gently, he placed Becky down and then, with another roar, he propelled himself on his knuckles and paws upon the harpies.

It seemed the *Ape Gigans* was vulnerable only to true beauty.

In panic, Talisa's sisters dropped their useless guises, launching themselves to meet the charging ape. They dropped on him from above, from behind, and head on, flailing at his eyes. They hooked him with their beaks and talons, biting deep into the flesh of his head and body.

The Ape peeled them from himself, tossing them as he had the men. But those whose necks he had not wrung, or whose vitals he had not torn free with his fangs, returned to bite and snatch and tear again.

Only Talisa had not joined in the attack — or changed her appearance. Skirting the edge of the battle, she was able to get behind the *Ape Gigans* and at what he guarded so valiantly: Becky Sharp.

Bruised and sore as she was, Becky managed to rise to her knees at the approach of her enemy and raised her fist to strike her. Talisa rushed forward, grabbing her wrist, and, putting her other hand over Becky's mouth, pushed her back to the ground, pinning her there.

"These ape creatures long plagued my kind —" Becky again heard the words in her head "— we had thought them long eliminated. Their resistance was always robust. To restore their strength, my sisters will require more than this dead human carrion the ape has let fall. You will provide fresh flesh and blood when they are done."

The *Ape Gigans*, flattened three more winged reptilian creatures. Yet there still seemed no end of assailants left to bite and rake him.

Rising, he now eyed the partially open pit which he had sealed long ago. He regarded the temple wall rising behind it, just as his adversaries hooked fast into his neck, into his abdomen, into the flesh above his right kidney. Roaring in anguish, he ran for the wall, springing upward, grabbing the top and propelling himself and the creatures which clung to him over the side.

Talisa smiled. "The brute in his torment has forgotten you, Miss Sharp, and seeks to escape his adversaries. T'would seem you drew the weak-minded of his lot."

Then the section of the wall behind the pit buckled, dust of ages first unsettling, stirring in clouds; then cracks showed in the masonry, and the first stones began to topple over into the pit . . .

From over the wall flew the screeching reptilian things who, unable to thwart the ape's purpose, quickly descended into the pit as the wall continued to crumble and spill into it behind them.

Talisa's eyes widened with realization. Releasing Becky, she scampered for the pit as fast as she could —

Too late! The section of the wall completely tumbled over the opening, leaving Talisa to throw her arms over her face against the rising plumes of dust —

— and then find herself suddenly before the *Ape Gigans* who stood hunched, bleeding and torn, swaying on his great knees. His amber eyes lit with anger at the last of his enemies, ready to deliver upon her full recompense for the grievances he had suffered lately from her kind.

Talisa shrieked, the sound of nails scraping slate. The ape lunged for her —

— and a long gun fired!

By chance, the ball grazed his gigantic head with only enough impact to steal his consciousness. His great form fell forward on top of the screaming Talisa.

Becky looked back to see an aghast Lidenbrock. "*No!*" he screamed. Then he was running with the gun toward the prostrate behemoth.

"Lidenbrock!" she cried out, trying to gain her feet against the pain. "She's dead! Crushed! It's too late!"

"Not to avenge her!" he shouted back, having now reached the *Ape Gigans*. In rage, he raised the gun's butt, ready to beat it to splinters against the colossal head before him.

"Stop, Professor!" Becky shouted, now to her knees. "You'll only rouse him! We dare not tarry — we must flee to the ship! I am weakened by the beating *you* participated in! You owe me your aid! *Now!*"

The end of the long gun hovered for long seconds, held ready still to strike, then, bellowing, Lidenbrock turned the gun so that now the barrel was aimed at the *Ape Gigans'* temple.

One great eyelid flittered….

His own eyes widening at the massive creature's first sign of returning consciousness, Lidenbrock immediately lowered his weapon, teeth pinching blood from his lower lip, eyelids beating back tears.

Groaning, he quickly turned and sprinted for Becky, gathered her up and began carrying her back to the ship, leaving behind the strewn corpses of fallen comrade and foe alike.

From over his shoulder, Becky watched the *Ape Gigans*, still except for the rise and fall of his great breast. Amidst her fear that he might yet rise and carry her away, never to escape again, she found herself strangely touched and wondering:

Why had he sealed the pit — two times now — and denied himself return to the world from which he came? Did he realize, as Talisa had said, that the rest of his kind were long dead? That, whether in this world or the one beneath, he was still ultimately alone?

Safely aboard Captain Marsh's ship, her bruises bandaged, Becky rested against the railing and regarded the island receding in the distance. There had been no sign of the *Ape Gigans* during their flight, though once out to sea, she had heard an inhuman yet despairing wail across the waters and far away.

Professor Lidenbrock joined her. He, too, stared silently toward the island they had left behind. Becky was surprised to discover that he, like she, had left it forever, abandoning that ingress to the inner earth.

"That way holds too much grief for me," he said. "Part of me died back there with her."

"Yes," Becky thought, "that part of you which she held captive."

"So let us not speak her name ever again," he said. "I never shall. But that does not mean I will forget her, or ever cease looking for another opening into the earth's center…perhaps the one that the alchemist Arne Saknussemm discovered. Though it becomes the work of my life, I am comforted that she, after a fashion, will carry on with me."

Becky looked toward the great stone dome of the island's tallest mountain that she had, of late, inhabited. Did the *Ape Gigans* wander about the cavern inside, an atavism beyond recall, a hermit memory taken residence in a long dead giant's discarded skull?

Becky wondered, did *she* in turn still stir inside the head of the *Ape Gigans*? It was unlikely he would ever see white skin again or other hair as radiant as her own. Perhaps, over time, she would seem to him some phantasm, something from a half-remembered dream. If such as he *could* dream . . .

From Becky Sharp's Journal: September 16, 1843

I found Lidenbrock fallen asleep at his table where he is working at translating the rubbings he took from the base of the *Ape Gigans*'s idol, before he — or more accurately, *Talisa* — had it blasted apart. My natural, feminine curiosity prompted me to read what he had written. I was quite shocked to see that what was inscribed on that dais centuries ago concerned me.

For it seems as the *Ape Gigans*'s bride, one who has absconded without fulfilling her term, I now owe him in lieu of myself any female offspring I may bring into this world. Or, as Lidenbrock has translated it, "If thou shall prove faithless to thy awful betrothed, holy unto the *Ape Gigans* be the first female of thy womb. In thy stead shall she fulfill your bond, for long is the reach of the *Ape Gigans*, unto the seventh generation."

Perhaps so, but I dare say his grasp is unable to extend into the next hemisphere! And I certainly shall have little difficulty avoiding his island domain for the rest of my preternaturally lengthened life.

No, the *Ape Gigans* shall never grasp me again, and as for his claim to any issue of mine . . . I dare say my adult son back in England would hardly satisfy him!

January 1, 1844

Today I at last escaped the Meonia upon the crooked streets of Tangiers. Swathed as a native woman and supplied with gold coins which I took from the Meonia's discretion fund, I have attached myself to a guarded caravan which should bring me safely to Safaqis and the resumption of my quest for Noot's caduceus.

To help insure that there will be no more distractions from this goal from

Disraeli and his superiors, Lidenbrock kindly bribed Captain Marsh to corroborate his account of my being carried down into the depths of the earth by one of Talisa's people immediately before the sealing of the pit by the *Ape Gigans*.

Lidenbrock would paint such a picture of the dangers of the island that Disraeli should be dissuaded from any further attempts to return there to unplug that passage to Kor's flame. And certainly from any attempt to merely recover me — especially given my alleged abductors' taste for human flesh.

So let the Meonia believe I have perished in the bowels of the earth. I have certainly buried myself deeply enough!

January 15, 1844

Reunited with Campbell at last, I discovered he has been able to confirm that Queequeg had indeed disembarked from the port of Safaqis but, unfortunately, to parts unknown. I found the rough dive Campbell was inhabiting unacceptable accommodations in which to rest, refresh, and consider our next move. Thus, I suggested we present ourselves to a nearby British colony as brother and sister missionaries to plead for civilized sanctuary among the heathens here on the Barbary Coast.

To this end, we made for the colony's vicarage. We were met with all alacrity and attentiveness to our needs by the vicar himself. He appears in his prime and quite strapping for a man of the cloth. I fancy he might have made quite a warrior-monk in Medieval times. We are to dine at his table tonight, though I dare say if either Campbell or myself is asked to say grace, we will do as well as this priest with the unlikely name of Padre Perditio.

Chapter Four: 1844 —
The Legacy of Captain Clegg

"Any cheer I may hope to offer two missionaries, fresh from their harsh toil in the evangelistic field of darkest Africa, will be woefully incommensurate with your efforts," said Padre Perditio as he led Becky and Campbell to the dining room of the vicarage. "Nevertheless, I hope the comforts of a warm dinner, a glass of port, and polite society will refresh you somewhat."

"I'm sure you will acquit yourself admirably," Becky responded and smiled reassuringly as the vicarage maid opened the door.

And then she laid her eyes on their other dinner companion for the evening.

"I'm sorry . . ." Perditio said, arching an eyebrow at her. ". . . Miss Sharp? You've gone pale. Are you unwell?"

"No, umm, just . . . getting over something. Nothing contagious. I had an unfortunate encounter with a tse-tse fly in the jungle. Haven't quite got all of the . . . tse . . . out of me, it seems."

"Please, direct the young woman to sit by me," the long-limbed man who had given Becky a start said as he rose from his chair. "I will be glad for her to take hold of my arm if she swoons."

"Thank you, kind sir," Becky said meekly, tucking her head in acknowledgement. The man, narrow of waist and broad of shoulder, twisted one of the tips of his moustache beneath which he flashed a toothy smile. He had ever been a charming rogue, had Donal McCormac, whenever Becky's path had crossed his in past times. Unfortunately, in their last criminal venture, Becky had left McCormac in the lurch.

"Miss Sharp, allow me to introduce Sheriff McCormac," said Perditio. "Sheriff McCormac, Miss Sharp and Mister Sharp have just returned from missionary work in the Congo. Sheriff McCormac keeps Her Majesty's order here in the colony."

"Indeed?" Becky asked in a small voice as she was seated.

"Oh, yes," Perditio said, as he and the other men also sat down to the table. "He struggles to keep the slave trade illegal here — though that pirate chap Clegg presses him hard."

Sheriff McCormac immediately took issue with the Padre. "Say, rather, the blackguard at hand has styled himself *after* the notorious Captain Clegg."

"Clegg?" Becky managed, wanting to keep the casual conversation going until she could fully get her wits about her again.

"Oh, a gentle woman as yourself would not know the tales of such scoundrels," McCormac said, keeping his delighted countenance beaming upon her. "Clegg's career ended in a well-deserved hanging a good fifty years or so back. His body lies unmourned in a grave at Dymchurch."

"But perhaps he is Clegg himself, back from the dead," Perditio said with a mischievous smile which didn't seem quite appropriate on a priest's face. "The last of his old crew told a former member of my congregation that Clegg had — at great price of an archenemy — some knowledge of Cuban deviltry . . . or was it Mayan witchery learned at the feet of his wife? Yes, that's right. And they say he has, via the same dark arts, summoned a deadly familiar to do his bidding, which on occasion animates a Guy Fawkes effigy Clegg has prepared for it — sort of a straw Golem."

"Balderdash!" Sheriff McCormac said, waving one hand as though to dispel the tall tales of Captain Clegg like so much annoying cigar smoke hovering about the dinner table. "I daresay it will *not* be this neo-Clegg's effigy that hangs, but the upstart blackguard himself, just as his namesake did at Rye!"

Conversation veered to less contentious topics, including the adventures of the missionaries in darkest Africa. Becky was a seasoned liar and had already instructed Campbell to let her do the talking about their exploits, so there would be no danger of his crossing her up.

Having recovered from her shock at discovering her old partner in crime was part of their dinner party, Becky warmed to the attentions of her audience and, in a moment of fateful inspiration, chose to embellish one particular adventure among the heathen by flourishing the image of Zervan Akarana (which she carried in her bosom). Becky claimed it was a fetish she had carried off as a spoil of sorts, after the natives had cast out their old god from their village.

"Amazing," Padre Perditio, said, indicating with a nod the tiny image she brandished. "I had no idea that Zoroastrianism had spread among the blacks in Africa."

Becky missed a beat, then said, "Well, of course it hasn't. In fact, I'm not familiar with that Faith at all. No, I was given this by a tribe of former Mithra worshippers."

"Indeed? Why, when you return to England, the antiquarians will have to rewrite the history books. Mithra worship has never been known to be extant in the Congo. You are certain it was Mithra?"

"Of course. This little chap is known to them as Zervan Akarana. 'Boundless Time.'"

"Since you have time in abundance, may I steal some of it from you, Miss Sharp, and trouble you for a turn about the drawing room with me?" McCormac asked with a smile. "When we all three retire there for after-dinner conversation, of course," he was quick to add.

Becky looked Campbell's way, pleading with her eyes for succor from the unwanted situation which was shaping up. "If my brother will permit it," she said.

Campbell, however, who was well into his second glass of port, was all too glad to acquiesce, and Becky felt with a returning sense of foreboding that she was on her own.

"Mrs. Oliver," Perditio said to his housekeeper, "you may leave the dinner dishes for now and join the couple in the drawing room. I very much wish to take Mr. Sharp out on the vicarage grounds and show off my aviary."

The housekeeper was glad to oblige. She had, in fact, some darning of the vicar's socks she could see to while chaperoning in the next room. Soon, Becky and the sheriff, arms linked, were having their turn.

"Well, well," McCormac said as soon as he and Becky were out of earshot of Mrs. Oliver, "how you have reformed, Rebecca. A missionary no less!"

"I could say the same of you, Donal McCormac. I never thought I would see you on the right side of the law."

"Why, Rebecca, don't you realize we've been attending a masquerade this evening? Excepting Mrs. Oliver, no one at the vicar's table was exactly as he seemed."

"Are you not the sheriff of these parts then?" Becky asked.

"Indeed I am. My credentials are immaculate. I have them of the real sheriff whom I met in transit to this port. Seems he couldn't hold his drink. Poor chap. I made off with his brandy as well as his credentials. Not that I left him empty handed in the exchange — I put a knife in his back before I tossed him off the train into the Punjab jungle.

"So, tell me, Rebecca, why did you not follow through with our deal? And don't tell me it was because you suddenly 'saw the light.'"

Now they paused before a large picture window looking out on the vicarage grounds, and thus had excuse to turn their backs to the chaperone. The sun was setting; gulls threw out their wild caws to each other and wheeled high in the sky, and the whisper of distant surf was just audible. The church, visible from the window, was the epitome of quaint, the whole moment incredibly picturesque — and entirely lost on Becky and McCormac.

"What I saw," Becky said, glaring at him, "were two officers of Her Majesty's armed forces as they swooped down on me in a back alley of Bath and informed me that the information that I sent to you in India had been intercepted. I never broke faith!"

"Yet here you are, walking free only four years later."

Becky glowered at him. "I am *not* free. I have never been more bound."

"By this fellow 'missionary' of yours? What are his circumstances?"

"He is a captain in Her Majesty's service. In fact, he was one of the arresting officers who gave me the choice of being carted off to Africa to pose as his sister — on some bit of intrigue of which he has not shared the details with me, so do not ask — or, being hanged. I did what I had to, to survive."

"As did I," McCormac sneered, and tugged her back into their stroll. "I had to flee India for my life when the rebels in the Punjab saw that I was not going to come through with that for which I had been paid so handsomely. I have a wound from that failed transaction which pains me yet."

"And you hold me to blame. Do you plan to expose me and imprison me for revenge? On what charge? Impersonating a missionary? And remember, you would be compromising the mission in which I'm involved. This is Her Majesty's business we are about!"

McCormac eyed her coldly. "So you say. But Her Majesty's throne is very far from here, where *I* am established as the law. I could at any time receive a report that a notorious traitor to her country — in the guise of a missionary — has arrived in my jurisdiction. Much unpleasantness could happen to you — and your 'brother' — before an official advocate could reach you."

Becky, who knew very well what McCormac was capable of, suppressed a shiver and met his gaze eye-to-eye: "Very well: what can I possibly do that could assuage this grievance of yours against me?"

McCormac smiled. "Ah . . . I thought you'd never ask."

"Well, now I have. So tell me! Out with it, man! Do you enjoy watching me writhe on the rack?"

Still grinning, McCormac reached out and made a quick, fond stroke under her chin. "The rack's the place for a wench as yourself. There . . . and in the bed."

Becky flinched from his caress. "I'm certain if *your* attentions are involved in either scenario, sir, one would be as pleasurable as the other."

McCormac's hand went to his chest. "Ah, Miss Sharp, you wound me!"

Becky leveled a coolly appraising stare at him. " 'The law!' Bosh! You're probably the notorious pirate Captain Clegg yourself! You're playing the game from both sides, I'd wager!"

"And you'd win. My position here *does* facilitate my personal continuance of the slave trade. But I am not this Neo-Clegg. No, in the masquerade we carry out here on the Barbary Coast, the villains go about as heroes, and the heroes as villains."

"Oh ho!" Becky allowed herself a caustic laugh. "The man Clegg opposes your continuance of the slave trade, and you publicly vilify him as the culprit responsible for it!"

McCormac gnawed his lower lip. "But your advent, Rebecca, marks the end of his interference in my schemes. I must find his base of operation, or that of his right hand, his 'familiar!' You will uncover this for me."

Becky's jaw dropped. "I? How am I supposed to accomplish this? I have no resources!"

McCormac dropped his gaze momentarily to her bosom. "You have a couple of resources which you carry on your person at all times. And, you have already supplied a third: this 'missionary' identity you've created for yourself."

"Really? I would suppose the third cancels out the first two."

"Except that your mark is a man of the cloth: the good Padre Perditio. He is involved with Clegg; I know it!"

"And you wish me to — what? Seduce him? A *priest*?! Even if I were to succeed, that would hardly guarantee me his complete confidence."

"My plan will thrust you into the heart of his double life, I promise you. And all you will have to do is provide a beautiful damsel in distress to appeal to that pusillanimous Padre's sense of chivalry."

"How? When?"

"Very soon," McCormac said, looking back toward the picture window. "Ah! The man in question returns with your 'brother' from his aviary. Let us finish our turn about the room. I plan to take my leave before the two of you. Give me a half-hour's lead so that I may prepare. At which inn do you lodge?"

"'The Crow's Nest.'"

"Good. Steer your brother to approach the inn from the back street. Do not fail me, Rebecca," and here he pulled painfully tightly on her arm so that she winced. "Remember white skin is traded alongside black and brown here on the Barbary Coast."

Becky followed McCormac's instructions, but as she guided Campbell back toward their Inn, she decided to try and share her predicament with him. Her pseudo- brother, however, was still drunk, and intent on sharing with her the wonders of Padre Perditio's aviary.

"Never seen the like, 'Becca," he slurred out. "An aviary . . . of crows . . . that talk! Damnedest thing I ever heard! They all have split tongues, see . . . Ha! They 'speak with forked tongue' as the red men in America say . . ."

"I've heard enough of Perditio's fabulous bird cage, Campbell! Now, listen to me: you need to know something about the sheriff —"

". . . a virtual chorus the Padre has in that cage: bass, alto, tenor, soprano, mezzo-soprano ... Padre Perditio says he's plannin' to replace the church choir with his crows! Extraordinary chap, the Padre ..."

"Yes, I'm sure. But I want to talk about Sheriff McCormac. I assure you, he's at least as colorful as your friend the vicar. Listen —"

"The catch is — they say only one word! They come when he blows his little whistle ..."

By this point, they were about to turn on the street behind their inn, and Becky concluded trying to counsel with Campbell was hopeless. And it was well she did, for they were barely on the back street when who should emerge from an adjoining alley but Donal McCormac.

"Look!" Campbell exclaimed with a smile. "It's the sheriff himself now! Speak of the devil and —"

McCormac's smile was as sharp as the knife he clenched. Campbell's stupor and surprise left him helpless as the blade sliced between two of his ribs and into his heart. He barely had time to register the shock of what was happening to him before he folded dead to the street at the mouth of the alley.

Becky leaped back to avoid the corpse collapsing upon her. McCormac unsheathed the knife from Campbell's chest and quickly pulled the body into the darkness of the alley. He emerged with his knife held at the ready. Becky's eyes started as she felt her face pale, and fear choked the scream in her throat: had McCormac overheard her attempt to betray him to Campbell?

In another moment McCormac was upon her, grinning wildly, pressing the flat of his blade against her cheek and bringing the point dangerously close to her eye. Then he slid the blade back, gently, leaving a trail of Campbell's blood on her face.

"Allow me to put a little color back into your cheeks, Rebecca," he laughed. He returned his knife to his side, then snatched out and ripped the shoulder from her dress, tearing until he revealed her cleavage. Becky leaped back, pulling the torn cloth back over her exposed flesh.

"Unhand me!" Becky commanded him, barely able to hide her fear.

"You'll forgive my sartorial enthusiasm, my dear, but the rags with which I've left you will serve our purpose more than a party frock fit for Victoria herself. You see, Becky, you are now going to return to the vicarage, your murdered brother's blood on your face, your dress rent from resisting a fate worse than death. All this, you will tell Perditio, occurred at the hands of slave dealers who bore you a grudge from your opposing their efforts in the jungle. They followed you here to take their revenge, and you barely escaped with your life, let alone your virtue!

"You will beg Perditio to hide you where no one will find you — and I wager, if he and his cohorts are not currently using it, he'll take you to the secret base from which they operate. There's certainly no place you'd be safer."

"Why, McCormac?" Becky asked him after a moment. "I had no affection for Captain Campbell; still, to strike him down without a care — what has this Clegg done to justify such ruthless acts?"

McCormac's eyes darkened. He reached into his breast pocket and pulled out a snuff box. "My right hand man had a frightful tobacco habit. Snorted the stuff so much that the tip of his nose was permanently stained brown. He tossed the snuff box to Becky. She caught it. "Open it!" he ordered her.

Becky did. Inside the snuff box was a small gobbet of flesh, brown stained about the still discernable nostrils.

Becky's mouth twisted with distaste. She shut the box quickly and tossed it back to McCormac who snatched it out of the air and thrust it back into his breast pocket. "The handiwork of Clegg's 'familiar!' They have taken all my best men from me, one by one, until I am the last left!" he spat.

"But they'll not find Donal McCormac meekly waiting for them. You find out what I want to know," he ordered, stabbing his index finger at her face, "and I will play no longer the part of the prey but rather the hunter! Clegg and his familiar have made a desperate man of me, Rebecca, and should you fail to give me what I desire, I will take my anger out on you!"

A frantic, insistent staccato at the back door of the vicarage summoned Perditio, still in his night gown, candle in hand. He was shocked to find revealed by the small, yellow light the distraught, disheveled Miss Sharp, her dress rent, her face blood stained.

"Merciful saints!" Perditio exclaimed. "Whatever happened? Who hurt you, lass?"

"Please, let me inside. Hurry!" Becky pleaded. "I don't know if they've managed to follow me!"

"Of course, of course," he said, standing back to let her enter and then securing the door behind her. "Whatever have you been through?"

This Padre was no frail, sedentary man, but a robust one, and Becky suppressed a smile of triumph when she saw his gaze drop more than once to her cleavage — and not, she wagered, to admire the figure of Zervan Akarana that rested there.

"It was terrible, Padre," Becky exclaimed, tears trembling on her cheeks. "This was no random assault on my person — or my dear brother's."

"Where is your brother?"

"My brother... Campbell... is dead at their hands," Becky said, clinching fresh tears from her eyes as she shuddered violently.

"My dear girl," Perditio said, tentatively stepping toward her. Becky quickly closed the distance, throwing herself in his arms, and the good Padre suddenly had the flesh of a woman's warm, heaving bosom pressed to his own. It was quite the rush she was giving him, to judge by the flush in his cheeks. Had ever a conquest been achieved so easily?

She pushed away from him after a moment and began to fumble with her torn dress. "Oh, forgive me, Padre! I am so embarrassed — those fiends barely left me with any clothes, as you can see. But... they did not... that is to say..."

"Shh... There, there, Miss Sharp! I understand. You need not be ashamed. But you said this assault was not random. Did you know your attackers?"

"Slavers," Becky said. "They've borne a grudge against my brother and me, since our preaching converted some of those tribal chieftains with whom they had heretofore trafficked."

"I will alert Sheriff McCormac immediately, of course!"

"That will do no good. You do not know these men! United in their fury, they are virtually unstoppable — especially by a backwater bumpkin sheriff!"

"My dear, our sheriff and his men are more than equal to the task..."

"It doesn't matter: by now the slavers are watching whatever paths would take me to him."

"Then *I* will go —"

Becky bunched her rags to her bosom. "And leave me alone and unprotected?" she asked, eyes wide, voice tremulous. "They may yet trace me here to your home in the meantime. Perhaps they're here already! Oh, they've watched Campbell and me like hawks since we've come to this city, I'm sure! Is there no place you can hide me? Where I can rest assured I will not be found?"

Perditio stared silently at the trembling girl.

"Please?" she breathed haltingly.

"Yes, of course. I will fetch some things you'll need. Food, of course, and a darning needle and some thread." He blew out the candle. "I know my way around this house in the dark. If they are watching, your assailants will have no idea of our movements. You stay here. And under cover of darkness, I promise to take you where no one will find you."

The Padre was true to his word. Becky soon found herself clinging to him on horseback as his steed's hooves kicked up the dirt, thrusting them forward into the night. Attached to the saddle, the bundle of provisions Perditio had supplied slung wildly, back and forth with the horse's charge. Soon, the dark village was behind them, the moonlit beach ahead, the surf's growing cacophony like applause from a

Chapter Four: 1844 — The Legacy of Captain Clegg

vast audience sympathetic to their flight.

Reaching the beach, they galloped along its edge, spray hissing out at them from the darkness, plastering Becky's skirt to her legs. She could see the shoreline rising into a range of cliffs. Perditio turned hard to the left, and then they were climbing. Becky consigned all landmarks to memory. She did, after all, have to be able to tell McCormac where the lair of Perditio and his friends was located, or she was as good as sold into slavery.

Now they were in a field of high grass whose long, large blades lapped roughly against their legs and lashed the horse's sides and belly. After they dismounted and pushed through on foot, the tall grass continued to snatch at and cling to them. Finally, they reached the remains of an old building all but covered by the undergrowth.

"An old mission," Perditio explained as he tied the horse to a remaining stone column, then detached the bundle of provisions from the saddle. "I discovered its location when I found parchments left in a secret panel by one of my predecessors to the vicarage." Now he was pushing back a section of the long grass that had been broken and folded over, to reveal a trap door apparently set in the ground but actually part of the old mission's floor.

A large key appeared in Perditio's hand, and he was soon turning it in the lock. Becky furrowed her brow: would he insist on locking her in, to keep her safe? That could complicate her getting back to McCormac. Further, without the key, how would the sheriff gain admission to the lair ... all assuming that this was indeed the entrance to the base of operations he sought.

Now Perditio pulled open the heavy door, and they quickly passed through the ingress, Becky first. The Padre passed the bundle of provisions down to her, then followed, pausing to close the door and lock it behind him. They descended warily some steps and, though in the dark, Becky was aware her surroundings were spacious. Perditio lit lamps and candles about the large chamber, and she saw Christian iconography all about: crucifixes, statues of the Madonna and Child and Jesus as the Good Shepherd, crook in one hand, lamb held to his breast in the other.

Becky bit her lower lip in disappointment: this was *not* what McCormac was looking for. She was as good as headed for the slave market already — unless she kept up her pretense with Perditio. Here, after all, was a refuge where she would not be found, where she might lie low until she could arrange passage off the Barbary Coast.

"This was a meditation grotto for the mission's priest, where he withdrew for prayer and fasting," Perditio explained. "I have found it serves my purposes as well ... such as now. I've been planning to spirit you away here ever since I saw your talisman at dinner . . ."

Becky went stock still, unsure of what she was hearing. "You were *planning* to bring me here?"

"I hardly imagined you to be so obliging as to come to me and save me the effort of thinking up some pretense. I had my suspicions about your career as a missionary, but when you pressed your bare, heaving bosom against mine, my doubts were confirmed."

"*Why* did you bring me?"

"First, your talisman, Miss Sharp. Zervan Akarana. I want it. Now. Give it to me."

Becky's mouth went dry, and then she bolted up the steps and began pushing futilely against the door she knew would be unyielding. But she *had* to escape. Else *all* would be lost . . . the whole *world* would be lost!

Perditio was rushing up the steps toward her. She turned and flailed out at him with her fists, but he easily grabbed her and threw her, kicking and pummeling him, over his shoulder. He carried her back down into the grotto, threw her onto a couch, and then he was atop her, grabbing at her person with intrusive familiarity —

— and then he had what he wanted: he snatched from her bosom the figure of Zervan Akarana.

"Come now, Miss Sharp. Your ruse has failed, and you and I both know . . ." and here he looked down at her, still lying beneath him on the couch, ". . . that this body in which you behold me is *not my own*."

"Get. Off. Of. Me," Becky said as, by degree, she struggled to regain her composure.

"Of course," Perditio said, hefting his weight from atop her. Becky began to rise from the couch. He reached out, grabbed her by the arm and pulled her back down, but this time only into a sitting position. "I didn't say you could get up. Now, tell me what it is your damned alien race wants from me *this* time."

Again, Becky was unsure of what she was hearing. "What are you talking about? I am *not* the one from Yith. *You are!* You just admitted as much!"

"No, my *human* mind inhabits a body *your* people gave to me."

Becky frowned, but managed to restrain her temper. "I am not given to repeating myself, but perhaps you are hard of hearing, so I will make an allowance this time and tell you again: I am *not* a 'Yithian.'"

Perditio held up the figure of Zervan Akarana. "This says otherwise."

"I told you where I got that —"

"You told me a load of nonsense. You claimed you had this of an African Mithra worshipper, and that you knew nothing of Zoroasterism . . . while giving the Zoroaster name for the god represented by this idol. For future reference, for any other subterfuge you *round*-headed, *stalk*-necked, *lobster*-clawed, *three-eyed Cyclopean monstrosities* may be planning — (here Perditio caught his breath) — Mithra worshippers called this lion-headed chap 'Aion.' Your ruse is thus exposed, so stop denying that you are not of this world."

"Because I made a mistake in comparative religion? *Pardon moi, Monsieur 'Je sais tout'!* And a Cyclops only has *one* eye!" Becky snapped back.

Perditio scowled. "*Pardon moi, mademoiselle,* but 'cyclopean' is an adjective meaning 'gigantic' — which accurately describes your true, girthy Yithian proportions."

Becky put her hands over her ears, rolled her eyes, and shook her head side to side. "Do I have to say it *again,* man?!"

"A falsehood does not become truth by stubborn repetition!"

Becky exploded: "*Fou! Vous etes sans cervelle!*"

"I understand everything you say, *mademoiselle!* My previous parish was just across the channel," Perditio said as he tucked Zervan Akarana into an inner coat pocket. "I dealt with the French on a regular basis."

Becky paused. "The English channel?"

"It could hardly have been any other: my parish was at Dymchurch-Under-the-Wall."

The expression on Becky's face immediately told Perditio that he had been far too forthcoming. Looking at him sidelong, Becky said, "Donal said that the pirate Clegg was buried at Dymchurch."

Perditio shifted his weight on the couch but met her gaze. "Yes, *fifty* years ago! And it's 'Donal' now? How long have you and the good Sheriff McCormac been so familiar with one another?"

"He's no friend of mine," Becky said. "Nor yours."

"And I will bring my dealings with him to a close in my own time."

Becky raised her hand to silence him. "Donal —"

Perditio arched an eyebrow at her.

"— *Sheriff McCormac*, then! He believes you are connected with his enemy, the man calling himself Clegg. Is it a coincidence that your last parish was where the original pirate's body was buried? I think not!"

"On the contrary: life is full of coincidences."

"But I daresay this isn't one of them, is it? What was it you said about Clegg to McCormac at dinner? You said Clegg had obtained knowledge of some sort of

Mayan sorcery — power to raise the dead? To raise *himself?*"

"I was merely baiting McCormac. Really, Miss Sharp! To seriously suggest witchcraft in this enlightened age —"

Becky was clearly having none of it. She leaned toward him. "Who *are* you?" she asked. "Who are you *really?*"

"Miss Sharp, the body of Captain Clegg had resolved to dust before you were even born."

"Yet here you are. Here . . . *we* are. Look, I am not telling you anything new when I say that there are powers beyond human ken in this world. If not sorcery, then . . ." Becky leveled her gaze with his. If ever there was a time for her to try honesty, this looked to be it.

Now Perditio was leaning forward. "Are you admitting, then —"

"I admit to an association with the Great Race of Yith. But I am not one of them. That would be impossible. They attempted to possess me in the past, but my brain chemistry would not allow it. Because of this, I am useful for carrying out the purposes of some secret faction among their ranks when they do not want others of their race to know what they are about."

Perditio narrowed his eyes, lowering them as he considered her words. His quick flush confused her until she realized where his gaze had wandered. Embarrassed he might have been, but his eyes still lingered on her cleavage.

"I assure you," she said, slightly tucking her head and smiling under half-hooded eyes, "that was not some alien thing that embraced you back at the vicarage. Not one bit of me. Including those bits of which you have, perhaps, become fond?"

Her coy eyes had been skillfully scanning Perditio's coat for the impressions that gave away in which pockets he had secured the idol and the key to the grotto door. Having located them, she now made her move. "Do you really believe a — how did you say? — *round*-headed, *stalk*-necked, *lobster*-clawed, *three-eyed Cyclopean monster* could ever feel as much a woman as *this?*"

Then Becky closed the distance between them for a second time, pushing herself eagerly and firmly into him. Simultaneously, he seized her curved, soft body tightly to his own, thrusting his mouth forward to meet hers. She grasped him, her scurrying hands feeling his waist and torso passionately until she had located the idol and the key.

But Perditio gently captured her hand just as it was about to reach into his pocket, and, raising it between them, stroked her slender, delicate fingers. "You artful minx," he chuckled. "You are not the least lobster-clawed, are you? How could I have missed?" Becky laughed softly as well, and then smiled up into his face. In spite of her failed gambit, she was as pleased with herself as Perditio seemed to be.

"Now," Perditio said, "that is what I call a successful interrogation."

Chapter Four: 1844 — The Legacy of Captain Clegg

"It was nice, wasn't it?"

"Hmm? Oh. Not the embrace or kiss," Perditio was quick to correct her as he dipped a hand inside an inner coat pocket. "That was just for fun. I had already decided to believe you, when you expressed knowledge of the secret faction of the Great Race of Yith. I have had my own — involuntary — dealings with that rogue element.

"And I also know, from experience, how their mind transference exercises can sometimes fail to meet their intentions. Your brain chemistry explanation seemed perfectly plausible to me. I believe you were looking for this?" He tossed the figure of Zervan Akarana to her. "Don't worry. A gentleman doesn't kiss and tell. Certainly not a Padre."

Becky flushed. "A peculiar sort of Padre you are! You're no more than a rogue! Admit it!"

Perditio sighed and smiled. "I *am* Nathaniel Clegg, and I have escaped death twice. The first time by arranging a substitute to take my place on the gallows. In penance for my past brigand's life, I took a new identity and became the vicar of Dymchurch. I was completely reformed. But then, to minister to all of my parishioners' needs, physical as well as spiritual, it became necessary to become a rogue yet again.

"One of the Yithians took a fancy to my adventures and desired to experience something of the swashbuckling life. Thus, I soon found my own consciousness, from time to time, in the distant past from which the Great Race operates. I communed with them while there, though they saw to it that I remembered nothing whenever I was returned to my own era of the 1790s."

"Then how is it you remember now?" Becky asked coolly.

Perditio smiled. "It was not the Yithians' intent, I assure you. Please, Miss Sharp, relax. And I will answer all your questions."

"Somehow I doubt that," Becky said sarcastically, but settled back none-the-less.

Perditio continued: "It seems my physical brain was not up to serial possession. My mechanism began to misfire. And as my brain was robbed of its sanity, the Yithian who possessed me became unwittingly entangled in my gray matter. Bereft of my brain's cunning, it proceeded to lose my life at the hands of an old enemy."

"Which left you in the distant past without a body," Becky said.

"Quite an embarrassment for the particular Yithian possessing me. Upon my body's death, Its consciousness rejoined Its own body in the past. *My* consciousness, however, could not be allowed to linger there; it had to be returned, or the Yithian authorities would want to know why not. The Great Race's entire time travel experiment could be halted if my case were known and the possibility of Yithians damaging human hosts became an issue.

"So my possessor was driven to approach unofficial channels. It covertly contacted the rogue element of the Great Race for their aid, threatening to expose their activities if they refused."

"Why couldn't your possessor simply travel back in Its own past and abort your series of possessions before they began?" Becky asked.

"Something about such action generating an extraneous amount of temporal thesis/ antithesis/ synthesis/ antithesis *ad infinitum* that would strain the multiverse beyond what it could bear.

"No, it was much simpler to move my mind into a new human host, some fifty years away from the temporal scene of the crime."

"And this was Padre Perditio, whose body you took."

"I know not to whom this body belonged. He was a faceless wretch who was destined to shuffle off this mortal coil under a heap of other bodies in a plague of cholera. But he was not quite dead, at least not to the Yithians' science.

"Human consciousness, however, does not easily adjust when it transfers from one host to another. One beneficial side effect, however, of the contents of my brain becoming unsettled was that my knowledge of the Great Race and my time among them resurfaced. Do you know that I actually had a friend, a human friend, there in the primordial past? Another transembodied consciousness of a chap much like myself —"

"Oh? Was he a rogue, too?" Becky sniffed.

"I was going to say 'with a nautical bend,' but, yes, he was a rogue, too. One who lived over fifty years after my own time. We would be contemporaries now, though, of course, we would never be able to recognize one another, even were we in the same room, because we've never actually *seen* each other.

"Well, my new body was brought to health and my mind acclimated to it. It was during the Yithians' ministrations that I noticed a peculiar token which I was able to later identify as an icon of Zervan Akarana. I recovered, chose the name 'Perditio' in homage to my past life, and since my arrival on the Barbary Coast five years ago, I have fought those who still practice the slave trade."

"I'm not keen on the mechanics of all this," Becky began, "I tend to confine my thinking to three familiar dimensions, but in giving you a new life, the Yithians introduced someone into time who should not be there. Do not your actions, your mere existence, create serious complications of some sort?"

"I overheard those who tended to my recovery speak of a possible, undesirable rippling out effect, resulting in a thinning of the temporal walls that could bring about a crisis just after the first quarter of the 20th century. But the Great Race spoke of having a plan to address this contingency."

"Yes," Becky said slowly. "I'm quite sure they do . . . and I'm 'it.'"

"What do you mean?"

"I mean, you have had a strange history with these time straddling creatures, while I have a past, present and a future. Sit back, Perditio or Clegg or whatever you call yourself, for I have a tale that will make both your ears ring. And I do not doubt you will bring me under your wing when you have heard it."

A half hour later, Becky had finished recounting her adventures, from her first meeting with the late Captain Campbell on the back streets of Bath up to the pursuit of Queequeg which had led her to Perditio's doorstep.

Perditio sat quietly when she was done.

"Well?" Becky asked. "Do not say you do not believe me —"

"No, no," Perditio was quick to assure her. "It is not doubt that I feel. Rather, I am so totally . . . aghast at the dilemma my continued existence has brought about. All creation veers toward annihilation because of *me!*"

Becky clucked her tongue and chided, "My, my . . . your ego just grows larger and larger, doesn't it? This is all the Yithians' manipulation! You are only the victim of their machinations — and their arrogant belief that they can compensate for any eventuality that would emerge from their tampering."

"And it sounds as though the worst possible eventuality *has* materialized," Perditio mused gloomily. "When this Tulu creature awakens at that weakened temporal point my existence has created, it will have opportunity — which it most certainly will seize — to merge all parallel realities into one doom! Tulu will *be* the universe!"

Perditio drew a deep breath and looked away. "Perhaps," he said, after a moment, "if I were to take my own life —"

"No!" Becky immediately interjected. "I need you," she said. "You and your years at sea, to help me trail down Queequeg. He is a sailor, remember? And, besides, the damage is already done, and I'm certain as sticky as our situation is, the Great Race knows that the scenario they've engineered has the best chance for succeeding over any other plan. Do not think for one minute that they would not have killed you themselves long ago, if it were the most propitious tactic to take."

Perditio reached out, stuck his thumb under her chin and slightly lifted her head back. "You would kill me yourself, wouldn't you, you vixen, if it meant the possibility of sparing yourself your coming confrontation with Tulu?"

Becky turned her head slightly, away from his thumb, and looked at him soberly. "Indeed I would, because it is in my own best interests. My life is most precious to me; not yours, nor the multitude of fools who mill about this planet."

Clegg's expression became suddenly contemplative. "Perhaps my own motives are no less self-serving. In my actions, I seek penance for things done in the flesh — my own, that is. Which brings us back to the moment at hand . . .

"I cannot abandon my plan to crush Donal McCormac's slave ring once and for all. You care for yourself? Then perhaps you should learn to have a care also for those wretches who on the next tide will be carried to an existence of misery in America, never to see their homeland or loved ones again. Because I will not help you in your task, Rebecca Sharp, until you have assisted me in completing mine."

"How can I be of any assistance to you? I cannot betray Donal! Then *I* would be the one sold into a life of wretchedness!"

"You shall have no need to betray him. I intend for you to give him what he wants." Here Perditio smiled, reached into his pocket, and produced the key to the door above:

"You will provide the good Sheriff with that which he most desires: ingress into the lair of the dread pirate Clegg!

Chapter Five: 1844 —
Bane of the Barbary Corsairs!

On the return ride to the village, Becky again clung tightly to Perditio. The embrace was different this time than on the journey to his grotto. She had intended seduction before, in how she had grasped him, moved her hands over his chest, and placed her head on his shoulder so that he would occasionally feel the softness of her cheek, the warmth of her breath.

Now her hands locked around his waist, and this time they did not wander. She lay the side of her face between his shoulder blades and was surprised to find herself feeling the sense of security she had experienced — on occasion — with her husband Rawdon, when they lay together in bed.

He had been her pawn, but in contrast to the man before her now, Rawdon had adored her. It was only when he had caught her in what would be her final tryst with Lord Steyne that he — rightly — had humiliated her. His devotion, then, was done away with forever, as he returned the contempt she had always held for him. They had never spoken again.

There had been little security in the years since Rawdon — but life had taught her early on that you could count on no one but yourself. She learned this when her mother left her. Despite all her promises to the contrary.

She had still died.

Was that why she could never fully give herself to Rawdon's care, even at his most tender, his most solicitous?

How strange, then, that she was allowing herself to trust Perditio. She had accepted his plan. She would give McCormac the key and the directions to Perditio's secret base, then return to the vicarage and wait for him.

Nice, for a while, to have the weight of the world lifted from her slim shoulders.

Face still pressed against Perditio's broad, strong back, Becky slept.

Perditio's housekeeper had an old frock she wore for cleaning, and back at the vicarage, he gave it to Becky to replace her torn dress. Then, taking one of the vicarage horses, she rode directly to Sheriff Donal McCormac's rooms, located on the harbor wall.

She was shown to the study, and, entering, was immediately taken aback: a tall, bearded Arab in dark robes and turban stood in the room, a sheathed, curved sword at his side, his gaze austere; still, she saw desire light in his eyes as he studied her face and figure. This was an interest she did not welcome at all, and her instincts screamed for her to flee —

— and then she saw McCormac, a brandy in his hand and a cigar in his mouth. Apparently noticing the misgivings in her expression, he was quick to reassure her: "Rebecca! No cause for alarm, my dear. This is my business associate: Omar bin Othman al-Hazad. He will be transporting the cargo with the next tide. Am I correct to assume that we need expect no interference from Captain Clegg?"

Becky focused her attention on McCormac, though she could still feel the heat of Omar bin Othman al-Hazad's gaze from across the room. She produced the key and smiled.

"If Clegg is indeed connected with Padre Perditio, then this is what you need to assure that he never trouble you again."

McCormac flashed his toothy grin and eagerly snatched the key from Becky's fingers. "And you can direct us to the door that goes with this key?"

"I watched the landmarks carefully. I can give you accurate directions, I'm certain."

McCormac pulled open a desk drawer, took paper from inside and thrust it on the desk top. Quickly closing the drawer, he then slid the ink bottle from its place and beside the paper. A pen already slanted up out of the bottle's opening. "Come, come," he bid Becky eagerly. "Sit down and write them here. Be quick, girl."

He then pulled the chair back for her. Becky cast another uneasy glance at Omar bin Othman al-Hazad, who still had not spoken but continued to regard her with an unnerving mix of cruelty and desire. Then she turned her back to him and sat down to write. For a few minutes her pen quickly scratched over the paper, with occasional pauses to dip the nub again into the ink.

Once she was finished, McCormac snatched it up from the desk and gave it a quick, frantic read with a running commentary of confirming, mumbling ramblings: "Uhm-hmm. Yes. I know the very spot. Yes . . . Yes . . . Door in the ground of the ruins of a burned out mission, eh? Oh-ho! Who would expect anything less colorful from old Clegg, eh?" Satisfied he looked up from the paper. "You have done well, Rebecca."

Becky rose hesitantly from the chair. "Then, my debt to you is paid? Our business is done?"

"Oh, indeed, yes. Our business is most assuredly concluded." He then nodded toward Omar. "The wench is yours," he said.

Betrayed! Becky's eyes widened with fear and anger. In the next instant, the Arab had flowed across the room in a flurry of his robes and laid eager hands on her, grasping her by the waist to him and violently caressing her strawberry blond hair.

"Unhand me!" Becky demanded, but al-Hazad continued his harsh fondling until her hair had fallen down. Then with callused fingers, he eagerly stroked the fair, soft skin of her face.

"Seems Omar has taken a fancy to you himself. You see, he is officially here to procure you for a sultan for whom he occasionally is a courier. Chap's a bit of a rough lover, Becca, but I reckon you're familiar with all that," McCormac said.

"*McCormac!*" she shrieked. "Make him take his hands off of me! I've done what you required —"

"Indeed you have, Rebecca, and that is why you are still living. Unfortunately, you know that I have killed an agent of Her Majesty's service, and so I cannot just let you go walking about freely. Fortunately, the sultan for whom Omar is procuring you is a bit tired of all the almond-eyed, mocha-toned lovelies who currently fill his palace."

Omar tossed his enraged prize over his shoulder and began carrying her out of the room. "Sold me into — a — a harem?" Becky spat out at McCormac, her face red and a silvery-blue vein swelling on her forehead. "You lying, backstabbing —"

"Sorry you don't have the, uhm, 'pedigree' to rank higher than the sultan's concubine. But Omar himself is still a wife or two short of the limit the Qur'an allows. He seems intrigued enough by your fair skin and gold hair to look over your 'deficiency' in other areas. Perhaps if you play your cards right . . ."

And as his screaming, swearing ex-partner in crime was carried away, Donal McCormac made his own preparations for his rendezvous with the man calling himself Captain Clegg. With the pirate and his associates destroyed, McCormac expected little trouble in re-building his slavery ring.

Within the hour, still under darkness, McCormac and two henchmen were headed for the lair of his enemies. He found the landmarks easily; Becky had recorded them well and accurately. He half-expected to find himself somehow betrayed by her and her directions, something that would give her the final comeuppance.

But all followed as she had placed it on the page. At last they reached the grassy field she had described. Dismounting and carrying his lantern high, he eagerly led his men through the tall grass ... yes, there were what looked to be the remains of a building ... the mission, if Becky had not played him false.

And then he cried out in triumph: there was the cellar door in the razed floor of the mission, leading under the ground. He quickly placed the key into the lock and turned it. There followed the sound of tumblers releasing. Eagerly, McCormac reached to turn the handle and open the door — and then thought better of it. If Perditio's partner indeed styled himself after the infamous Captain Clegg, would he not be prepared for the event of unwanted intruders?

McCormac beckoned one of his henchmen forward, indicating that he should open the door. The man hesitated, but McCormac's threatening countenance prodded him on. The henchman pulled the door upward and outward, and leapt away. McCormac waved him to come back and handed him the lantern to examine the passage yawning below.

The stairway it revealed was apparently clear. McCormac sent both of his men on before him, and they began to descend into the darkness beneath them, the man in lead carrying the lantern — which McCormac was counting on drawing any initial fire that might erupt out of the dark.

But they passed down the steps without resistance, and soon they stood on the grotto's floor. The door above, which remained open, had granted them moonlight along with that of the lantern, but now they saw ensconced torches which they lit.

The figure that suddenly loomed in the room before them seemed to take a menacing step forward. But before any gun was fired, they all realized that had been but a trick of the flickering shadows and torch light. What they were looking at was merely a straw dummy wearing a brim hat in the fashion of the 17th century. Yet, McCormac's men remained ill at ease.

"'Penny for the old guy?'" one of the henchmen said jokingly, a feeble attempt at levity. "Looks like the Padre's a bit early for Guy Fawkes day."

"He must be," said the other, eager to believe his cohort's explanation. "Would be a bit of a funny spot for a scarecrow, wouldnit?"

The simulacrum in question hung erect on a pole. Its head under the hat was made of brownish burlap. It wore a full cloak that reached to the ground, enfolding the figure. Its arms were crossed over the chest, each hand holding a small, wicked-looking scythe.

From the open door in the earth above their heads now came the high call of a bird, yet its voice was eerily quasi-human as well. Louder and louder the voice grew until the bird itself flew down the opening and the basement's acoustics echoed and magnified its cry:

"CLEGG! CLEGG! CLEGG!"

One of the nervous henchmen fired his gun at the bird, sending the ball ricocheting along with the caws of the crow off the stone walls about them. McCormac ducked and swore.

Unharmed, the crow now came to rest on one of the effigy's shoulder. There it sat, its head bobbing. "Clegg!" it cawed out one more time.

"You fool," McCormac snapped. "Listen to what the bird is saying: it's *his!* It knows this place. Aye, it seems the good Padre Perditio is indeed in league with the man calling himself Clegg. Becky, I could kiss you — though I'd have to push aside the swarthy beard under which your mouth is no doubt smothering by now."

McCormac allowed himself a moment for a self-congratulatory chuckle. All was going amazingly to plan. Soon he would have this "Clegg" and, with any luck, the good Padre as well.

The men with him were still dubiously eyeing the mannequin: with the breeze from above, the dry straw rustled like the rattle of a snake.

"They say," the man who carried the lantern said, as he continued to watch the straw man from a space, "that Clegg has a familiar that appears sometimes in a crow or a whole murder of crows, and other times moves about in an effigy Clegg made for it."

"Stop talking nonsense," McCormac snapped. "That thing doesn't *need* to move about: it's made the two of you piss your pants just by hanging there! Now, look for somewhere to hide yourselves. Then we'll douse the lights and take this so-called 'Clegg' by ambush."

The men had left the door open in case they needed to make a hasty retreat. It would have to be shut, of course, lest Clegg or Perditio know that something was amiss. McCormac had turned to mount the steps to this end, the crow from the mannequin's shoulder flying ahead and out the opening, at which point the door began to close on its own from above.

McCormac dashed upward, but found the shut door now unmovable, a great weight seeming to lay on it. A chill wind blew through the grotto and the torches flickered into darkness. A sonorous voice reverberated off the stone walls:

"WHO DARES ENTER UNBIDDEN THE LAIR OF CAPTAIN CLEGG?"

At the sound of the voice, McCormac's men's eyes trained immediately on the mannequin.

"It *is* alive!" the one holding the lantern gasped.

McCormac looked down in disbelief to see the mannequin's arms, that had been heretofore crossed over its chest, were now uncrossing, opening, and opening with them the cloak that hung beneath the burlap face.

"Don't stand there, you fools! *Shoot!*" McCormac shouted.

"PRESUMPTUOUS TOADS . . . YOU WILL NOT LEAVE HERE

ALIVE!" the voice sounded again.

Now the dark shape under the cloak stood open and vulnerable. One of McCormac's men aimed his gun at the effigy's chest as the other held up the lantern —

— and a shrill, high whistle drilled McCormac's eardrums. He pressed his palms to the sides of his head —

— and his man fired, but the piercing sound made him wince, and, his aim thrown off, the ball passed harmlessly over the straw man's shoulder. McCormac's other man dropped the lantern as the whistle also vibrated through his head.

The shrill tone apparently had an effect on the effigy as well, for, as its cloak and head fell away, the body exploded outward in bits of black, an ersatz chorus taking up the cry:

"CLEGG! CLEGG! CLEGG! CLEGG!"

Wings, beaks, and claws thronged McCormac and his men, the latter covering their eyes and dashing blindly up the steps. There, they joined McCormac, who repeatedly rammed the unyielding door with his shoulder but was constantly having to stop and fling his arms about to wave off the shrieking birds that darted for his eyes, his nose, his cheeks.

Swearing, he dove over the side of the stairs to escape, leaving his men, who were now pounding against the door, the focus of the birds' relentless thrashing. The crows scratched blood from the hands the men threw up to protect their faces.

McCormac scooped up the dropped lantern, casting the crows' shadows over the walls and seeming to multiply, in a disorienting kaleidoscopic effect, the number of flapping black shapes. The birds continued worrying, pecking, tearing his men, who finally retreated down the steps, the crows flocking after them.

As soon as they reached the floor, the door above flew open of its own accord. Another shrill whistle pierced their ears, and, like large bits of ash riding currents of heat up a chimney, the crows flew up the stairway and out the door.

Seeing the door remained open after them, one of McCormac's men sprinted wildly up the stairs, not waiting to be sealed in this chamber of horrors again. He did not even pause to reload and powder his gun whose ball he had wasted firing at that first crow which had flown into the grotto.

"Stop, idiot!" McCormac shouted after him. "Don't you see that's what he *wants* you to do?"

The man wasn't having it, and neither was his fellow, who followed him. The first lackey out the door found what appeared to be the effigy from below, reconstructed and looming before him, scythes raised —

"Clegg's familiar!" the man gasped out, just as the blades slashed forward, slicing his throat from each side.

"Who Dares Enter Unbidden the Lair of Captain Clegg?"

Blood jetted from his neck as the simulacrum used its upper shoulder to shove him aside. The criminal's cohort reached the top of the stairs just in time to see the marauding Guy Fawkes figure pushing away the bleeding body. The man started to dash back down the steps, but Clegg's familiar reached out, snatching him with both hands and heaving him through and clear of the doorway in the ground.

To do so, it had had to drop its scythes. It now tried to secure its grip with one hand on its writhing opponent, while grabbing with the other at one of two other small scythes that hung at each hip.

As it twirled its victim around by his lapel, the straw man suddenly saw McCormac standing at the top of the steps in the open doorway, two pistols at the ready.

The first ball fired. The living mannequin swung the adversary with which it struggled into the projectile's path, killing McCormac's man instantly. Then, using the suddenly limp body as a shield, Clegg's familiar rushed McCormac. Another ball fired, taking off the ear of the corpse, and then the dead man was colliding with McCormac, the familiar pushing it on, so that McCormac lost his balance and went down backwards.

Now, with his dead lackey atop McCormac and the animated Guy Fawkes effigy atop the corpse, they all slid down the steps together, the corpse acting as the straw man's buffer, McCormac serving as a sled of sorts. His head struck every step on the way down, so that he repeatedly saw flint sparks swimming against a veil dimming his eyes.

The threesome came to rest at the bottom of the stairway. Instantly, the living effigy was up, hefting the corpse along with it, then thrusting the body aside. Then it turned a still-stunned McCormac onto his stomach and mounted him again, digging its knee into one of the rogue sheriff's kidneys.

The thing's voice was sibilant as it demanded of McCormac: "Where issss Rebecca Ssharp? I heard you chuckling that ssshe wasss in unfriendly handsss. Who hass her? My massster will want to know thisss!"

McCormac stammered, trying to buy time: he had seen a dropped pistol laying just within his reach. He stretched his fingers toward it, ignoring the pain of the knee pressing into his back —

Down dropped the straw man's scythe, slicing off all four fingers of McCormac's outreaching hand.

McCormac howled in pain, blood spraying from his open wounds. With inhuman detachment, the familiar snatched his other hand by the wrist, splaying the fingers out flat.

"From thisss point on," it hissed, "yer wiping yer arsssse with your *left* hand. Ifff you would like to continue to enjoy that option, you will tell me what I wisssh to know NOW!"

McCormac sobbed, "I gave her to an Arab slave trader —"

The simulacrum drew back the hand that clutched its scythe. "Ssshe's to be ssold, then? Where?"

"No! She's sold already! She's on his ship. He's taking her to be a concubine to a sultan. Please! I've got to stop bleeding! I . . . I think I'm going to faint . . ."

"You'll awaken lessss four *more* fingersss if you ssswoon before you tell me what I want to know!" It lowered the scythe aside and shook McCormac by the shoulder. "What isss her dessstination?"

"D'halzabar. . . please make the bleeding stop now . . ."

And with that, Donal McCormac passed out.

Clegg's familiar ripped McCormac's shirt sleeve to make a tourniquet, applied it, then slumped the man over its shoulder and headed deeper into the grotto. There, the living effigy set McCormac to the ground for a moment to open a sealed portal. Immediately, the breeze off the sea rushed through, and the rhythmic sound of surf thrashing stone was audible.

The straw golem drug McCormac inside, closed and resealed the portal behind them, and then hefted its burden to its shoulder again.

The narrow passage stretched for a quarter of a mile, then opened up into an enormous cavern, set within one of the sea side cliffs. The ocean ran in deep, creating a natural, hidden harbor.

Even at low tide, there was always abundance of water to buoy the majestic ship for which they were headed. Its masts rose like red woods, reaching into the cathedral expanse of the cavern and still clearing its ceiling by far.

Emblazoned on the ship's side was this legend: *Imogene II*, named after the daughter born to Clegg by a Mayan princess. The ship was alive with men who were anxious that they not lose the tide, eager as they were to finally crush the slave ring of the Barbary Corsairs. Their interest was not completely altruistic, laced as it was with the venomous desire for revenge. For Clegg's ship was manned by former slaves whom he had freed from that same ring.

It was the First Mate, Hadithi, who first saw the straw man emerge from the tunnel, bearing over its shoulder the source of Hadithi's and the others' misery. Hadithi had been the esteemed storyteller of his tribe before McCormac's slavers had wiped his people from their place. At the sight of the crooked sheriff, his lips curled back, and his hand went to his sword's handle, but his fear of Clegg's familiar, the product of Mayan witchcraft, stayed Hadithi's hand. Clegg had made it clear that, for the moment, McCormac was his creature's special charge.

So Hadithi turned instead and called to the men: "Weigh anchor!"

Chapter Five: 1844 — Bane of the Barbary Corsairs! 73

Becky Sharp was no stranger to lock and key, so she regarded the manacle and chain which joined her foot to the wall of al-Hazad's cabin with a familiarity which long ago had veered into the province of contempt. Already she was at work, with a pin from her hair, on the restraint chafing her ankle.

Omar had dressed her in a brief silk loincloth that hung at knee's length, and a filmy bodice of the same material. This was further indication that he was indeed having second thoughts about handing her over to the Sultan of D'halzabar. And once he saw her in her scanty garments, he had begun again his rough lovemaking in earnest.

As she picked the lock, Becky smiled at the memory of the scratch across his face she had dealt him. He had slapped her hard in return, but it had been worth it, as she knew the conspicuous mark she left would humiliate him in his and his men's eyes, though the latter would not dare speak of it. Still, she knew she was fortunate that he had been called topside at that moment, and his violence could proceed no further.

The lock on her manacle clicked, and she released her foot. She took a robe and turban from Omar's clothing, managing to get her bounteous hair under the latter. Keeping her head low, she ventured out on board. She did not know how long she could avoid recapture on this ship, with nothing but endless sea surrounding her, but she intended to find out.

In Becky's favor, all attention was focused on the ship, the *Imogene II*, closing in on the one that bore her. Her heart leapt at the sight of the British vessel — and then it sank just as quickly, for her disguise could cause her to be mistaken as one of the Arabs. Yet she dare not shed it and reveal herself until the opportune moment.

A distant crack sounded, like the thunder of a long-frozen lake thawing, accompanied by a flash and a billowing cloud of blue smoke from the *Imogene*'s side. A high screech grew louder, and a cannon ball crashed through the Arab ship's railing, furrowing the deck and spitting splinters. Becky raised her robe to protect her face, but not before she was pricked. The ship reeled; men swarmed over the deck, grabbing at rigging, pulling oars, and though Becky was jostled about as she tried to find a place of refuge, no one had time to give her a second look. She was safe, in a fashion, under cover of battle. Now she just had to survive.

Omar's ship returned fired. Their cannon ball smashed into the upper reaches of one of the *Imogene*'s masts. But the ship, like the one Becky was on, was moving more by men at the oars than by the wind, and so the *Imogene* continued its steady gain on its prey.

But this prey had its *own* fangs, and Omar gave the command to let the *Imogene* move in closer, and then they would fire again, when they could place with greater accuracy a cannon ball directly into the galley.

When the *Imogene* neared the desired range, Omar's men fired a round of arrows — for distraction as much as to kill their nemeses. And al-Hazad himself moved to light the cannon . . .

Then a hitherto unnoticed blanket of black that lay over the *Imogene*'s deck lifted into the air, separating into individual bits of ebony in the process with a riotous sound of cawing and screeching. Airborne, they came together again and immediately descended on Omar's men in a torrent of feathers, thrashing wings and claws, darting beaks — all screeching in terrible chorus:

"CLEGG! CLEGG! CLEGG! CLEGG!"

Omar's hand never touched the flame to the cannon's fuse: he dropped back, raising both his hands to cover his face. His archers fired at the assaulting crows, and though the Arab's men were unable to aim and were practically firing blind, chance and the sheer mass of birds granted that some crows were struck. An erratic hail of small carcasses followed, here and there beating the water and decks below — dead birds then pulped underfoot into feathered jelly by sailors having no time to watch their step in the melee.

Becky, of course, was not exempt from the crows' attack, and she was compelled to seek shelter between two overturned life boats. Though she suffered pecks and scratches, she took heart at the bird's battle cry of their master's name.

Becky raised her head to see the *Imogene* coming alongside Omar's vessel. Grappling hooks were cast and the enemy ships were joined!

Then her pulse quickened as she recognized the man barking orders to the men of the *Imogene*: he was none other than Padre Perditio, but he no longer dressed as a priest. He wore a wide brimmed, feather-plumed hat, and a red military jacket tailored to fit from broad shoulder to lean waist. Tight, white breeches were stuffed into knee-high leather boots. A brace of pistols was tucked in his bright sash, and at each side hung a small scythe.

"Captain Clegg himself," Becky said softly, impressed in spite of herself with the dashing figure Perditio cut. He had told her of his past, of course, but now to see him in his proper milieu . . .

The man who once had been Captain Clegg and now was again cried out: "It's cutlasses now, me hardies!"

At his word, his men swung from their rigging onto the enemy vessel, steel clashing steel, sword against sword. Clegg himself swung over the ship's side, holding the line with one hand, firing a pistol with the other.

Chapter Five: 1844 — Bane of the Barbary Corsairs!

He tossed it aside, landed in a crouch on the deck of the slave ship, then sprang erect with a scythe in each hand. Pressing into the mob, he slung his blades left and right. Men reeled before him as he cut a bloody swathe through the tangle of their bodies.

Becky watched, her bosom swelling and falling tumultuously. He was headed her way, though there were still men between them. She might yet be struck down, mistaken as an enemy by any of Clegg's men. Neither did she dare to reveal herself as an escaped captive, for Omar's men were also about her.

Then she saw that Clegg was veering away from her in the jostling throng. Her chance might be lost forever — So she threw aside the robe and turban she had taken, and as her reddish blond hair tumbled over her shoulders, she leapt atop the upturned hull of one of the life boats between which she had taken refuge.

"PERDITIO!" she cried.

Clegg's head snapped around upon hearing his alter ego's name. All battling near-by paused at the sound of a female voice. All were startled at the sudden apparition of the near naked woman with flesh like snow ruddy with the dawn, and reddish gold hair that hung to her waist. She looked like a Nordic chooser of the slain, strayed from her native northern clime into the heat and swelter of this southern battlefield.

Further, Becky felt something radiating from her, some tingling of her skin she had experienced in the flame of Kor. No radiance was visible, but *something* was affecting the men close by. The battle about her stopped as they all gazed upon her. For a moment she hoped the power to strike them down, which Ayesha had promised her, had at last emerged. She raised her arms —

— but no lightning flew from her hands. And now she could see that the reaction among the Arabs was something quite different from that of the English men and Africans. As the initial shock of her revelation subsided, the Arabs cried out as one:

"Unclean! Unclean!" they shouted. Their public — if momentary — attraction to the epitome of all that should be hidden was abasing. Angrily, they surged forward, a riotous mob, ready to rend her.

But the Westerners and Africans among Omar's crew, as well as Clegg's men, were galvanized to protect her. The battle was rejoined, but in this part of the arena, the objective had changed.

Captain Clegg had needed no extra nudging to come to Becky's aid. In fact, he had begun pushing his way toward her while the others still stood stunned.

But someone else was quickly encroaching on Becky, and faster than Clegg: Omar bin Othman al-Hazad. Becky's emanation had reached out to him as well, vexing the scar she had put on his face until it was a searing crimson, burning fresh humiliation into his flesh.

His curved sword was drawn, and in his wrath he hacked all before him indiscriminately, his own men as well as Clegg's, so that *he* might be the one to hew Becky into chum before all and thus avenge his honor.

From her raised platform atop the overturned boat, Becky kept her eyes trained on Clegg and the succor he represented, oblivious to Omar nearing her from behind. The tangled mob thronging at her feet, including her defenders, hindered her rescue.

Eyeing those men favorably disposed toward her, she shouted out, "Get me to him!" and pointed at Clegg, who was still pressing in as well.

Her allies beckoned, holding out their hands in an offer to bear her. Becky tossed herself into their arms to be carried above the mob —

— just as Omar leaped atop the small boat on which she had stood. Angrily, he cursed, and dropping his sword, he reached out and grabbed Becky by her legs, and began pulling her back to him —

— Becky glanced over her shoulder, and cried out at the sight of who had seized her. But there was Clegg before her, just within reach. She strained forward as his hand reached out for hers, their fingertips all but brushing —

— and Becky's hand dropped, dipping into his sash, and snatching from it a yet unfired pistol —

— just as Omar succeeded in pulling her to him. He grasped her from behind with one arm while drawing a poniard sheathed at his side. Raising the hand in which he held the dagger, he roughly jostled Becky around so that he might see the terror in her eyes as he plunged his blade into her —

— and Becky turned, the pistol clinched in both hands, and fired point blank into Omar's face. The ball slammed into his cranium, penetrating his brain, and Omar bin Othman al-Hazad, he whom men had once called the Raptor of the Sea, fell dead to the deck.

Becky collapsed with him, landing on top, face to face with Omar's fixed, perplexed stare and the leaking crater in his forehead. She immediately sought to regain her standing, but discovered the corpse still held her in its death embrace. Her mouth twisting with distaste, she peeled away the dead hands.

Then a pair of knee-high leather boots were planted on the deck beside her, and the strong arm of Captain Clegg was grasping hers, pulling her to her feet.

"Are you all right, Rebecca?" he asked.

"For the moment, it appears," she said, noticing the slavers around them had lowered their weapons, at loss with the sudden death of their leader.

"Then let us extend the moment," Clegg said, grabbing up Omar's dropped sword. In a moment, he had, with both hands, heaved the heavy weapon over his head and brought it down across the dead Arab's throat.

Clegg looked around to see which of his own men were nearby. "Hadithi! Give me your spear! Bos'sun, Sexton — come!" Then: "Becky, stick close to me."

Holding their blades at the ready, Clegg's men made a protective circle around Becky and their captain, who speared the decapitated head and hoisted it high. His men moved with Clegg as he bore Omar's head over the press of the battle. Greeted by the gruesome sight, Omar's crew became distraught, some leaping over the side of the ship rather than face the fearsome justice of Captain Clegg.

Others tossed down their weapons immediately. Some still fought on, their arms growing weaker, their swords heavier, as their own, inevitable doom descended by degree upon them.

A few of the slavers were able to get the life boats over the side; fearing to wait to complete their lowering, they cut them loose into the brine and leapt in after them. The *Imogene*'s cannon balls shattered some of these escape craft, but, by design, Clegg allowed some to escape: a few, after all, must live to tell the tale.

Becky was escorted to the *Imogene* by Hadithi and quartered in the Captain's own cabin. On entering, her eyes immediately fixed on the straw Guy Fawkes effigy suspended on a frame in the corner. She noticed Hadithi regarded it warily, as though it were a pacing watchdog; then he exited the room. Becky walked up to the dummy, mumbling incredulously the words "Mayan sorcery *indeed*" as she reached out and tilted the figure's hat at a jaunty angle.

Then her eyes riveted on the silk sheets, plump pillows and downy mattress of Clegg's own bed. Though the man himself was absent, his presence hung over the room, and she felt again that sense of security she had, clinging to him on the horse ride back to his parish. Once again, she allowed the burden of her quest to slip from her shoulders, and pulling back the covers, she settled into the bed and slept comfortably and in a civilized manner for the first time in months.

She awoke to a tickling sensation at the tip of her nose. Stubbornly, she tightened her closed eyes, swatting the air before her face. The tickling persisted. Her eyelids finally flew up, and she beheld a smiling Clegg sitting by her, the plume of his hat hovering just beyond her nose.

"Get off," she said, pushing the feather away with a playful sulk.

"Did you rest well?" Clegg asked.

Disregarding decorum, Becky yawned, and, instead of covering her mouth, stretched her hands out at arm's length before her, the yawn turning into a sensuous moan as she crooked her head to her shoulder and smiled. Then, straightening her head and dropping her hands by her sides, she said, "It was delicious."

"You might be interested in knowing that I slept on a pallet on the deck."

"How awful for you," Becky said with a grin. Then: "I am grateful. For everything."

"I could not abandon you to the fate the late Donal McCormac intended —"

"Wait!" Her hand reached out and grasped Clegg's wrist. "Donal is *dead?*"

"I killed him."

"When? How?"

Clegg arched an eyebrow. "You sound as though you have a care."

"Of course I care! I wanted to see! I hope it was slow and painful?" Her eyes shone, and she leaned in toward him eagerly.

Clegg raised her small, delicate hand to his lips and kissed it. "After we freed the slaves, McCormac and his gang were chained below deck, piled like cordwood, just as they did their pitiful victims. Once, one of his slave ships bound for the United States sank, the fleeing crew leaving the slaves chained below to drown. A couple of well-placed cannon balls into the slaver ship saw to it that McCormac and his Barbary corsairs were dealt the same fate."

"And what is to be my fate, oh Captain Clegg?" Becky said, reaching out, taking his hat and playfully putting it on her own head. She lowered the brim partially over her eyes and tilted her head up to regard him.

"Madame, I am at your service, just as I promised you: together we will find this Queequeg and his pagan fetish."

Becky locked her arms around Clegg's neck, drawing him closer to her warm body. He joined the embrace; their lips eagerly sought and found each other. A sudden caw arrested her attention, and she drew back her head, looking toward the corner where the straw man stood, a crow on its shoulder. She nodded toward it.

"So *that's* your infamous familiar," she laughed. "Why, it can't even frighten a crow!"

"Let's just say he's an old friend. Now retired. I think I owe him a long vacation at sea."

He moved to kiss her again. Becky drew close, then drew back with a startled little cry.

"What is it?" Clegg asked.

"Your straw man . . . I could swear it just moved!"

"And what did you expect? It *is* Mayan sorcery, after all, Miss Sharp, and you *are* in the lair of Captain Clegg."

Chapter Six: 1848 —
Shadows Out of Time

From Becky Sharp's Journal:
May 19, 1892

The events of over forty years ago seem as but yesterday to me, for, indeed, to my mind, they *are*. Those were the days Captain Nathaniel Clegg and I scoured the seas together, in pursuit of the elusive Queequeg. More than once we missed him by mere days. But the world is vast, and a few moments' time may be all that is needed to guarantee paths that might have crossed shall never join. After four years of fruitless pursuit, we received a lead that he was en route to the New England coast of the United States. We raced to catch him.

The way was perilous, for Mocha Dick, the great white whale, terrorized with impunity the seas through which we were compelled to pass. And, indeed, when we saw the massive shape on the horizon, looming out of the sinking sun, we were certain we were met.

Then, while still at a range distant enough that the huge, aquatic creature's features were indistinct, it dove under the water, semi-emerging about a mile and a half away, churning huge foaming waves in its wake.

Nathaniel Clegg was ever loath to flee a battle, whether man to man or 'twixt man and beast. But we had heard surviving victims speak of Mocha Dick, and he knew it unlikely the *Imogene* would come out the better of such an encounter. Even in the best case, we would lose precious time and miss, once again, Queequeg and his talisman.

Escape, however, was not an option: the beast was gaining too fast. Clegg ordered the cannons turned on the quickly encroaching monster. Twin geysers shot high in the air from the back of the slick creature. Clegg's men gasped in awe and fear: it seemed Mocha Dick was so large he required *two* spouts, whose issue touched the sky in angry hot veils of steam.

Clegg commanded the men at the cannons to hold fire until his order, when he deemed the whale close enough so that chances for missing their target would be slimmer. He was certain there would be no time to fire a second volley.

The stars were appearing in the darkening sky above us, and the failing light revealed Mocha Dick now only a half-mile away. Then, just as the men moved to ignite their powder, a flash of blue-white light as bright as midday issued from

Mocha Dick.

We were all blinded, and the cries of the terrified men chilled me, for they were hardened by life at sea and would take the *Imogene* through a squall as though it were just all in the course of a day. But here was a terror that had penetrated their world from one beyond all the natural laws that they understood.

After a long moment, we were able to squint and peer into the unabated diamond light, and gradually we became accustomed to the glow which continued to engulf our ship. More than one fire had begun when some of the men at the cannons had dropped the flame they carried. Fortunately, these flames were easily put out, and the creature, which had stopped a quarter of a mile away, no longer seemed intent on attack.

I heard Clegg swear out loud only twice in our time together, for he was never completely shed of Padre Perditio. This was the second. He had snatched up his spy glass and was looking at the thing that hovered in churning water just beyond us.

"What?" I demanded. "What do you see?"

He shook his head in disbelief and handed the glass to me. "An . . . Indian," he answered. Eagerly, I plugged it to my eye, and I gasped at what I saw:

This was no living creature which had pursued us! This was a large, metal plated vessel of some sort, and standing out of an open hatch at its top, a swarthy, turbaned man in eastern robes waved a white flag!

In the other hand, he held a megaphone to his mouth. He shouted out through it, "CAPTAIN CLEGG, WE COME IN PEACE!"

I fired a quizzical glance Nathaniel's way. "Friend of yours?" I asked as he snatched the spy glass from my hand and raised it again to his eye.

"LOWER A BOAT AND COME OUT TO ME! AND BRING MISS SHARP! SHE HAS AN OLD FRIEND ABOARD MY VESSEL!"

Clegg immediately lowered the spy glass and looked at me. "On the contrary, it is you he seems to know. Any former lovers in the Punjab? Calcutta, perhaps? Now would be a good time to let me know . . ."

"You buried my last connection with India yourself, four years ago."

"And Donal McCormac has been picked to the bones by fish and tide by now."

Then, the Indian with the megaphone spoke again: "I AM NO ONE THAT YOU SHOULD FEAR. DO YOU RECEIVE MY MEANING, CAPTAIN? I AM *NO ONE!*"

Clegg's jaw went slack; he immediately raised the glass and again peered through it at the strange man. "It can't be!" he exclaimed. "He . . . he was *Polish!*"

Clegg suddenly lowered the telescope and smiled. "Of course! Becky, do you remember my friend — the human friend — I told you I had in the distant past, when the Yithians held my consciousness hostage? *That* is he!"

Suddenly, I shared his epiphany. "Then, he is as you find yourself now: his consciousness has been transferred into a different body. In his case, from a Pole to an Indian."

"That must be it. And if there's a friend of *yours* aboard — I dare say he, like you, is involved with the Great Race. We have allies, Rebecca!"

The crew of the *Imogene* remained dubious of the man and his undersea vessel. It was unnatural that man should travel that way, and the first mate Hadithi was particularly adamant that we should not enter it. Reluctantly, he lowered over the ship's side the boat bearing Clegg and myself.

As we rowed closer and closer, I was able to discern more of the undersea vessel. I could see it reached a good six yards before the open hatch, and extended immeasurably behind it. I could even see, in the bright, icy light the vessel cast over the water, the individual rivets which held its metal-plated hull together.

Soon the front of our boat was bumping against the undersea vehicle's bow. As we came alongside, two other Indians emerged from the hatch, and we observed that they moved over something of a metal walkway that extended from the hatch and over the exterior of the vessel.

One of the men helped me from the boat, though in the breeches and boots which were now my regular attire, I was as sure-footed as any man. His fellow took the rope from Clegg and secured our boat to the bow.

"Welcome, Miss Sharp," the Indian captain of the strange vessel greeted me, bowing. Clegg, however, he embraced heartily. Clegg returned the hug warmly as it was given.

"Nemo, my friend," Clegg said. " 'No one' indeed — no one better, I always said."

"It is Prince Dakkar now, Nathaniel. At least, that is the name of the man whose body I now inhabit. I know you as well find yourself in a body which is not your natural one."

"My consciousness was transferred to a host in the future," Clegg said. "Yours, it seems, was moved into what would be the recent past for you, correct?"

"All will be explained forthwith, I promise," Dakkar said, "but let us depart from this night wind and cold sea spray. Below, all is warm and ready to receive you."

We followed him down a ladder by which the hatch was accessed. We passed into the belly of the vessel, which Dakkar had named *Nautilus II*. He told us he had lost — here he caught himself and smiled — *would* lose his first submarine (as he described the vessel) twenty years in the future to this very day.

I would have thought such talk cracked at one time, but I had come to accept without question what the Yithians were capable of in the realm of Physics. If only I had reminded myself of what they were capable of in dealing with human lives — my own included — I should have never stepped aboard the *Nautilus* that fateful evening. Nor would I have allowed Nathaniel to.

We stepped out of the wide passageway into an opulent dining room. At one end of a long, glossy table gleaming amber under an electric chandelier, sat my old friend, the Magus. He had traded his ridiculous powdered wig for an equally ridiculous sea captain's hat, askew on his head as his wig had been.

I looked about the walls: they, indeed, were draped in the mercurial salt treated fabric which had lined the Magus' cell in Bath. Here, we were safe from any monitoring by those Yithian authorities he and his co-horts wished to avoid.

"Ah, Miss Sharp," the Magus' eyes lit at the sight of me as he rose from the table in greeting. "Welcome, my dear. And Captain Clegg. You and I have business to which we must attend, sir."

"And what business would that be?" Clegg asked, as I sat and the others followed.

"Quarantine."

Clegg's eyes narrowed. "Sir, we cannot afford to be detained, not now of all times! Not when we are so close to —"

"Indeed, Captain Clegg, *we* shall not be detained. *You* shall be. Miss Sharp shall continue on. Without you."

Fire flew in Clegg's eyes, and he was halfway risen from his chair before I could place a firm, restraining hand on his arm. "Don't be foolish, Nathaniel," I cautioned him.

He shrugged me off, but returned to his seat. "What need do I have to be quarantined? You creatures cured me of the cholera that all but killed this body long ago. I am fit, and ready to fight, and have promised Becky Sharp my aid. I do not break my word without cause."

The Magus regarded him coolly. "Nathaniel Clegg, it is not some biological contagion that demands your removal. You, sir, remain a temporal anomaly. Your continuance in this time stream is weakening the walls between parallel realities which simultaneously exist —"

"Yes!" Clegg snapped. "Becky filled me in years ago! Because of what you've done to me, all probabilities stand to collapse into one doom when this Tulu creature emerges in the next century. Believe me, I considered suicide when I heard —"

"It is well that you did not harm yourself; you have been of much assistance to Miss Sharp. That is why we have run the risk of your discovery by Yithian authorities this long. But we are now fastly approaching a point in space-time at which you *must* be slipped completely out of the temporal continuum."

"'Slipped'?" I asked. "Don't you mean 'smuggled' to cover the evidence of your colossal cosmic blunder? I'd wager you've arranged that the collective backs of the Yithian authorities will be turned at this moment of 'space-time.' Am I correct?"

The Magus leaned forward in his chair. "You are indeed, Miss Sharp. And do I hear in your voice a note of recrimination? Be glad for the latitude we've allowed Captain Clegg up till now. It was not by accident that we located 'Padre Perditio' where he could assist you."

"Pure altruism, was it then? I think not!" I retorted. "You were covering up the death of Nathaniel's proper body by slipping his consciousness into another one across time!"

The Magus sat back and templed his fingers. "All according to plan. We reasoned the past history you both shared with our race, once discovered, would strengthen the bond between you two, as it obviously has. Look at you, Miss Sharp: you're ready to go to war for him, aren't you?"

I admit I colored at that, and my tongue seemed to shrivel in my mouth. A vulnerability exposed. This, I did not like, and I was immediately cross with Nathaniel Clegg for being the cause.

"Silent now, are you?" the Magus asked, lowering his hands to his lap. "Please remain so, and I will be happy to explain all. As I told you when we met, Becky Sharp, those humans with your unique brain chemistry tend to be few and far between in earth's history. So, we have to manipulate the others, as we have Clegg here, whom we would have do our bidding."

"You sound as though my death was planned," Clegg said. "You know well that it was *not*. You were scurrying to cover your scaly arse when you shuffled me through time; *that's* what it was all about."

"And we took advantage of our error so that you might serve us elsewhere. And not just in the aid of Miss Sharp. You see, Donal McCormac was never intended to come to the Barbary Coast and begin his slave trade."

"Not 'intended'?" Clegg asked, incredulous. "What? Was McCormac another of your mistakes? How many of us are there?"

"Well, since you've asked," the Magus said, "your friend Nemo over there, for one. As with you, his brain could not take the strain of Yithian possession, and it was under this resulting mental collapse that the possessed Nemo sent the first *Nautilus* to the bottom of the sea in a maelstrom he was *supposed* to survive. Again, as with yourself, this left Nemo's own consciousness stranded in the past, compelling us to find a new home for it."

"And Donal McCormac?" Clegg asked.

"McCormac was not ours. To the contrary, he was to die at the hands of another of our agents in India, so as not to hinder Miss Sharp's progress, for we had foreseen her path was going to cross his, and he would not be favorably disposed toward his old partner in crime. Unfortunately, our man was sloppy, and he became McCormac's victim instead. So we needed you to clean up the slave trade our error allowed him to perpetrate. Which you did admirably, 'Padre Perditio.'"

I found my voice then. "Exactly how many holes do you have in this dike?" I asked. "Even the little Dutch boy did not create more holes by seeking to plug the one!"

"And we have far more than ten fingers at our disposal, Miss Sharp, and our reach is exceedingly further than a mere child's arm span," the Magus answered sternly.

Clegg looked at his old friend. "Nemo . . . I take it you are to be quarantined with me, since you were placed into the body of this Indian prince Dakkar, who, I assume, at the time, must have been as near a corpse as the body I now inhabit was."

"Not at all," the Magus spoke up. "Your Polish friend's consciousness was 'put to sleep' and placed in the mind of a fully functioning Dakkar. But both wills were strong, and it resulted in a split personality, one not knowing of the other's existence. Under the Nemo persona, he created a new *Nautilus*, which we are aboard now. It would serve our purposes, so we allowed it."

"But wait," Clegg injected. "Nemo, your primary self, the one the Great Race robbed you of, exists concurrently with your Dakkar incarnation. Magus, wouldn't the authorities you wish to avoid notice such a paradox?"

"They *would*," the Magus answered, "but Nemo's consciousness comes from a reality parallel to this one; it is there that the events of his life are actualized. In *this* reality, that of Prince Dakkar, Captain Nemo exists *only* as a character in the novel *Twenty-Thousand Leagues Under the Sea*, which will be published in 1863."

"You moved me through time," Clegg said. "But you shifted Nemo from one entire *reality* to another. Such an action must have created more of a stress to the fabric of the multiverse than your dealings with me have caused."

"Indeed."

"So my existence alone is not all there is to the weakening of the temporal walls that will enable Tulu's bid for absolute dominion," Clegg said, a look of relief passing over his features.

"As I said, it would have been a mistake for you to kill yourself. Now, we have prepared for you a haven —"

"You mean 'prison'!" I interrupted.

"— a place cordoned off from all temporal cause and effect: an uncharted island around which we have warped time and space. As you have guessed, Clegg, you will not be alone . . . not forever, at any rate. You and Nemo will be comrades again, but first, as Prince Dakkar, he has to play a part in the Sepoy Mutiny nine years hence."

"You mean, Nathaniel will be in solitary confinement for nearly a *decade*? Intolerable!" I said, rising from my chair. "I will not allow —"

"Becky Sharp, it is done already."

"Oh? It is not as though I have no card to play."

The Magus smiled. "And what exactly would you accomplish, should you cease to be our agent? Suppose you forsake your mission and take Clegg from us now. You could have a life with him, but, eventually, he will die, while you will live on, only to suffer the dominion of Tulu. Then, too late, the full weight of your sacrifice will come crashing down upon you. You are a survivor, Becky Sharp. First and foremost. Has that changed? I think not."

I was dumb struck. Not that he expressed knowledge of the threat of Tulu or my life's extended longevity — I realized long ago that had been the Great Race's design in sending me to Ayesha's domain in the first place. No, I could not speak because I could not deny what he had said — yet I wanted to. It was absurd! Had I not admitted to Nathaniel when we first met that I would kill him if it would spare myself?

But in the four years since, I had grown accustomed to playing the part of his lover; it was a part of which I had allowed myself to become fond. Too fond, it seemed, for it stung that the Yithian could dismiss our relationship so easily. I hated the Magus then; I wished to forcibly wipe that triumphant grin from his face.

And then Nathaniel Clegg arose, rescuing me from my embarrassment.

"Am I to understand by my continuing on with Rebecca, I would compromise the invisibility that is necessary for her to complete her task?" he asked.

"Indeed. And she has much service yet ahead. Though if she gets herself into more trouble, we will not be moving you — or anyone else — across time to aid her. From this point on, she must be truly, completely on her own."

"How will she get to America? Aboard the *Nautilus*?"

"No. Rather, aboard your ship, Captain. A trip aboard the *Nautilus* would be quicker, but that way lies a . . . vortex of power, capable of bending time and space. This is not of our doing, nor that of the cult of Tulu. Indeed when Tulu — and we of Yith — came to this planet, this vortex was here already. We have never understood it, other than it isn't natural, but if whoever is behind it is aware of us, they seem indifferent to our machinations.

"Still, we cannot be certain. Since it is doubtful we could mask the temporal anomalies surrounding Clegg and Nemo from these others who warp time, we find it prudent not to risk revealing ourselves by venturing near them.

"Beware, Becky Sharp, for indifference may throw off our plans just as effectively as active opposition. You must not enter the United States' mainland via the Hudson River. Be certain, Captain, that your men understand that."

"I will be able to speak with them, then? Before –"

"You must make them understand that the completion of the delivery of Miss Sharp to the New England states is a sacred trust which they must not break. As long as *you* understand you must not break faith with me that you will return to the *Nautilus* immediately thereafter."

"Of course," Clegg said, his face grave. "You forget my propensity for self-sacrifice. Did I not say I would have ended my life years ago when I believed my continued existence alone was responsible for the doom of all?"

"Yes. But in the interim you have developed an attachment you did not have then."

Clegg looked at me. "Magus, you have made it clear that my continuance on this adventure could sabotage Becky's mission. I will not be responsible for that."

The Magus slapped his palms together and smiled, apparently satisfied. "Very well, then. Go back to your ship. Issue your new orders to your crew. Say your good-byes. We wish to be on our way by dawn."

Our trip back to the *Imogene* was a silent one. For my part, not acknowledging vocally the imminent separation was a comforting form of denial. I hoped that Nathaniel had a plan, that this was all a ruse, that he would order his cannons turned on the *Nautilus* . . .

But I knew it was true, all that he had said. In four years, he had never given me reason to doubt his devotion to my cause. Clegg truly had been useful to me. And now that that usefulness was done, that he had, in fact, become a liability, was it not in my best interests that he be eliminated? Had he not said as much himself?

Upon our return to the ship, he roused his crew and announced that he would be joining his friend on the *Nautilus*. He then appointed Hadithi as his successor as the captain of the *Imogene*. It was his will that Captain Hadithi and the crew bear me to my destination, even though his path must diverge from ours here.

But his men were having none of it. Expectantly, they looked at me, of all people, for the truth, for they knew he would die before he allowed himself to be separated from me.

"Your captain is sparing you a confrontation you cannot win," I suddenly announced.

"Rebecca! Don't —" he injected.

"He is going into captivity!" I shouted above him. "The very thing he saved all of you from!"

That provoked an angry roar from the crew, and they were already turning the *Imogene*'s cannons on the *Nautilus* in their captain's defense before Clegg could calm them. He explained that this confinement was in accordance with his own will, that he had become a danger to me, whose friendship they knew he valued over all others. He assured them this voyage on the *Nautilus* promised to correct all that.

Why he had no time to make them understand his circumstances, his crew knew that Clegg had ever been truthful with them, and thus did not doubt that this danger was real. Further, he left the impression that he would return some day, and I hope he was forgiven this one lie, for he told it to spare them . . . and me.

Then we retreated to our cabin, where he collected some of the books he loved. I stood apart, unable to assist him in this task. Finally, I spoke:

"What the Magus said back there, in the *Nautilus*' stateroom, that my own survival was my first interest —"

"— was the truth," Clegg quickly interrupted me, looking up from a bundle he had put together. Never before, in all the years we had shared it, had that chamber seemed so large, the space between us so great.

"You see," he continued, "at the very beginning of our time together, after your initial attempted ruse, you told me plainly that you would kill me if it would spare yourself. And as you have always been truthful with me, Rebecca, I have never expected any more from you."

Nor should he have. The man was no fool; that was why I respected him. And yet his words struck a softness in me I had not expected to find. As much for my benefit as his, I paused to explore it.

"Did I not announce to your men what was going to happen to you? So that they could stop your being taken?"

He looked at me, his expression a wounded one at my attempted defense.

"You speak as though you truly expected your actions to change the situation. You knew that I was already committed to go with the Yithian, for reasons I made clear back on the *Nautilus*. Your attempt to rally my crew to my aid was merely an empty gesture, to draw their admiration and thus continue the illusion that you have ever been on anyone's side but your own. Please, Becky, we have always had so much respect for each other; don't lie now, at the end."

An empty gesture, an illusion — is that all our time together had been?

No.

I realized it. No.

I sat down, stunned. Yet, what would it profit either of us were I to succeed in assuring him now that my regard for him was no lie? It would only exacerbate the solitude he must now endure. A fight with the *Nautilus* was indeed one the *Imogene* would lose. I had been foolish to attempt to rally his men to his salvation. As the Magus had said, "It is done already."

So, I did not speak; he placed a hand on my shoulder in passing, and then

Nathaniel Clegg was gone from my life.

I sat in silence, dry-eyed, for a long time, thinking. Finally, there was a knock on the door. I bid the person enter. It was Hadithi.

"They have departed, then?" I asked without looking up.

"Yes."

"Then, you are captain now."

"Only in his absence, miss. You will keep the cabin, of course. Keep it ready for his return."

"Yes," I said. "I shall." Then I rose to my feet. "Hadithi, I think I know a way to get him back. But it is ultimately up to you."

He stepped toward me, eagerness in eyes yellowed by a long-ago battle with jaundice. "Of course, Miss! Are we to pursue, then? We'll go at once —"

I raised my hand to silence him. "No, no. We cannot resist the power of those who have taken Nathaniel. Not alone and unaided, at least. Clegg told you not to enter the United States by way of the Hudson River, didn't he?"

"Yes'm."

"He was relaying the orders that were given to him by the Yithians."

"The *who?*"

"The ones who have taken him. There is something up the Hudson that they are wary of. A source of the kind of power we'll need to rescue Nathaniel, I'd wager. So, we will continue to the United States' coast, but then it is up the Hudson!"

"But Queequeg . . . the fetish . . . the fate of the world, Miss! What of all that?"

"We'll see to it in due course. Whatever is up the Hudson may help with that as well. But first we'll look to your captain's welfare, I swear!"

Smiling, Hadithi hurried out of the cabin. There was no more that I could do for now, and though it was morning, I had not slept all night. I crossed over to the bed.

"I will show you," I murmured into Clegg's pillow as I fell asleep, "I will show you, that you were wrong about me . . ."

Our journey to the New England coast was without further incident. Mocha Dick, it turned out, was of no consequence. Apparently, he sported in other waters while we made our way through the olive-green Atlantic. Whatever reason we were spared further complication, I was thankful. The winds were good, and the men bent to the galley's oars with a single-minded purpose: to secure the key of freedom for the man who had freed them all.

When the rocky coast of the Northeastern United States became visible, the oar men's efforts doubled. They worked in unceasing shifts, and before long we were in brackish waters, which meant fresh river water was mingling with the salt of the ocean.

Not long afterward, we entered the mouth of the Hudson. The *Imogene* drew much interest from those manning the vessels among which it now cruised, as well as those people along the shore. Quaint Dutch cottages were mirrored on the river. Men, horses, and carriages traveled along crooked cobblestone streets sprawling up from the piers and quays into the hills where more cottages could be glimpsed.

We passed by other towns and settlements, though we took no time to satisfy the curiosity of those whose skiffs and barges drew near and slid alongside us for a pace. Indeed, a vessel manned by a predominantly black crew, apparently under their own command, was a novelty even in the northern states.

Add to that, these were *flamboyant* black men with colorful plumes sprouting from their hats, gaudy baubles hanging from their ears and noses, and shirts and breeches of clashing hues. With my baggy clothing and my hair pulled up under my hat, I was taken for a white man, all according to design: were a lone white woman to be spotted among so much dusky skin, we would invite investigation, even in this abolitionist state. And we could brook no delays.

Finally, we left the villages and settlements behind, observing only an occasional, solitary, buckskin-clad trapper along the shore. Once we found ourselves amidst a small sporting fleet of canoes, propelled by red men who incessantly alternated their oars from side to side, skimming from the water's surface the wet leaves which clung limply to the wide blades of their paddles. We had arrived among the Kaatskill Mountains in the fall, the trees conflagrant over the Hudson River a luster with autumnal hues.

These American Indians found Clegg's pirate crew as colorful a novelty as we did them. Where the river diverged, they propelled their canoes around a bend, headed with their catch for dark huts we could see in the distance, smoke rising into the chilled air. We took the other watery path. One Indian in the rear of their party laid his oar across his canoe, turned, and beckoned emphatically to us, seeming to indicate that we should go that way no further.

Then thunder cracked in the blue, cloudless sky, emanating from the direction in which the *Imogene* was winding. Thunder fallen from a clear sky? Hadithi and I looked at each other.

"The power source," I said, and he nodded in mute agreement. "And I'd wager that gesticulating red man there is aware of something unnatural in that direction of which he wishes to warn us, though his primitive mind can't grasp exactly *what*. I only hope *I* can. Enough, at least, to save Nathaniel."

When the native saw we were intent on maintaining our course, or just did not understand, he turned back to paddling and hastened after the others of his fishing party from whom he had drifted apart.

We sailed on.

From that point, our voyage was punctuated periodically by further bursts of thunder in the clear sky. It became evident the noise emanated from a still distant range of the mountains which seemed to shift in size and color even as you gazed upon them. We would have to quit the *Imogene* and travel on foot to reach our destination. So Hadithi and I and a handful of volunteers rowed ashore and began the long trek over ground.

After three days ascent, we suddenly found our compass' needle spinning crazily. Should we continue onward, we might become hopelessly lost, unable to return to our ship. My hope was that this vortex we sought was under the control of beings who may help us find our way back, whether they agreed to use their power to succor Nathaniel or no. There were no guarantees, of course, and becoming lost and starving to death were definite possibilities.

After the ordeal of the hike, the men's enthusiasm was waning. Clearly, they wanted to turn back. Even the faithful Hadithi seemed to waver —

— and then the little man appeared in the woods, far away enough that, admittedly, his exact features were indistinct. But I perceived a stout, dwarfish fellow with a bushy red beard and a bulbous nose, dressed in earth colors.

"Do you see him?" I asked Hadithi.

"Sure do, Ma'am."

"I think we should approach him."

"He'd be filling, that's for certain."

I laughed. "Not quite ready to turn to cannibalism yet," I said. "Besides, there's not much to him."

Hadithi continued to gaze in the hairy dwarf's direction. "'Not much to him?' Miss Sharp, that's the *biggest* hare I ever seen!"

"That's not a rabbit, you booby!" I chuckled. "It's a man. He's rather hirsute, I admit, but I'd think a bear cub would be a more apt comparison."

"No ma'am," Hadithi insisted. "That's a rabbit. A big Jack!"

He'd half-way raised his pistol to take aim when I caught his forearm and lowered it again. "Don't shoot, you fool!"

At that moment, the dwarf put his hand to his mouth and hallooed, "Becky Sharp! Becky Sharp!"

"Did you hear that?" I asked. The other men had noticed too, and shifted their weight about uncertainly, looking at me expectantly. I, of course, was as taken aback as any of them. Could it be that the beings connected to this vortex were — the Magus' belief otherwise — already familiar with the Great Race? Did they know of my mission? And if so, did they intend to aid or oppose me?

I put my hand to my mouth to call back, and this time it was Hadithi's turn to take my arm and lower it to my side. "Don't do it, ma'am," he cautioned. "It's a trick."

"And how on earth can you know that?" I asked.

"I knew there was something prodigious about that hare; I just didn't know *what*. We'd best just pay him no mind; let him go on along. Nothing good could come from truck with such as that!"

"That is *not* a rabbit!" I protested. "It's a man and he knows who I am! I'm going to him —"

"No, miss —"

"I have a knife. You can hang back with the men. Just keep your powder dry and watch for my signal."

I headed for the dwarf, both hands in plain sight, one hovering near my sheathed weapon. The little man beckoned, then turned and scurried into the undergrowth and out of sight.

"Wait!" I shouted out. "Where are you going?"

I could see the tall grass move, marking his course. "I do not understand! You called me; I came!" I shouted. "Why are you running?"

And then my decision was made: I would pursue.

"Don't do it, Miss Sharp!" I heard Hadithi shout behind me. "That rabbit'll lickety-split into a briar patch where you won't be able to follow, once he gets you lost!"

"It's *not* a rabbit!" I yelled as I gave chase. Soon I could no longer hear Hadithi, and I had also lost sight of the hairy dwarf.

I stopped, spun around, and shouted, hoping my men would hear me as well as my quarry. "Why did you run from me? You called my name!" I said. "Why did you do that, if you did not wish to *parlez* with me?"

And then a disembodied voice, as though the trees and rocks were speaking:

"The story-teller was going to throw metal at me. I called to you so that you would stop him."

"How did you know my name?"

"What is important is that you do not know mine."

I paused. "Will you not show yourself? You know I do not mean you any harm; I could have allowed my man to shoot you anyway."

"No," the voice answered. "You would not. You want something."

"Yes," I said, "I need your help. You have power over time, do you not? I need to partake of that power."

An eerie, disembodied tittering from all about me was the only response.

"WILL YOU DO AS I ASK?" I shouted, my poise shattered at last.

"I will give you power over time," the voice answered but volunteered no elaboration.

"Well?" I asked into the deepening silence.

And then the thunder sounded again. Not distant this time, but all around me. I felt the vibrations up through the ground.

I followed the thunder.

Followed it to a deep ravine made by a long-dry riverbed, from which the noise emanated up toward me. I hesitated, thinking that perhaps I should call for Hadithi and the others, or go back and find them before moving forward alone.

But the little man seemed wary of Hadithi and his ability to "throw metal." Reluctant to help me as he was already, reintroducing the *Imogene*'s new captain into the scenario might frighten the dwarf away. Calling for him — and the others — then, was clearly not an option.

Further, if the men now sought me, they were doing so without a working compass, and were just as likely as not to have already wandered away in the wrong direction. It was doubtful they remained in ear shot by now.

Thus, I determined to go on alone. I began working my way down the bank of the dried river ravine, trying to keep my footing, but quickly losing it, and sliding the rest of the way.

The heels of my hands were slightly scraped. Otherwise, I had only received a good dusting. Brushing myself off, I followed the dry riverbed; as it took a turn, I could see that I was coming to where, apparently, the water long ago had tumbled over a rising, rocky precipice.

Where the riverbed widened at the base of the now dead waterfall, it formed a natural amphitheater. And then something totally unexpected met my gaze. I paused, squinted, uncertain of what I was seeing:

There was a small group of squat, stocky men, dressed like the dwarf who had led me here. Though these sported Flemish style hats, I could see shaggy hair at the backs of their heads, but none matched the color of his red beard. Any further attempt at identification was impossible with their backs turned toward me, engaged, as they were, in playing at ninepins!

To my astonishment, each time a ball struck the pins, the sound of thunder reverberated down the ravine, taunting the dry riverbed with a promise it had no intention of fulfilling. There were several large, wooden barrels between the men and me.

"Hello?" I raised my voice in vain to speak over the racket they made, for hardly had the cacophony of one blow to the ninepins completely subsided, than the pins were rearranged already, and another strike was in progress.

I strode forward, intent on making my presence known, when suddenly a small, stubby fingered hand clasped my wrist from behind. I turned to find the red bearded dwarf I had followed cackling at me. He pointed toward those playing ninepins and shook his head slowly, but emphatically, from side to side so that I would understand that I should *not* interrupt their play.

Then he walked to one of the barrels; I saw a valve was tapped into its side. He turned it and filled a cup that he had produced apparently from nowhere. This he handed to me, indicating that I should drink.

"I need access to your vortex. I need to know how to use it," I said loudly, trying to be heard over the ninepin thunder. I made no move to take the cup.

He smiled toothily up at me, but did not answer. Had he even understood me?

"Power over time," I shouted.

Still grinning, he nodded his head in agreement and held the cup up to me again.

Wishing to be diplomatic, I took it this time and drank. What I had intended to be a gesture of civility was quickly superseded by my unexpected discovery of a genuine taste for this drink. Wild and robust it was, and like nothing I had drunk before. I was compelled to throw my head back and down all at once the complete draught. After living four years among pirates, I had fallen out of ladylike manners and taken on their habits as though a swaggering Jack myself.

Wiping my mouth with the back of one hand, I returned the cup to the dwarf. Grinning, he indicated by nod and gesture that I could have another draught if I should like. I nodded in agreement —

— then suddenly my skull seemed to swell to the size of a cathedral's dome and my mind — myself — dwindled to miniscule size inside the expanse of my own head. I staggered and fell. My eyelids felt weighted, and when I finally managed to pry them open again, I saw the dwarves were still bowling. And still it thundered, so I tried to cry out over it to alert them to my distress, but my speech was slurred.

One of the dwarves actually turned from the game and saw me, I suppose, for the first time. His face registered neither urgency nor novelty. In fact, his expression was entirely unmoved, as unmoved as the face of the rocky precipice behind him, against which he set his ninepins. He turned back to his game. The last thing I saw, though it may have been but a drunken fancy, was a prodigiously large red hare with a cup of the brew in his paw. He toasted me.

I awoke with the foul taste of a long sleep in my mouth — sleep and the loathsome coating that elfin broth left on my tongue. There were no stocky little men, no ninepins, no thunder, no barrels, no . . . rabbit. I was in full possession of my faculties, and seemed none the worse for the wear from the beverage's effects —

— oh, how I would that it were so!

There was no sign of Hadithi or the *Imogene*'s crew. Knowing I could not rely on their succor, I decided to follow the river bed in the direction whence I had come. As I walked, I ate some dried jerky from my belt's pouch to refresh myself.

Then, casting my glance upward, I noticed something that made me stop in my tracks:

The leaves of the trees, which had been vivid gold, rosette, and orange the day before were now all green!

An incredible panic took me, and I ran down the riverbed, only sliding to a stop when I reached the spot where I had come down the embankment. It was now grown over with vines. As I used them to pull myself up the side, I determined to try for the direction of the ship; there was a chance, wasn't there, that I may find it? Certainly, Hadithi and the others could not have given up on me. Not yet!

Reaching the top of the embankment, I then ran like a mad woman through the woods, resilient branches lashing my face. I ran through a swarm of gnats and my eyes stung with the mites, but I did not pause to wipe them away. I tripped once over a log, flying forward by my momentum over the forest floor. I rose, ran, all the while shouting at the top of my lungs for Hadithi and the others — collapsing at last into a heap at the base of a group of birches.

I convulsed, sobbing, tears stinging my bleeding face. It was that cursed brew! The dwarves had drugged me, and I had effectively hibernated through the fall and winter, like a bear in its den. Yet, I had lain exposed to the elements. I should have been covered under snow for months. And I had gone into my long sleep with less than an inch of fat on my body. What had I fed off all that time?

Suddenly, a robin on a branch of the elm broke into song, and I began to laugh as uncontrollably as I had sobbed. Those dwarves, they had used their mastery over space and time to remove me from their effects. Just as I had asked, I was given "power over time." No doubt that devil's draught had enabled my body to survive.

But I had been brought no closer to Nathaniel.

He was gone. As beyond my reach as he had ever been. And now the *Imogene* was no doubt gone as well. They would not have endangered the ship and crew by spending the winter here. I was, for the first time in many years, completely on my own. Melancholy weighed heavily upon me. And this time I shed tears instead of sobbing them. Tears for departed comrades, for friends … and one who might have been more.

But that opportunity, it would appear, was now long passed.

Irrevocably passed.

This bitterness now, I reminded myself, was the result of relying on others. It was a lesson I thought I had learned well long before. But I had been a fool. Well, never again.

I spent a long time under those elms, laying my recent history to rest, making peace with myself. Soon the sun was high above. And I rose, speaking as a mantra a line of poetry by Milton, one of the few beautiful things from my time at the boarding school: "Tomorrow to fresh woods and pastures new."

How "fresh the woods" were, I had not a clue. I arrived, after a day's journey, in a small village, where I learned the year was now 1892 and the date the 19th of May! Seeing my shock, the villagers were most kind to me, providing food, a bath, fresh clothing and shelter in an inn. It seems these people are well aware that strange powers lurk in the Kaatskills, and apparently have done so since the mountains' formation. "Manitou" the red men call it, a trickster spirit. Hadithi was right about that rabbit. I should have listened to him. Or the Magus. As it was, I had not helped Nathaniel and lost time precious to all.

Queequeg — is he still alive? Of course, it is only his icon that I need. Tomorrow I take whatever road will carry me the quickest to the New England port cities. I am over forty years late, but I am not likely to find a fresher lead between here and there.

Chapter Seven: 1893 —
Queequeg's Fetish

The thin, tall man stopped outside the two-story house on the *Rue Etoile de Mer*. He checked the pistol concealed in the inside pocket of his bright green and yellow checkered waistcoat, then drew his black frock about him against the early evening chill of Paris in late winter. Ivy green gloved hands clasped his cane which he partially separated to reveal an inch or so of the gleaming sword blade inside its casing. Satisfied he could open it smoothly and quickly, he snapped the pieces back into one whole.

Then he mounted the steps, grasped the door knocker and rapped a quick, metallic staccato.

"Enter. The door is unlocked." A woman's voice summoned him inside. As he turned the knob, pushed the door inward, and entered, he thought of the card left at his club, addressed to Sir Rafe Congleton. It stated the writer knew his secret, and wished to negotiate for something in his possession. The handwriting was a woman's. But was it the woman the card claimed her to be?

He had last heard her voice, briefly, as she bid him adieu from the street before his former home in London. The timbre of the voice that beckoned him now *could* be that of the person she claimed to be, a former operatic Contralto, allowing that her supple vocal chords would have grown comparatively coarse since their possessor's retirement.

"Hello?" the woman spoke again. "Please, Sir Rafe. Step inside and close the door behind you: you are letting the evening fog inside. I will be in the parlor at your immediate right. The parlor door is open. You can see me clearly and will be able to survey the room in its entirety from the hallway. I promise you, I have no desire to harm you. To the contrary, you have always had my admiration."

The tall man smiled. Thanks to her extended speech, he now had his answer as to the woman's identity — at least he knew who she was *not*.

"You are not Irene Norton, nee Adler," the tall man said as he stepped into the parlor doorway and faced the woman seated before a large fireplace. She had positioned herself so that the back lighting would obscure her face. "You never could be, of course. Irene Adler is dead."

"The same is said of you, 'Sir Rafe,'" the woman said. "Yet, here you are. Why shouldn't Irene Adler live as well?"

"Perhaps she does. But you are not she. I'm afraid your speech betrays you, young lady. Irene Adler was a Yankee, born and bred, while your *sotto voce* reveals someone whose formative years were spent in the environs of Soho."

Abandoning the American voice with a silver tinkle of laughter, the woman said, "Perhaps 'Sir Rafe' would prefer my French accent? *Je parle très joliment maintenant, non?*"

"Much improved. Near perfect Parisian, as a matter of fact."

"My mother was French."

"*Très bien.* But you did not summon me here because you craved an audience before whom to perform your linguistic gymnastics, did you, young lady? I am much more interested in testing your other areas of expertise. In particular, what do you know about me?"

"I know you are *Monsieur Le Grand Détective* who took an allegedly fatal plunge a few years ago. But, as you know, there are those who know better — among them, the surviving members of the Moriarty gang."

At this the tall man quickly reached inside his waistcoat and drew forth the pistol at the ready.

"*Non, non, Monsieur Le Grand Détective,*" the woman said. "I have no intention of betraying you to them. We are alone here. I courted the secret from an old enemy of yours — I think you know whom I mean. The old goat was eager to get at my firm, soft bosom, and would have told me anything for the paradise I appeared to offer. But I have since cut ties; neither he nor his men have trailed me here. No, I merely wish to propose an exchange between you and me."

"Am I to assume your bosom for my —?"

Again, the laughter. "Really, detective — I understand that Irene Adler is the only woman for you — were *any* woman to obtain your heart. I have information about her I'm certain is missing from your own files."

"Pray tell: what is this that you have learned, Miss —?"

"Rebecca Sharp. Please, step inside and I will tell you. Have a seat here by me, by the fire."

"I would prefer to remain standing."

"Very well. I dare say you will seek a chair on your own volition when you hear what I have to say about the one who got away. It seems 'escape' was her *modus operandi.*"

"I know of her checkered past . . ."

"I mean *before* she was an adventuress, long before her scandals began."

"She was born in New Jersey in 1858 —"

"Wrong on both counts, *Monsieur Le Grand Détective*. The woman you knew was born in the Confederate states over ten years earlier. She was not 30 when you met her, but a well-preserved 40."

"Bosh! There was no trace of a southern accent in Irene Adler's voice!"

"As there was British in my American accent? Ah, but you would agree that Irene Adler was a much more accomplished chameleon than I, would you not? You just did not consider that her 'true' identity was yet another mask."

The man calling himself Sir Rafe Congleton colored. He cleared his throat. "Of course, such is not without precedent. Irene Adler has outwitted me before."

"*Monsieur Le Grand Détective* would care to hear more, then?"

"Please."

""Very well: to escape her milquetoast husband, she faked her own death — in childbirth, no less — and relocated to New Jersey with the aid of a loyal friend, a former Union-blockade runner. Though her actions would be scandalous if exposed, she, apparently, just did not give a damn.

"She emerged after a few years of voice lessons, enabled to realize her long denied dream of becoming a diva of the opera."

"There's more?"

"Indeed. But, Sir Congleton, if you would care to read it, you must give me something *I* desire."

"Ah. *Quid pro quo.* Here, I suspect, is where matters are about to become most interesting."

"Not at all. You must simply contact your brother — yes, I previously dealt unsuccessfully with the executor of your estate."

"Contact him . . . for what purpose?"

"To deliver into my possession a paperweight I suspect sits gathering dust on your desk in your rooms on Baker Street. An African savage's idol, which you purchased from a salvage auction of wreckage which had washed ashore from the sunken whaler, the *Pequod*."

"Yes. A fetish with a most colorful history."

"'Sir Rafe'. . . you do not know the half of it!"

Indeed, *Monsieur Le Grand Détective*, with all his powers of the mind, could not begin to suspect the full history of his paperweight, but Becky knew better than to offer him a complete account. He would only conclude that she was mad, and, perhaps, after the more than half-century that the pursuit of this fetish had taken from her, she *was* a bit cracked at that!

She had arrived at long last in the port cities of New England. As she suspected,

Queequeg was long gone from there. Worse, he had left on the ill-fated *Pequod*.

In a tavern in the whaling village of Nantucket, Becky subsequently interviewed the sole survivor of the sunken ship. The survivor — call him Ishmael — confirmed what she dreaded: Queequeg and his idol had both been casualties when the mad Captain Ahab's vendetta against the legendary Mocha Dick doomed his crew.

"I suppose, then, it lies at the bottom of the sea," Becky bitterly mused aloud, taking a shot of whisky to dull the edge off the futility she felt. "But why stop there? It may as well have gone straight down to Hell — Hell or R'lyeh, whichever comes first."

Ishmael took advantage of Becky's distraction to indulge himself with an appreciative stare at the wench's ample bosom. These days, he was little more than a barely-tolerated, old wharf rat, so when the pretty new bar maid had fluttered her eyelashes at him, he was more than a bit receptive. "Actually," he said, and licked his lips, "it washed ashore with other wreckage of the *Pequod*."

Becky snapped from her gloomy reverie and pinned Ishmael with her stare. Her hand shot out and clamped his forearm. "Do you know where?"

"Easy, lass. It was years ago. Salvaged and stored away in a warehouse in England while the rights were argued over. Captain Ahab's widow finally took possession and auctioned it all off in lots, including all personal effects. As the only survivor, I was the verifier of authenticity."

"And Queequeg's fetish —?!"

"Aye, it was auctioned off . . . hmm, it would be near ten-years now. Those were better days, I can tell you. I cut a swaggering figure for the ladies, with my adventurer's past. There's still a lot of that adventurer in me," he said, openly ogling her bosom this time, "— if you receive my meaning."

Becky's top front teeth pinched her lower lip, biting off her contempt. "Were you there for the auction?" she insisted. "Do you know who placed the winning bid for Queequeg's fetish?"

"No. I have no idea."

"But you know the auction house? Yes? And there would be records?"

"Certainly, girl. But it is a reputable business — they won't be compromising anyone's privacy."

Becky arched an eyebrow at the admiring Ishmael. "I assure you, I have much experience compromising the 'reputable British.' Now, give me the address . . ." She winked. ". . . and I'll take you in the back room and show you my ankles."

Of course, if there was a reputable Englishman immune to Becky's brand of compromise, it was *Monsieur Le Grand Détective*. Even after she learned that his "death" was no longer an obstacle, his lack of passion for the fairer sex was ... until she learned of the one woman he admired.

She had gambled his interest was an abiding one. If that were the case, his curiosity would certainly render the notebook on Irene Adler (which Becky had obtained from the Diogenes cabal of *Le Grand Détective*'s brother in exchange for inside information concerning the criminal organization that had outlived Moriarty) of more potential worth than any paperweight — exotic though it might be.

Her gamble paid off — though *Monsieur Le Grand Détective* added that the exchange price should also include her silence concerning the truth about his "death." She agreed, and soon his brother had delivered to her a non-descript package.

She opened it and then held at last in her hands the first objective corroboration of the Staff of Noot's existence: the statue that made its headpiece.

As Ishmael had described it, Queequeg's fetish was a "hunchback." But Ishmael must have never looked closely at the figure. Not exactly a "hunchback," it was more a sitting figure, with hunched shoulders. A closer inspection revealed a head resembling an octopus with its tentacles drooping like drowsing serpents on a lazy Medusa.

So that was in her possession now. There remained only the staff to reclaim, and that would have to be soon. Here it was, already the last decade of the 19th century, and Noot had prophesied that Tulu would rise not long after the first quarter of the 20th.

Chapter Eight: 1893-1894 —
Cette Femme-La Qui Sont Etre S'Obeit

From Becky Sharp's Journal:
March 1, 1893

Having received the headpiece of Noot's caduceus, I now hasten to Africa for the final portion. I can only hope that the lost city of Ophir, the last known location of Noot's staff, has remained undiscovered and the staff I covet undisturbed. Though it is beyond hope that the old shaman who knew the way still lives, his young acolyte could be alive — though he would now be about the age his master was when I met them both in the early 1840s. Was the way to Ophir passed on to him? Will he remember me? And, if so, what will he and any other elderly survivors think of my still-youthful appearance?

May 31

I have returned to the African village today to find it much changed. The tribe has immensely benefited from its Christianizing a half-century before. The thatched huts have been replaced by European style houses. Well maintained roads, on which horses and carriages are not rare, connect this village to others. There is even a combination post office and general store. A church and hospital have been built, manned by priests and nuns who appear to truly care for the people to whom they minister.

My white skin, then, is no longer the novelty it was when I was first here. I have come as a missionary, on my way to yet-to-be evangelized fields. A few of the elderly have taken a second glance at me, but did not seem to be able to place me. Of course, I was here only briefly fifty years ago. I am hoping, however, that here is at least *one* who committed my appearance to memory, who has never stopped looking for my return.

I removed my bonnet in front of the General Store, by which it seems everyone manages to drop by to socialize some time during the day. Though white skin is not unusual, no one seems to have my particular hue of golden hair, nor to wear it down in public. The sight of my reddish-blond locks cascading over my shoulders should gain me some notoriety, including, hopefully, the attention of any who might yet watch for me.

June 1

It is now just before sunrise. I did not have to wait long to get a response to my unfurling of my hair. At midnight, there was a tapping at my window. Opening it, I peered out with a lit candle and was greeted by an old man who held a staff but did not lean on it. He asked,

"Is it you, Becky Sharp? Have you returned the Tulu to this faithless people as you promised my master fifty years ago?"

"It is I," I said. "I have your idol. But what of its pole? Did your master pass on to you the way to Ophir before he died?"

"Under torture, he did. The old fool thought he might endure until your return even when it became apparent to all that he would not. I had to give him much ... persuasion.

"But enough! Will you come with me now, and bring the fetish?"

"And how do I know that you will not dispose of me as you did your master once you have from me what you desire?" Becky asked.

His laughter was like the rattle of bones in the hand of the witch doctor about to roll them. "You are the handmaiden of Tulu. Your eternal youth is a sign that his power is with you. I would not dare attempt to harm you. Besides, you promised to be my old master's priestess, and when he died, right to you passed to me."

I shuddered at what that implied. But at least it seemed he would see to my protection.

I dressed and we departed, I bearing with me, wrapped in a cloth, the icon of Tulu, *Monsieur Le Grand Détective*'s paperweight. It is odd the vast degree that separates the value that may be attached to the same object. One man's god is another man's geegaw, I suppose. I followed the spry old man into the jungle. He knew his way, guiding me at some length by only what starlight shone through the closely entwined branches. Finally, in the distance, I could see torches.

"Where are you taking me?" I asked the shaman.

"Our cult has grown in your absence, though we have had to meet secretly by night. There are followers now from several villages. When we return from Ophir, we shall conquer more than my tribe."

I am no prude, but what I saw that night when the idol of Tulu was unveiled before those followers is something that I dare not commit to paper. Would that I could erase the scene of those orgiastic rites from my mind. It was almost enough to put me off sex for the rest of my preternaturally lengthened life.

Fortunately, no one attempted to touch me; not even the shaman dared molest me publicly, for as Tulu's handmaiden, I was as close to being a vestal virgin as I am ever likely to be.

None must suspect that I plan to betray them *and* their god. Since I do not know the extent of the old shaman's ability to read English, this will be my final entry for the foreseeable future. I cannot risk drawing his attention to my diary, as I surely would since he and I shall be all but joined at the hip for the journey ahead. A revolting arrangement, but one I must endure —

— at least as far as the journey *to* Ophir. I have no intention of returning with the shaman back to his cult. I think I shall have to smother him in his sleep, lest he report my treachery (the cult of Tulu, I have been made to understand, has a reach that extends over the world). Since he jealously guards the knowledge of the way to Ophir, he will actually facilitate my plan to do away with him, for we shall travel alone.

From Becky Sharp's Journal: Date Unknown

I write again after months in the jungle. I have lost all track of time. The Congo shaman is dead, but not by my hand. It looks as though I would learn my lesson about participating in an attempted *coup* in these lost cities, for the effort always seems to end with me imprisoned, as I am now, in Ophir.

When we had at last broken through the jungle and entered the environs of Ophir, the fool shaman thought that by waving the icon about, the people of the city would fall before us. Especially when paired with the white goddess gambit that I represented. But instead of bowing in obeisance before Tulu's image and my fair skin, the wild men of Ophir descended upon us, seizing the idol and slaying the Congo shaman on the spot.

When the strange beauty of my reddish-blond hair spared me from being killed as well, I thought I might well make my "white goddess" bid after all. Alas, it seems the people of Ophir *already* have their own fair-skin priestess, who, upon seeing me at a distance, rushed upon me, knife held ready to strike. Her men held me fast, and when I saw there was no hope of escape, I looked steadfastly upon the woman who would soon strike me down, flinching only at the last moment.

But the raven-haired priestess drew up short and lowered her knife. She reached out and firmly turned my face back toward her own. She studied my features with a mild astonishment, an expression that suggested she was expecting someone else.

Though I was a prisoner — to be sacrificed, when the stars were right, to the idol of Tulu I had carried to Ophir — the woman came to visit me regularly. She was obviously intrigued by me for reasons I could not understand, but which I was sure I would come to learn. The mastery of language was an old strength of mine, and soon we two could communicate well enough.

This priestess, it turns out, is desperately in love with an outsider, a wealthy plantation owner from one of her Majesty's African colonies. Unfortunately, the man for whom she lusts is married. In fact, she had first mistaken me for this man's wife, and thanked Tulu for bringing her hated rival into her power.

Now I turned this mistake that had nearly cost me my life to my advantage: "Might not your beloved make the same mistake?" I asked. "I will assume his wife's identity and lure him to you . . . if you return to me the fetish of Tulu — and the staff to bear it."

The deal was struck, and the priestess has promised me guidance through secret passages which run under ground and open far from the city.

She has also passed on to me a certain pouch.

"Inside," she said, "are some of the herbs which have been in the possession of the priestesses of Ophir since our ancestors traded with the merchants of old Egypt. They may be brewed into a special tea. Eight herbs will steal my beloved's mind and make him your obedient slave. See that he drinks the tea daily, so that he may remain under your control, and then mine, when you relinquish him to me."

As for the trip at hand, however, once I am through the secret tunnel and back in the jungle, I will be left to my own devices. Which makes my getting those herbs across the African wilds and brewing them into a tea for the object of the priestess' desire very unlikely. But if I and the rest of the multiverse are to survive the coming of Tulu, I cannot but try.

Thus, scratched and ragged and soiled, a lost Becky stumbled by chance across a British safari. A lone white woman so far from civilization, she had no trouble convincing them that she was a missionary who had escaped the very savages she and her dear, martyred husband had meant to evangelize.

Upon her return with the safari, Rebecca Sharp thus became a person of interest among the British colonies of Africa. And who should invite her home to tea, but the priestess of Ophir's hated rival, Lady Eugenides?

Born Odette St.-Claire, Lady Eugenides had achieved her notoriety by becoming the bride of the celebrated feral child of Africa. Odette St.-Claire was a banker's daughter who had come with her father to Bloemfontein, Africa where diamond mining was burgeoning. That was when her path crossed that of the feral child, by now a grown wild man, who immediately fell in love and therefore entered the civilized world, earning a peerage in service of the Queen during the famous "Affair of the Mad Mullah."

When Becky met Odette face-to-face, she understood how the priestess of Ophir could have mistaken her for this woman. She would see to it that, at the crucial moment, Lord Eugenides did as well.

Over tea, Odette said to Becky, "I must apologize for my husband's absence. He is away in London, arguing in Parliament for the preservation from British colonization the very area of Africa in which you were discovered, Mrs. Sharp. His love for the indigenous flora and fauna — to say nothing of the people — has made him determined that it remain untouched by white men."

He means other *white men*, Becky thought.

"We have much in common, Mrs. Sharp," Odette continued. "Of course, I've never had to endure what you have — your poor husband devoured by those savages, yet you found grace to nurse those of the same tribe suffering from a cholera outbreak. Amazing! If anyone were to ever eat *my* husband — of course, that's not likely, is it?"

The ladies' laughter lightly pealed in chorus across the clinking of fine china.

"No, indeed not, Lady Eugenides."

"Please. Call me Odette."

Becky smiled and toasted Odette with her tea cup. "Then you must call me 'Becky.'"

"We might be blood sisters, based on appearances," Odette said. "And I have so longed for a sister, all these long years in Africa. Even since I wed. Rebecca . . . Becky, may I ask a favor?"

"Certainly, Odette."

"You said earlier that you've spoken French since childhood . . ."

"Yes. My mother taught me."

"French happens to be my husband's preferred language."

"Indeed?" Becky's tea cup stopped on way to her mouth and she arched an eyebrow.

"I know it must seem unlikely — as if anything about his life were 'likely.' Still, it is his tongue of choice, and I'm afraid I have been selfishly remiss in mastering it. He will be away for another three months. Would you consent to be my guest during that time, and help me prepare a surprise for my husband?"

Becky smiled. "*Avec plaisir*," she said.

Odette did not notice that Becky had found something to learn from her as well. She had been watching how Odette handled her cup, how her upper lip slipped over the rim when she sipped. Becky was already drinking her tea the same way...

The former feral child of Africa, the Lord Arboreal, returned home to find his wife absent, his house empty. The scent of her perfume was all there was of Odette to greet him. He lit a candelabrum against the on-coming evening. All appeared in order, but it was very unlikely that she would have ventured far from home with his return imminent. He had sent out a runner to inform Odette he had arrived on the continent, and she would have known he was less than a day's journey away by the time she received the message.

Something was not as it should be ...

His hand quickly drew the long knife sheathed at his side as he inhaled deeply: another scent, beneath the perfume — the acrid tang of blood.

The slight light was all his honed eyesight needed to ascertain that there were no visible blood stains. Cleaned, then? No scent of soap...

Suddenly his eyes lit upon a note on Odette's desk. He snatched it up: yes, it was Odette's handwriting. The note said that she had had a guest of late, one she had not told him of because she wished to surprise him. Would he not join her now, for his surprise, in their private paradise?

Lord Eugenides was both relieved and annoyed. Was Odette's guest waiting with her at their jungle trysting place? If so, he or she would delay the breaking of his long sexual fast. Then animal passions receded, impelled by a chilling realization:

The mingling odors of perfume with blood, as though to drown out the latter's scent: it was his wife's method, when she was self-conscious of her time of the month. But Odette would never venture beyond the compound's safe parameters during her menses. She knew the danger of the blood scent attracting a lion. Odette had put herself at risk for a romantic gesture? Unthinkable! And if Odette's guest were female, it was unlikely that Odette would have not inquired about her cycle before taking her into the jungle and endangering them both.

The note then, was forced, and his wife taken against her will. Sheathing his knife, he ran outside, catching the blood scent in the air as he stripped himself of encumbering outer garments. He could *not* be too late! He would find his wife before one of the great cats did — and if there *were* captors involved, any predators would have *them* in her stead!

The trail unfolding itself to his olfactory nerve was indeed leading in the

Chapter Eight: 1893-1894 — Cette Femme-La Qui Sont Etre S'Obeit

direction of their arboreal bier, where Odette said she would meet him.

A woman's shrill scream tore the air as he leapt and hurdled the twelve-foot high fence that protected the compound. He landed, crouched, and with his wild blood-cry, sprinted, running faster, intensifying all into the final thrust needed to gain their trysting place.

Suddenly, he caught the sight of a fear-crazed woman, trapped in the bier, shrinking away from the great lioness climbing the tree towards her. He only had time for quick impressions: blond hair, bare long limbs, fair skin glowing in the gloom... his mate's flesh exposed and vulnerable to Shenitha the lioness' mutilating tooth and claw!

To cover the remaining distance, Lord Eugenides leapt like Shenitha herself in a series of bounds, the last of which carried him nine feet up the tree, his body colliding with the lioness'. It felt like slamming at full speed into a frozen-hard side of beef. But this carcass was warm with life — dangerously so.

Eugenides wrenched the lioness off the tree, locking his muscular legs around the mass of writhing muscle of the cat's trunk. One arm caught her under the chin, tightening on the beast's throat, while his free hand drew his knife.

As they fell to the ground, he strained to press his thighs together and was rewarded with the sound of cracking ribs. Hoping he had punctured the lioness' lungs, he stabbed with the blade at the back of her neck, but the predator's thick muscles resisted penetration.

Then the two hit the ground, Eugenides beneath the creature, the impact of its weight crushing the wind out of him. The jungle cat flailed with her hind claws at his legs, scratching deeply...

Now he struck again with his knife. He pressed the edge of the broad blade into the soft underside of the lioness' throat, drawing back with the full strength of his brawny arm and shoulder to slice, steadily, until he felt the blade hit the spinal column. The lioness' head, all but severed, folded, collapsing forward by her skull's own weight.

Eugenides thrust the carcass from atop him and rose on his badly scratched legs, coated with the thick, sticky blood of both the lioness and himself. Exhausted, he managed to bellow his triumph while he swayed on his feet. He scanned the trees above...

Yes! Odette was unharmed, gracefully descending the boughs, her nigh naked white form like an angel's coming down to him. She wore the tatters of a blouse that failed to cover her midriff and barely contained her copious breasts. Around her hips was a tiny loin cloth of the same material as the blouse: these were the lovingly preserved scanty rags which were all she had had to clad herself when they first met.

Perspiration stung his eyes, blurred his vision, but, of course, it could only be Odette. It was just that her long hair, unpinned as it was, obscured her face as it fell about her. On the ground now, she walked toward him, hips swaying with her familiar feminine grace. He could smell the same perfume from the house, and there was still the scent of blood under it. And other predators stalked the jungle —

"Odette," he began. "Quickly! We must . . ."

Hair still hanging about her face like a veil, she held out a cup to him. Where had that come from? She insisted he drink from it:

"*Ah, mon pauvre amour! Tu es blessé à cause de moi! Vite! Vous devez boire, mon amour!*" she exclaimed.

Even wounded, with his animal instincts alerting him that the danger was not over, Eugenides' civilized self couldn't help but be charmed. Odette was speaking flawless French, and her accent was perfect Parisian. The sweetness of the gesture, the time and effort that would have gone into its preparation, touched his heart.

Keenly aware of her nearly naked breasts so close to his bare chest, he reached out and took the offered water. He was, after all, quickly dehydrating from his ordeal. Spent, he drank deeply . . .

And then Lord Eugenides knew no more.

A few simple commands were all it took to confirm the jungle man was under Becky's power. That established, she leaned against a tree, broke into convulsive sobs, and vomited.

She could have died . . . *would* have died . . . except for this man she was going to make the love slave of the priestess of Ophir. Her identity as his wife had been feigned, but not her screams of terror.

The real Odette was currently also in a zombie-like state, having unknowingly drunk the Egyptian tea during yesterday's elevenses with Becky. Becky had ordered her to hide herself in a disused barn on the other side of the compound. By the time the effects of the drug had worn off Odette, Becky planned to have taken her husband deep into the jungle, guided by Eugenides own map pinched from his study.

The handwriting on the note Eugenides had read *was* that of his wife. Her intended seduction of him had been Becky's suggestion. Over their three months together, she had gradually teased out the necessary details from Odette: their special trysting place, and where she kept the prized rags she'd been wearing when she had first laid eyes on her savage lord.

As her sobbing subsided, Becky turned and looked again at the man who had saved her life. She had drugged him regardless, so as not to lose her only chance. But could she now keep him in this state of half-existence and make him the plaything of the priestess of Ophir? He had given her what she valued most — her life. How

Chapter Eight: 1893-1894 — *Cette Femme-La Qui Sont Etre S'Obeit* 109

could she repay him by separating him forever from *his* greatest possession — his wife?

She wondered if she might allow the effects of the tea to wear off, to tell him of all that was at stake. But how could he, even with the experiences of his own *outré* adventures, believe so fantastic a tale as that of Tulu and the threat to the multiverse?

Further, if she admitted her trickery — of him and his beloved Odette — what chance was there that he would ever trust her? And the priestess still held the cult objects she required. If she suspected Becky had turned against her, could even the prowess and power of such an ally as this man guarantee they would be delivered into her hands?

Becky thought long on this as the jungle shadows deepened around her.

Three days later, Becky and Lord Eugenides were on their way to Ophir. In the interim, she had been forced to return with him to his house to allow him time to recuperate. Under the influence of the tea, he had yielded to her ministrations to his wounds. Becky had realized that, unhealed, he might not be up to the struggle if they encountered another predator in the jungle.

Further, this wait allowed the time necessary for nature to jettison the undesirable biological encumbering of her menses, leaving her more fit for the rigors ahead as well.

By her design, the house servants were still away — Becky had suggested Odette give them a few days off to allow for continued privacy with her husband. Of course, the truth was Becky hadn't wished anyone to find Odette until she and Eugenides were days deep into the jungle.

As it turned out, she needed that time to nurse the wounded jungle king. During this convalescent period, she had made Odette continue to drink the tea to maintain her stupor, keeping her locked on the other side of the compound.

Now, Becky and her thrall were not as far along as she had hoped they would be. Further, she had not given Eugenides any more tea since the previous day. She would have to decide soon if she would administer another draught. Could she risk the effects wearing away to the point that his iron will could shred apart the fog that currently shrouded his mind?

She suspected he might have done so already, except when he gazed out through that fog, he still believed he saw his wife, whom he trusted without reservation.

Thus, he did not struggle against his state as he might have, and, to assist the ruse, she had dressed in Odette's clothing during their stay at the ranch house.

Now Becky wore again his wife's scanty garments, those in which she had greeted him at the trysting bier. They allowed for freedom of movement, and made the African heat more tolerable.

She was still not certain she should allow the tea's effects to fade. Could he ever trust her? Regardless, he had saved her life . . .

And then the decision was taken out of her hands.

"Lord Eugenides!"

Becky froze, and she commanded Eugenides to be still as well. Her heart pounded: was she found out already? Had someone discovered Odette in her zombie state, and come looking for her husband? What would they do when they found him in the same condition? They would insist that he return home for his own health, reuniting him with his wife . . .

They could not go back to the compound. Becky had been certain to carry a knife on this venture into the jungle, and her hand went to its pommel. She wished for a pistol; then any problem presenting itself could be resolved quickly, but she had never really learned to handle one, even during all that time as a buccaneer. That would have to change.

Crashing through the high jungle growth, cutting out a swathe with a long blade, came two Arabs. The older of the pair, who had called out Eugenides' name, looked eagerly towards the Lord Arboreal. Were these friends of his? Becky almost wished they were enemies. She could then turn her powerful thrall upon them with no regard, and she could use her knife as opportunity presented itself. But could she order Eugenides to strike indiscriminately at his friends — taking a chance of wounding them for life or perhaps even killing them?

Becky moved her hand away from her weapon and knitted her brow in self-contempt: why should she have a care for the consequences of Lord Eugenides' actions?

The men now stood before her.

"You're not Odette . . ." the man who had spoken before said, surprised. "Who are you? And what the devil is the matter with Lord Eugenides?"

Becky sighed. Apparently, they had no idea that Odette was in a condition similar to her husband. Having ascertained that she was not Eugenides' wife, the Arab who had spoken and his young companion now felt free to openly regard the voluptuousness her scanty rags revealed. For the first time she felt as near naked as she was. It had not bothered her at all when she'd been alone with Eugenides, even before she took his mind, when she had drawn her body near his.

"I am a missionary. My name is Becky Sharp," she said. "I have been the captive

Chapter Eight: 1893-1894 — Cette Femme-La Qui Sont Etre S'Obeit

of savages and would be so yet if not for Lord Eugenides. He was taking me back to the British Colony. We were swinging through the trees — I clinging to his back — when a vine on which we hung broke away and we fell. Ever since, he has been in this dazed state. Are you his friends?"

"Aye, *I* am," said the Arab who had spoken, careful now to keep his eyes level with Becky's. "I am Hassan. Lord Eugenides and I fought together against the cult of the Black Pharaoh when its power held all Cairo in fear. I owe him my life, and I am completely at his service now."

Becky slowly inhaled, feeling a hardness show in her eyes that she did not wish Hassan to notice. So she nodded toward his still silent fellow, who had not ceased to look at her body appreciatively. "And who is your companion? He lacks your manners."

Hassan turned sharply toward the other Arab. "Son of a jackal!" he barked. "Eater of swine! Avert your eyes from the woman's nakedness!"

"Forgive me, my uncle," the young man said, dropping his gaze to the ground and stepping back.

"My apologies, Becky Sharp," Hassan said, turning back to her. "This is my worthless nephew, Cahmesh. He was educated at university in Cairo and in the ways of the modern West, but became an addict of hashish and fraternized with occult societies. For my sister's sake, I have promised to rehabilitate him.

"I will be glad to lead Lord Eugenides home and you to the English colonies you sought. You are fortunate we found you — you are going in the opposite direction."

Becky managed to smile graciously, but her face flushed with her displeasure. Fortunately, it was easily accredited to the heat, and her reluctance was not noticed as she allowed the newcomers to alter her path. By sunset, they were a quarter of the way back towards the Eugenides plantation. Further progress, Becky could not allow. It was crucial that she keep the jungle king under her control.

And so, that night, Becky told Hassan and Cahmesh that she could prepare a medicine she had learned from the natives which could, perhaps, speed Eugenides' recovery. Satisfied that the Arabs believed her explanation, Becky went to work. When the tea was brewed to satisfaction, she took the cup from the flames. She was startled, then, to see she was, once again, the object of Cahmesh's intent scrutiny.

"Is that the medicine for Lord Eugenides, or do you prepare tea for yourself?" he asked.

He eyed the herbs that clung about the mouth of the pouch in which she carried them. Becky anxiously pushed the remnants back inside the bag and drew the string tight.

"It is for me," she said. "I have other herbs for Lord Eugenides."

"Cahmesh! Progeny of a jackal!" Hassan shouted, turning from his watch of the dark jungle. "Do you trouble this woman again? Go to sleep!"

"Yes, uncle," Cahmesh said meekly and turned away from Becky. His uncle then turned his attention back to the jungle. Becky kept an eye on Cahmesh, and, when she was satisfied that he slept, she gave the tea to Eugenides, and he drank.

Becky soon heard Cahmesh snoring softly. The pouch of herbs was safely in her hands. Lord Eugenides was close by. All it would take would be a call for aid if Cahmesh attempted anything. An inviting pallet of grasses had been prepared for her, and her eyes were weighted with the fatigue of tramping through the jungle all day.

Soon she was sleeping.

She awoke just before dawn, to the sound of Hassan shouting:

"Cahmesh! Worthless child of my sister! Where have you gone? Answer me!"

Becky quickly stirred to full attention. She anxiously ferreted about her pallet, and discovered, as she feared, that the pouch of herbs was not to be found! She immediately reported this to Hassan.

"Cahmesh! Eater of swine!" he bellowed out to the jungle sky. "Thief! When we find you, you and I are done! Do you hear me? Done!"

"Lord Eugenides! Rise!" Becky commanded her thrall. She had gathered up the pallet Cahmesh had left behind and now put it to Eugenides' nose. "Breathe deep, my lord!" Then she mounted his back, locking her arms around his strong neck. "Find the owner of that scent! Go! Quickly!"

Becky cried out as Eugenides instantly sprang up into the limbs of the trees and began swinging them both through the branches. She gripped tighter. At least they were leaving the slack-jawed Arab behind, so his friendship with Eugenides would no longer be an imposition on her schemes. And as for his nephew, when they found him, she would have no problem in ordering Eugenides to break his neck.

Thin branches and leaves whipped her face. She buried it into Eugenides' shoulder, enjoying the feel of her skin on his. The sense that they were flying she found exhilarating. After a while, she chanced to raise her head —

— just in time for her forehead to strike a hard branch stretched out into their aerial path. As unconsciousness swallowed her, she felt herself begin to fall.

She came to, staring up at the branch-latticed sky. The sun was high, the jungle a cacophony of life around her. Her head throbbed. There was no sign of Eugenides. Her arms were stinging with numbness, and she found she could not move them.

Adrenaline jolted her, but her arms still resisted movement. Were they broken? No, she was bound. And then an unwelcome revelation imposed itself between her and her view of African sky:

"Cahmesh!" she shouted and began to writhe upward to her knees. "Release me, now! I will scream for Eugenides, and he shall kill you —"

Smiling, Cahmesh shook his head. "The jungle lord is far gone by now. Even if his keen ear hears, I shall have plenty of time to make my escape — with you."

Becky's jaw dropped. "Escape with me? Where are you taking me? What do you want with me that . . . that you cannot satisfy here, then leave me behind?"

"Abandon a woman to the wild? I am not as discourteous as my uncle thinks. Besides, you are an infidel who has defiled the sacred secrets of the cult of Nyarlathotep."

Becky had now made it to her feet. Her eyes widened with incredulity. "'Defiled sacred secrets?' I have no idea what you are talking about!"

"Do you deny that you have taken on immortality?" Cahmesh demanded of her, his voice rising.

Stunned, Becky was silent for a moment. He could only be referring to the flame of Kor. "How do you know —?"

"How do I know?" He held up the pouch, shaking and rustling the dried herbs inside. "Did you not tell me that these were brewed for yourself?"

"Y-yes," Becky said with stammering lips as she realized the agent of immortality to which Cahmesh referred was not Kor's flame but Ophir's *tea*.

"Have you stolen the herbs, then, for yourself?" she asked.

Cahmesh's features hardened. "Commit sacrilege as you did? Affront Nyarlathotep, the Black Pharaoh? Nay! Well do I know the fate of the wretch who did so dare, he who was Unnamed, and I will not share his fate with you."

"What . . . 'fate?'" Becky felt her mouth go dry.

"You will be entombed alive."

Becky started. She could survive for hundreds . . . maybe thousands . . . of years inside a dark crypt. That would *not* be her fate! She began to scream for Eugenides, for Hassan, for succor from the nearest cannibal if need be. Even that fate was softer than what Cahmesh planned for her. Panic took her, and she bolted for freedom.

He easily overtook her. "No, no, Becky Sharp, my little 'missionary.' You have picked the pocket of the gods! Do you think you can now escape their judgement?

"Now, you will come with me. And you will give account for your sin when I seize control of the cult of Nyarlathotep."

"Please, Cahmesh! Why can't you let me go? You have your leaves; no one will know of me unless you tell!"

"Oh no, Becky Sharp. The eternal eye of the Black Pharaoh sees all. Now, while you were unconscious, I have brewed some tea for you — you know the recipe, I think."

Becky struggled against him as he began to drag her toward a steaming vessel on the coals of a burned-out fire. "No! Don't do this, Cahmesh! Please!" she begged.

"But you've taken it already, yourself. What do you fear?"

"You know! Too much will take my will . . . my mind . . . from me!"

By now, Cahmesh had wrestled her to her knees on the ground by the vessel of tea. He took it in one hand and moved it toward her mouth. Becky darted her face away. With the other hand, he grabbed her by the chin and pulled her mouth back.

She strained against him, but he was too strong. She pressed her lips tight together and set her jaw. Cahmesh pinched her nostrils closed, and, after long, torturous moments, when her mouth gaped wide for air, Cahmesh poured the draught down her throat, then tossed the vessel aside. He was quick to clamp her jaws shut before she could spit it out, and manipulated her head back to assure she swallowed —

— and then Becky Sharp knew no more.

Chapter Nine: 1894 —
The Hand of the Black Pharaoh

She came to in darkness, her limbs possessed of a warm drowsiness; thus, she felt no inclination to struggle. Her eyes were open wide, yet all was still dark. Cahmesh had apparently stored her somewhere. At least she was not yet the victim of his cult. She had to work against the seductive lethargy, to struggle against her bonds —

She concentrated, trying to remember what had happened to her up to this moment. The leaves had held her mind in a torpid miasma, but she retained impressions: their trek through the jungle ... then a series of caravans ... Cahmesh presenting her as his property whenever someone questioned ... no one expressed moral outrage; it seemed slavery was acceptable in the company Cahmesh kept.

She hoped, wistfully, that Lord Eugenides might come for her. Surely, there had been time for the effects of the tea to wear off him. But he was no doubt entrenched back at his compound with his wife — who would also be recovered by now from her drugging at Becky's hands. Becky realized aid from that quarter was unlikely, and, besides, it would not go well for her if Lord Eugenides ever laid eyes on her again.

If she managed to escape, how would she now, without Eugenides, obtain the cult items she needed to defeat Tulu? If she could not, then escape was pointless. She would die with the rest of the world. Her preternaturally extended life would matter not a whit —

— then she remembered the occult council she was brought before, how Cahmesh had presented her and the tea leaves. How they had come upon her, took her, binding, wrapping her body —

— placing her into the sarcophagus, sliding closed the heavy lid —

Becky screamed and frantically writhed, finding her limbs constrained. It was too late to escape! She was *already* entombed alive —

— alive for centuries yet to come, which in all their slow passing, would never bring her succor.

Too late. All too late.

As her initial rush of panic subsided, she remembered the power of the flame of Kor inside her. She strained to draw it out and blast away the sarcophagus that held her, but she felt only the faintest tingle which quickly passed.

Becky began to cry, her cocooned body trembling with sobs. She cursed Lord Steyne, and his entire alien race, for bringing her to this fate. But for that trinket of

Zervan Akarana with which Steyne had "graced" her... Better to have died years ago, as the prostitute Campbell and Black had pulled off that back street of Bath, hung as a traitor to her country. Such a fate would have been softer.

"Zervan Akarana" — boundless time was indeed hers.

She gladly surrendered to unconsciousness.

Each waking yielded only further failed attempts to raise the potency of the flame within her. Where she was, there was no passing of time, just a long, hellish, eternal now. She wondered if the world outside was still there, if Tulu had yet come.

Regardless, for her, there would always be darkness. Always more darkness. No lack of it, nor lack of time to contemplate the vanity of her life.

She found herself dreaming of the deliciousness of fresh air, remembering the sea breeze on her face when she and her husband Rawdon had traveled to Bath. The *first* time she was there, as a young bride, long before the degradations she would suffer in that resort town. Then she was with Clegg on the deck of the *Imogene*, feeling the warmth of the sun...

... and gasping in gulps of fresh air. She opened her mouth wide as though tasting it.

And then her eyes flew open.

"Yes, she's alive," a familiar voice announced. Strong arms embraced her, lifted her out and to the cool stone floor of the tomb. She could see the man was robed and turbaned and bearded. Her concentration on him quickly slipped away as she felt the mummy bindings begin to be unwound. She could begin to move her limbs...

Her rescuer paused a moment to remove his hot, constraining eastern attire, then pluck away his beard — and she dared not believe what she saw: Eugenides! She began to cry, to sob with ecstasy with the relief she had known she had no right to hope for, but had never ceased to hope would come.

The bandages were now loosened enough for her to reach upward toward Eugenides, wanting to lock her arms about his neck, desiring human contact, *his* contact —

Another man, a true Arab in eastern attire, stepped into her field of vision.

"Amazing!" said Hassan. "She lives! Then... she *has* partaken of the herbs. She is immortal!"

"The witch is probably too evil to die," Lord Eugenides growled, stepping back from her beckoning arms. "Get up," he commanded her coldly. Grudgingly, he passed her the scraps of clothing that she had taken from his wife. "Your limbs are free enough for you to finish unwrapping yourself. Then cover your body with these."

He turned his back to her while she dressed. "When I found Odette's clothing discarded in this tomb, we knew Cahmesh had brought you here. Hassan had told me the legend of the Unnamed, how the cult of the Black Pharaoh had him buried alive for stealing the same herbs you used on me. It stood to reason you would suffer the Unnamed's fate…the difference being that you might still be alive in that sarcophagus if partaking of those herbs had made you immortal."

"You came… for me?" Becky asked.

Lord Eugenides, back still to her, coughed a dry, contemptuous laugh. "I came to aid my friend Hassan to recover those cursed herbs and stop the revival of this cult of the Black Pharaoh … *and* its weapon of destruction from coming under his nephew's control.

"As for you… I didn't believe one whit that those herbs could endow you or anyone with eternal life. I only agreed to open your stone coffin to assuage Hassan's fear that you were in distress inside it. *He* is the one you should thank for your rescue."

Becky touched his arm, gently pressing it to turn him back around to her, hoping now that she was again in his wife's clothes, she might see some trace of affection by association. "But you're not sorry you found me?"

His upper lip curled. "You're not her. I'm only allowing you to wear her clothes because that is all you have. I promise you, I will have you out of them as quickly as possible."

Becky stepped closer to him. "I eagerly await milord's pleasure, then."

Eugenides, she noted with a sense of triumph, was actually blushing.

She pressed on: "I can wait a long time for you, my lord," she said, "In fact, *I* can wait for ever how long it may take. In time, my lord may very well come to better appreciate what only *I* have to offer him. For, have you not already considered the possibility that, having drank the tea, you may now possess the same preternatural longevity as I?"

Flustered, Lord Eugenides only narrowed his eyes at Becky's suggestive comment, then turned away from her and addressed Hassan instead. "We need to get her away from here to safety."

"Do you wish me away for *my* safety, or your own from having to be near me?" Becky asked and smiled up at Eugenides when he looked at her. With an expulsion of breath and a quick shake of his head, he turned back to Hassan.

"The sooner she is removed from this scenario the safer we *all* shall be in this dangerous enterprise. Then we'll return to deal with the Black Pharaoh Cult. Permanently, this time."

"My friend, she will only be safe if she remains with us," Hassan said. "The cult has many spies. If one recognizes her as their escaped victim, they will certainly recapture her. In fact, as long as the cult survives, they will never cease stalking her until they have returned her to that sarcophagus. She has pilfered immortality from their god Nyarlathotep. She will *not* be allowed to enjoy it."

Eugenides stroked his chin. "There is that, I suppose. My major concern is that whoever might catch her will know she didn't crawl out of that sarcophagus on her own. If that were to happen before she gets far, her escape might compromise the secret of our activity here upon our return."

Becky's eyes had widened at Hassan's words, and her breath to quicken: return to that eternal darkness? Bound alive forever? There would be no chance of escaping her adversaries a second time, of that she was certain.

"No, Lord Eugenides, your initial estimation was the correct one after all," she said. "You must get me away from here *immediately*. I . . . I will not go back to that," she pointed at the sarcophagus and shuddered. "I'll gladly take my chances alone in this heathen city, in the desert . . . *anywhere* is safer than where I am now, in *their* very lair!"

Eugenides noted her trembling, and Becky could — almost — see pity in his eyes. Then his countenance hardened again. Clearly, her best interests were secondary here.

She sprang for the tomb entrance —

Immediately, Eugenides caught her, spun her around as she struggled to be free.

"Stop it!" Eugenides said, shaking her so that she bit her tongue. The sharp pain brought clarity to her panic addled mind. "You would risk alerting them to us before we can derail their engine of destruction? Then not only we but uncountable numbers would suffer. Do you ever think of anyone but yourself?"

Becky now ceased her struggling and looked at him, her mouth open but mute. How could she expect him to believe that her escape meant more than saving herself? That whatever this cult's weapon, far less would die from it than those who would perish at the coming of Tulu, whose conquest was assured if she were recaptured and rendered helpless again?

A sense of loneliness pressed in on Becky, greater than any she had felt since she climbed down the Kaatskills alone. It was much worse, having someone with her, feeling his company, and yet, at the same time, feeling terribly apart from him. She wanted to share her terrible burden, but Eugenides' face told her he would never believe her, never trust her . . .

She bit her trembling lower lip and nodded her head to indicate that she would consent to his will. She turned and quickly flicked away the beginning of tears from her eyes. Why did Eugenides' disdain sting her so? All too well, she had come to understand the priestess of Ophir's overwhelming sense of desperation for him.

Having gathered her wits, she turned back to her unwilling companions. "I will not put you at risk. I see that I will always be in danger unless this cult is wiped out. What is your plan?"

"It is simple, actually," Eugenides said. "We will sabotage their weapon of destruction. It is hidden here, in another one of these sarcophagi."

Suddenly, Lord Eugenides' nostrils flared, pumped the air. "Wait. There is something, an odor . . ." He locked his eyes on Becky. "That wretched tea you served me . . . someone is brewing it."

"Cahmesh took the herbs from me," Becky said. "But, that means he's here, or some other cult member is brewing them . . . ." Her bosom heaved, and though she did not run this time, her fear of recapture and what would be done to her was no less present than before. Eugenides reached out and grasped her upper arm. "Steady, girl."

Amazing, the strength she drew from his mere touch. She reached over to lay her other hand over his —

— and Eugenides jerked his hand away, as though a snake struck at him.

"Hassan, Rebecca . . . follow me," he ordered. Unsheathing his knife, he slipped off his shoes to pad ahead barefoot into the tenebrous reaches of the vast tomb. Guided by his keen sense of smell, he uncovered a passageway of sorts: a fissure in the stone. He beckoned, and, pressing his back against one wall of the passage, began to slide through. Becky and Hassan followed.

It was far too close a fit for Becky. Pressed between unyielding slabs of stone became too much like being in the sarcophagus again. She began to breathe in deep gulps, gasping audibly for air.

"Silence," Eugenides hissed back at her. Becky tried to obey, but the fear was swelling tightly within her breast, and soon she found she couldn't breathe at all.

There was light visible ahead now, an eerie blue. Eugenides was sliding towards it. She was quick to follow, but his hand reached back, making her stop short as he himself slipped free. She knew not to burst out of the passage, knew the need of stealth and surprise —

But seconds stretched into infinities. The swelling in her lungs was smothering her, as surely as though an incubus sat crushingly upon her breast. She closed her eyes and saw flickering white sparks against the dark. She was passing out. She had to be free — *now!*

Becky shot out of the opening and fell to her knees, noisily swallowing great draughts of air. Above her, she heard Eugenides snarl, "You little fool!"

Becky looked out upon a vast, subterranean chamber. Its high, domed ceiling, far above reach, had a circular aperture that opened on the desert floor. Through this opening, the azure moonlight shone on the chamber's floor below. There, twelve black-robed, hooded figures stood before a stone altar.

Behind it, wide stone steps ascended to a giant idol in the form of a man: this was Nyarlathotep, the Black Pharaoh.

The obsidian, monolithic deity's arms were crossed over his breast, an ankh in one hand, a wicked looking flail in the other. Under an ebony, diamond-studded headpiece, his black face's expression was cruel. The idol seemed to wish the empowerment to lift the heavy stone arms from his breast, heave the pillars of his legs down those ancient steps, and thrash to bloody shreds with his flail anything whose mere presence gave him offense.

Beneath Nyarlathotep, before the altar, a closed sarcophagus stood on end. Before it, on a tripod arrangement, a glazed, earthen pot was suspended above an open flame. Vapors wafted up from what crackled there. Stirring the pot with a ladle, in dark ceremonial robes, regal in spite of himself, stood Cahmesh. He smiled at the entrance of Becky's party.

Then he pushed aside the stone lid to the sarcophagus, revealing a mummy. Tall and broad shouldered, his body had been powerful. The unwrapped, wizened head was the color of ash.

"You sought the weapon of our cult. Behold him now, you fools!" Cahmesh shouted. "Behold the Hand of the Black Pharaoh, 'The Unnamed!' We have already brought him back to life through our knowledge of that which is written in the *Kitab al-Azif!*"

He dipped into the tea with the ladle, held the spoon to dried lips which suddenly cracked, then pursed, trembling to life, parting to receive the liquid.

"Now I have brewed a tea of many herbs in this pot. Not only has it placed him under our complete sway, having partaken of such a large quantity, this mummy shall become unstoppable! Aye, he shall rend all the world before him as papyrus!

"Do you think I did not know of your efforts? I allowed you here, so that your blood will be spilled before Nyarlathotep to initiate the chaos which now ensues upon the world!

"Kill the infidels!" Cahmesh shouted to the Unnamed, and pointed at Eugenides and his uncle. "But spare the woman! She must be returned to the exquisite torture of eternal darkness! Perhaps — yes! A companion to relieve *your* long loneliness — *if* you serve Nyarlathotep well!"

The mummy dashed forward, striking aside several of the cult who had not suspected such speed from him. They struck the dirt floor hard and did not move, blood pooling under their heads.

"Becky," Eugenides said. "That tea you used to control me as Cahmesh controls the mummy . . . Would this brew of many herbs increase my strength as well?"

"I suppose . . ."

"Then it seems my course is clear. You know what to do after I have drank. Run, Hassan, my friend, there is nothing you can do!"

"No! That mummy is too fast . . . I will occupy him or you will never reach the tea!" With that, the brave Arab drew his long knife and dashed forward.

"Hassan! Don't —!" Eugenides shouted, reaching out to restrain him. But Hassan

"Behold him now, you fools! Behold the Hand of the Black Pharaoh!"

slipped by and the mummy was now upon them. As Hassan drew back to strike, the mummy reached out, seized Hassan's head, and twisted it effortlessly around. With a sickening snap, Hassan suddenly found himself regarding Becky uncertainly from over his own shoulder blades...

Becky screamed as the eyes flickered closed and Hassan's chin dipped to touch the top of his spine.

Eugenides swore in anger. He wished to avenge Hassan's death then and there, but, lest his friend's sacrifice be in vain, he continued his dash for the vessel containing the tea.

Meanwhile, Becky attempted to elude the mummy until Eugenides could engage him. She ran toward the altar. The mummy would have caught her easily enough at his superior speed, but the Hand of the Black Pharaoh took pleasure in lingering over Hassan, working the head till he might wrench it from the body.

His nephew had laughed at his uncle's death and now brayed at his body's mutilation. Anger flushed Eugenides' face, and he hurled his knife into Cahmesh's throat: it sank in to the hilt, inches of blade protruding through the back of his neck. He tumbled, grasping at the knife, and as his body fell, he knocked over the tea urn —

Eugenides' quick reflexes saved it. He snatched it up, and drank quickly — and far, far too much. A fire lit in his skull, and he was only aware of the glazed pot dropping from his hands to the floor as though it were happening far away.

Becky, meanwhile, had scurried up the steps with the mummy behind her. She had managed to put the idol of Nyarlathotep between them, and, by circling it, keep it there. She looked down at Eugenides and shouted, "Attack the mummy, milord! Destroy him!"

But Eugenides' expression told her to expect no succor from him. His face was twisted into a wild grin, eyes twin lights of a single, joyous, homicidal purpose. And Becky was the focus of that insane gleam.

Eugenides began mounting the stairway.

Becky looked on in disbelief: why had he become a menace to her and no longer her thrall? Then she saw the fallen tea urn and realized Eugenides must have drunk a deep enough draught of the potent liquid to push his mind and body beyond her control.

Distracted by this new, unexpected threat, Becky momentarily forgot the mummy. A moment was all he needed. He caught at her, pulling her to him and heaving her up, struggling, into his arms.

Then the mummy saw Eugenides ascending the steps. He effortlessly threw Becky across one shoulder, and, with his free hand, pushed against the back of the heavy statue of the Black Pharaoh. At first, the deity seemed to resist, unwilling to be thrust from his high place —

— then the idol toppled, fell forward, face flat, as though the god made obeisance, and began sliding down the steps into the path of Eugenides.

Becky, still held over the mummy's shoulder, turned her head back over her own. "NO!" she screamed. She could *not* lose Eugenides —

The jungle chief did not leap aside, but crouched low, waiting for the idol to reach him before he jumped straight up —

— and came down atop the still moving statue. In the next instant, Eugenides sprang to full height, sprinted the length of the skidding stone image, then leapt from it, the idol sliding away beneath him. As the image of Nyarlathotep continued its journey down the steps, Eugenides landed on its former base.

The typically impassive sphinx face of the mummy suddenly shone with anger. He discarded Becky from over his shoulder as though she were a weighted sack. Becky landed on her back and immediately began disengaging herself from underneath the feet of the now wrestling adversaries, receiving a hard kick to her ribs in the passing.

Becky examined her reddening side gingerly with her fingers. Nothing broken. She appeared sound. For the moment.

That would change, once the fight was resolved between Eugenides and the mummy. She knew she was the prize, and whoever won, her fate would not be a pleasant one. Regardless, Eugenides represented the best wager. If he should defeat the mummy, his own madness would, hopefully, eventually die down.

If she could only avoid him until then.

Her eyes fixed on the urn of tea. Did any remain?

She rose to her feet, ready to run down the steps, but the struggling Eugenides and mummy continually blocked her way in their weird waltz, weaving randomly along the platform. She dashed forward, and they veered into her path. The mummy snatched out at Eugenides and caught Becky's long, reddish blond hair. She cried out as her scalp was pulled tightly. She couldn't separate herself, entwined in their death grip, and they were now all stumbling sideways together toward the platform's edge.

Closer they drew, closer . . . then, but one quarter-inch more, and her body would drop over the side. She hung onto the edge by her toes. If the mummy continued to grasp her long hair, and she fell, either her hair would tear loose at the roots or the weight of her own body would effectively snap her neck . . .

Then the struggling titans in their death dance swayed back onto the platform, dragging Becky with them. The mummy released her hair to land a blow to Eugenides, and Becky dropped to her knees. The impact hurt, but, seeing her path momentarily clear, she ignored the pain, rose immediately, and sprinted down the stairs, eyes again on the container of tea.

Reaching it, she stepped over Cahmesh's corpse and found a pint's worth remained.

That would not be enough to keep Eugenides under her influence for the long journey back to Ophir. She looked atop the steps — to her alarm, he was being strangled, held by the throat at arm's length by the mummy.

Eugenides grasped that arm with both his hands, muscles working, his face swollen red and sweating copiously. It looked as though Eugenides' head might suddenly shoot from the mummy's grasp like a clinched, wet bar of soap. A heaviness of despair dropped deep into her stomach: he could *not* die! Not for the world's sake . . .

. . . not for hers.

Then the Lord Arboreal wrenched loose the mummy's arm from its shoulder. Quickly, Eugenides detached the still grasping hand from his throat, threw the arm aside, and dove into the reeling mummy. He fell with the feral man atop him, striking, tearing —

The battle, Becky saw then, was decided. The buoyancy she felt immediately yielded to the gravity of her situation: Eugenides would think nothing of ripping her to pieces as he did the mummy.

Becky quickly searched Cahmesh's robes. Yes! There were more herbs on his person: he had kept them close, for they were his source of power over the cult. She also found a pistol on the hip of one of the dead cult members whom the mummy had dashed to the floor.

Armed, and with the pouch of herbs tucked in her loincloth and the pot of tea in hand, she sprinted up the corridor that led to the desert's surface, fearful that at any moment she would hear the rapid paddling of Eugenides' feet hurrying death upon her from behind.

With a shout of exultation, she emerged onto the moon-lit desert floor, amidst the ruins of a fabulous city. Other robed cult members and their slaves were breaking camp hurriedly, wishing to be victims neither of their own secret weapon run amuck nor Eugenides.

Waving her gun, Becky forced one follower of Nyarlathotep to dismount from his camel and flee on foot. Transportation obtained, Becky now needed a guide back to civilization. She caught one of the cult's slaves and forced him to secure the camel.

Looking back at the entrance to the underground chamber, she saw a heavy stone positioned to seal it. She pointed at the stone, keeping the gun aimed at the slave, and nodded emphatically. He understood, and he and Becky together rolled the stone in its prepared groove, closing the opening.

That would not be enough to keep Eugenides in. Becky looked about. Among the ruins of the city, she found much broken masonry. Pointing at one piece of hewn marble the size of a boulder, she forced the slave to push it across the ground and slide it into the groove to block the rolling away of the stone.

"There," Becky thought, "if that will hold Eugenides until his madness passes, until I can bring him again under my influence . . ." Seeing the cult's camp was now deserted except for herself and the man she had forced into her service, she found some rope and tied him. She then collapsed against the stone blocking the chamber entrance and, wearied from her ordeal, fell asleep.

A jarring thud against the stone woke her, the impact thrusting her forward and onto her face. The still-tied slave's eyes were wide, his tongue gibbering, with occasional high pitched yelps like a stuck dog. He clearly did not wish to be bound before the door when what was trying to get from behind it emerged.

Becky scrambled to her feet, watching the stone shake and quiver from the repeated impact which caused the sand before it to rise in veils. Strong as he was, Eugenides could not dislodge it.

Becky could hear his screams of rage from inside, and, remembering the opening in the desert floor that looked down upon the chamber, she scrambled to peer into it. Of the mummy, there were only parts and pieces scattered about. Eugenides rampaged about the chamber, howling as he tore in rage at the occult paraphernalia. He snatched up one corpse of a cult member, and, holding it by its ankles, he swung it about, beating the walls, altars, and steps, until the body was no more than a pulpy sack.

Apparently, he could not leap high enough to escape through the desert floor opening, and Becky hoped his drug addled mind did not remember the crevice through which he'd entered the chamber.

By the end of the second day of her vigil, Becky no longer heard or saw any sign of Eugenides inside his prison. There was, she knew, the possibility that he had found a way out, that he now roamed the vast desert sands that would eventually bury his bones —

— or was he capable of cunning in that state of mind? Possibly, he was trying to lure her in . . .

. . . or, he might be inside, simply collapsed out of view, his rage spent. He could be approachable now, in the desired weakened state in which he could be bent again to her will.

Becky untied the slave, but when he saw she intended for him to remove the stone, he refused. She was forced to risk a shot to persuade him. She might not know how to aim, but he didn't know that. The wild bullet ricocheting close by the slave's head came much closer to hitting him than she had intended, but that only sped his decision to yield to her wishes.

She then forced him into the passageway ahead of her. If Eugenides were indeed still mad, the slave would take the brunt of his attack and, hopefully, allow her time to return to the surface and escape on the camel.

As they entered the room, a foul stench struck Becky and the slave: the bodies of the dead cult members inside were now sun swollen and swarming with flies. Becky, of course, had been aware of their decomposing. She had shredded a blanket left at the camp to wrap strips around her nose and mouth as well as those of the slave.

Eugenides was nowhere to be seen. For a moment, Becky's heart sank, and she feared that he had indeed been able to remember and slip through that crevice in the wall by which he had entered —

Then she saw him, prone under the fallen idol of the Black Pharaoh, whose shade he had apparently sought when the desert sun burned down through the opening above. Becky had to stop herself from running to his side. Instead, she poked the gun's barrel into her unwilling servant's back and motioned for *him* to examine Eugenides — in case the savage lord should awake and think himself under attack.

It was only Becky's continued shaking her gun in his direction that prompted the slave to touch Eugenides and roll him over . . .

"Odette . . ."

"Stand back now, you fool!" Becky shouted at the slave, who had been looking her way inquiringly. Gladly, he stepped away, while Becky pulled away the scarf from her face and ran to Eugenides' side with the tea she had brought.

She dropped to her knees, lifted his head gently and laid it on her lap.

"Odette . . ." His eyelids fluttered, opened, and Becky could see he was trying to focus. She only had seconds to give him more tea, while he still thought she was his wife.

He had saved her life thrice now, from the lion, the cult, and the mummy. Could she restore him to the state of a thrall? But what choice did she have? By all indications, Eugenides would never trust her, so making a plan together seemed out of the question.

The harsh reality of the situation was the priestess of Ophir still held the cult objects she required to save the world from Tulu — a world that included Eugenides' beloved Odette. Surely, he would agree willingly to the price the priestess demanded if it was the only way to save his wife's life. Perhaps a clouded mind was merciful, under the circumstances.

"*Un autre femme-la qui sont etre s'obeit,*" Becky grumbled again as she gave Eugenides drink.

Two months later, a fire burst out on the eastern peripheries of Ophir's domain, attracting the attention of Ophir's sentries, who immediately began making their way across the plain.

But their priestess had seen as well, and, recognizing the agreed-upon signal, she took the secret, underground passages known only to her, thus reaching Becky and her captive a good hour before the sentries would. She carried with her the staff and icon of Tulu as well as a bag of gold for Becky's use upon her return to civilization.

The exchange was made, and by the time the sentries were regarding the cinders that were all that were left of Becky's fire, she was making her way with the desired cult objects back to civilization.

She had neglected, however, to tell the priestess of Ophir that she had been gradually decreasing the leaves in Lord Eugenides' tea, and that day had given him only water.

From Becky Sharp's Journal:
Not dated

Today I have accepted something with which I have been struggling since my latest emergence from the African jungle. I have long been uncertain of the complete effect those flames of Kor have had on my insides. And after so much time as Clegg's mistress, and no ensuing complications, I thought my glorified womb in a state inviolate to mere mortals.

But, of course, the words "mere mortal" are totally inadequate to describe the father. If anyone could strike a bull's eye, it would be him. "Lord Good Genes" indeed!

Chapter Ten: 1917 —
The Encounter on Great Pulteney Street

He seemed to have stepped out of the painting inspired by the *Rubaiyat* at the nearby Victoria Museum, this man in the turban whose olive complexion and beard with its texture of tightly coiled vines summoned images of a remote landscape both arid and lush.

Sâr Dubnotal's turban, puffy white trousers, and gold embroidered sash gave him an exotic appearance which was compromised only by his fashionable Edwardian frock coat and cravat.

El Tebib — as he was known in the East — and his massive Hindu manservant Naïni sat in an enclosed black carriage drawn by horses dark as pitch and driven by a soberly dressed man in a black top hat. Like a preternatural shadow without a source, the somber conveyance loomed in the midday sunlight that brightened Bath's Great Pulteney Street.

The carriage set by a row of homogeneously designed Georgian homes, which, along with the series of similar houses across the street, gave the impression of a single image repeated infinitely in a vast, open corridor of mirrors. The object of Sâr Dubnotal's quest had thought herself hidden among these residences indistinguishable from each other.

But little in this terrestrial sphere was hidden from the Great Psychagogue.

"Look, Naïni." Sâr Dubnotal did not break his austere emerald gaze, nor move other than to slightly raise his forefinger and then smoothly lower it. His manservant's powerful frame was cloaked in even more conservative Edwardian attire than his master: charcoal frock coat and trousers and black Stetson hat. Naïni nodded, his hand already on the carriage door's handle, awaiting the next command.

They watched a petite, shapely Gibson girl tentatively making her way down the row of houses on the opposite side of the street. An abundance of strawberry blond hair spilled from beneath a broad brimmed hat, the shadow of which veiled her eyes. Under a dark vest, she wore a high, white collared blouse clasped at the throat by a thin tie. Her full-length skirt was the cut favored by the "new woman": straight and sensible.

Sâr Dubnotal, still without breaking his stare, raised five fingers to signal Naïni to hold. The woman answered the physical description of their quarry, but she seemed not to know where her home was. But, of course, the similarity of a row of houses could disorient even those most familiar with the street.

Then the woman's chin raised at a sudden melodious chanting in the air. Sâr Dubnotal recognized the words, but he was compelled to keep his attention riveted on the woman herself and so let the chant recede into the background. She was now heading briskly towards the specific house they were watching. With the stakes so high, they could ill-afford to hesitate any longer.

Sâr Dubnotal flicked his wrist in the woman's direction and Naïni went into action. The pair expected no resistance for *El Tebib* had planned the abduction for the heat of the day, when the wealthy would be seeking fashionable salons indoors. Still, speed was paramount, as well as stealth. To that end, the giant was both quick and strangely ephemeral, as though carried along on the summer breeze stirring in the heat of the brick and mortar canyon that was Great Pulteney Street. His stealth was aided by the woman hesitating uncertainly before the house. She looked up at an open window from which the chanting came.

As she was about to mount the front steps, Naïni moved in behind her, one muscular arm lashing out about her waist and pulling her to him while his other hand pressed a cloth dabbed with chloroform over her nose and mouth.

The woman immediately went limp. The coachman cracked the whip and the carriage lunged forward to meet the Hindu. In the next moment, Naïni was lifting the woman into the carriage and the receiving arms of Sâr Dubnotal. Then, before the door was closed behind him, the coach was already bolting down Pulteney Street towards the bridge.

"It is her, master?" Naïni asked.

"I have never seen Helen Vaughan before," Sâr Dubnotal said, looking down into the beautiful, creamy face. He began to search her pockets.

From there, he produced a small packet of papers bound by twine which ran through a ring. *El Tebib* loosened the string and examined the jewelry. It was an ancient bit of Roman work. He found it significant that the front of the ring was shaped into a satyr's head. On the inner side of the band, his keen eye could make out a script in Latin: *DEVOMNODENT-MAVORS CAMVLOS*.

He cupped the ring, feeling strange eddies in the mystic fluids. Turning his attention to, and shuffling through, the papers, he came at last to a document of identification. He gave a sigh of accomplishment — together with the ring, there was little room for doubt as to the woman's identity.

Yet Sâr Dubnotal could not completely relax, for a spur of uncertainty remained lodged in his mind. His keen ear, which retained detailed information from even ambient noise, allowed him to recall the words to the song he had heard on the street:

Old King Cole was a merry old soul,

And a merry old soul was he;
He called for his pipe, and he called for his bowl
And he called for his fiddlers three.

Sâr Dubnotal initially had thought that the voice belonged to someone who shared Helen's dwelling, and that it had helped her recognize her own house, after a brief moment of disorientation. Yet, she had hesitated on the front steps, looking up at that open window instead of striding into her rightful home.

They crossed the bridge and soon were at the rear entrance of the Psychagogue's temporary lodgings near the Victoria Museum. Naïni swept the woman into his arms, then effortlessly carried her up the back flight of stairs to their flat.

The driver dismounted, removing his black hat to reveal blond hair. His face, though now in early middle age, radiated something of Sâr Dubnotal's own time-defying robustness — perhaps due to his being in the Great Psychagogue's presence almost continually since he was a child.

"You look troubled, master," he said. "Why?"

"Rudolph," said the Psychagogue, "I am no longer sure that this woman is Helen Vaughan. In our haste, we may have taken an innocent. Or much worse — Helen Vaughan knew we were in Bath searching for her, and is now long gone, while we have wasted time stalking an impostor..."

"Let us ascend," he continued. "Naïni should have her well restrained by now. We will come to the truth of this matter by whatever means necessary."

Upon reaching their floor, their ears were assaulted by shrill screaming that would soon summon the local constabulary if allowed to continue. Sâr Dubnotal raced down the hall: one thing they did *not* need was a red blooded English bobby bursting upon the scene to rescue this lovely flower of British womanhood, bound and at the mercy of him and Naïni — "dark heathens" both.

Now he heard Naïni screaming along with the woman. Reaching the still open doorway, the Great Psychagogue and Rudolph saw the Hindu standing beside the woman, whom he had successfully bound in a wooden chair, holding a bleeding hand. The same blood smeared the woman's mouth, open wide in wailing.

"Rudolph! See to Naïni's wound! Take him to his room, then summon our new friends with haste," *El Tebib* ordered as he crossed the room, plucking away the skull ornament that pinned his cravat. He stuffed the freed article of clothing into the woman's mouth as she desperately turned her head from side to side, all the time bellowing. Then, Sâr Dubnotal ripped apart her high collar, undid her tie, and wrapped it around her head, securing the gag.

The woman was now looking up at him, her eyes widening as she fully took in his strange, austere appearance for the first time. This initiated a new round of bellowing, but, this time, it lodged and rumbled in her throat.

When she was spent, the Great Psychagogue asked, "If you are through screaming, Miss Vaughan, might we talk now?"

Still eyeing him dubiously, she nodded "yes." He began to remove the gag, and, before he could pull his cravat from her mouth, she had spit it into her lap. Gasping for air and vehemently shaking her head, she shouted:

"I am *not* that *bitch* Helen Vaughan!"

"Exactly what the real Helen Vaughan would say in this position. My great tutelary, Ranijesti — blessed be he! — to whom nothing is lost in this world or the Empyrean beyond, and who is beyond reproof of error, says otherwise."

The woman's features trembled between an expression of rage and utter bafflement: "Your great Rooney-jesty — *what*?"

Sâr Dubnotal's eyes narrowed and his nose lifted in the air at this slurring of his master's name. "Ranijesti—that Bodhisattva who even now enjoys foretastes of Nirvana from his cell submerged in the earth of India…"

"You think I'm Helen Vaughan because a man *in a hole in the ground* on the other side of the globe told you so?" the woman responded, incredulity and contempt in her voice.

Sâr Dubnotal drew himself up and glared down at her. "Ranijesti directed us *where* to find Helen Vaughan. *This*," he produced the pack of papers bound with the ring, "says that you are the object of our quest. So, instead of bantering metaphysics, let us limit ourselves to the more mundane evidence, shall we?

"I adjure you to tell me why you are carrying these papers. If it's because you think you have killed Helen Vaughan and taken her identity, allow me to disabuse you of that plan: Helen Vaughan does not die so easily and remains a present danger. On the other hand, if you are her willing accomplice, planted to misdirect us while she escapes, I will see that you will bear the full penalty for this crime — after you have told us where to find her."

"You swarthy fool!" the woman snapped. "Your head is as brown as a hen's egg, but apparently nothing grows inside it! It was Helen Vaughan who murdered *me* — or, at least, came close — and took *my* identity. Not the other way around. *She* switched our papers! If you would ever withdraw your turbaned head from the 'Empyrean,' you might notice there's a war going on. With the Huns at the gate, I could ill afford to risk moving about England without some form of identification, and this was the only one available to me.

"I was at her home today because I have been searching for Helen Vaughan for two years to exact my own revenge on her, and to take back something that witch took from me. I did not know I was even on the right street until I heard that accursed song coming from the window…"

Chapter Ten: 1917 — The Encounter on Great Pulteney Street

"If you are not Helen Vaughan, then who are you?" Sâr Dubnotal asked.

"My name is Rebecca Sharp!"

Sâr Dubnotal studied the woman whose initial conflagration of outrage had now cooled to simmering indignation. He was not yet certain she was not Helen Vaughan and this tale of woe but a fabrication. He could no longer wait for Rudolph to return with their colleagues who could settle the matter. If she was an impostor, the real Helen Vaughan was free — though perhaps not yet far beyond Bath. A few minutes might make all the difference in her slipping beyond their grasp.

He began to move to the back of the woman calling herself Rebecca Sharp.

"What — what are you doing? Get off!" she demanded as he took her head between his hands. She thrust her head from side to side to try to wrench it free as he pulled back her blonde locks to examine her scalp. He ran his index finger along a long groove there.

She recoiled from his touch and shouted: "How *dare* you! *Don't touch me there!*"

Sâr Dubnotal did not answer, but crossed the room to open a drawer from which he took a large pair of scissors.

The woman's eyes bulged as he approached her with the sharp object. "What are you going to do?" she gasped out.

"Only the science of phrenology can quickly resolve the enigma you present, Miss Sharp — if that is who you are," the Psychagogue answered. "I have noted an irregularity in your skull — of which you seem very protective. Helen Vaughan is the Devil's child, and that may be your father's mark."

"You're mad!" she gasped.

"Even so, I have studied various specimens of human skulls in the development of my phrenology skills — skills for which, if I may say, I have demonstrated a high aptitude. Your skull shall now testify for or against you. To that end, your head must first be sheared…"

The woman screamed in face of this new humiliation and again struggled against her restraints, lifting the chair legs off the floor in her paroxysms, as the Great Psychagogue moved in to fulfill his declared purpose.

Suddenly, the door thrust inward. Sâr Dubnotal looked up to see Rudolph, Naïni, and the two men he had joined in their quest. One shouted out, "Stop! Whoever she may be — this woman is *not* Helen Vaughan!"

"Finally — someone *sane!*" Becky cried out. "Now will one of you help me rescue my child, now that this turbaned buffoon has sabotaged *my* efforts?"

Chapter Eleven: 1917 —
What Lurked Within the Artists Gallery

Becky Sharp delicately gnawed the broiled chicken breast and surveyed her new and exceedingly colorful surroundings. She was eager for some distraction from the bitingly disappointing report that the two men who had interrupted her head shaving had brought back from Great Pulteney Street. Helen Vaughan had once again absconded with her child. More, the condition in which she had left the house made it clear that she would not be returning.

For that, Becky hated Sâr Dubnotal. But she hated Helen Vaughan far more, and she desperately needed allies in what she had thought was a personal war with that wretched woman. The revelation that she was not a lone foot soldier in that battle gave her more hope than she had had for two years.

She was no longer in the room in which she had been bound, but in the largest one in the flat. Its dimensions were necessary to contain Sâr Dubnotal's entourage, along with a number of guests who had traveled from all over County Somerset to break bread with the renowned Psychagogue.

Becky had bathed and now wore a fresh dress from the wardrobe of *El Tebib's* medium, Gianetti Annunciata. Frankly, the woman gave Becky the creeps: her pale visage suggested the disturbed, emaciated faces of medieval iconography. Becky did not relish wearing a gown — no matter how resplendent — that had rested against the flesh of a conduit to the dead. She couldn't help an occasional, writhing shrug of her shoulders, thinking that she had felt a residual ghost creep over her skin.

Naïni, had recovered and apologized for his role in her mistaken abduction. Becky had not apologized for the bite.

In a corner of the room, a dwarf, perched on a box atop a stool, tossed some chicken to the enormous dog that stood before him. He leaned forward to wipe his greasy fingers on the dog's coat and affectionately tousled the fur of its neck, saying, "Bon Eustache. Bon chien."

Whatever was inside the box thumped against its lid and sides, as though trying to kick through. The dwarf glared harshly at Becky when he saw her staring at this unexplained phenomenon to which no one else at this bizarre soirée was paying attention.

In the middle of the room, before a draped painting on an easel — to be debuted at Sâr Dubnotal's salon that night, before being displayed at the Victoria — two men from the Order of the Golden Dawn were attempting to engage the

Chapter Eleven: 1917 — What Lurked Within the Artists Gallery

Great Psychagogue on a topic that was apparently paramount with them. A blond man named Rudolph stood beside *El Tebib*. Becky had noticed that he seemed to make a point of being always as close to Sâr Dubnotal as possible, never removing his adoring eyes from the pompous fakir.

"Sycophant," Becky hissed under her breath, continuing to chew her chicken, watching and listening to the conversation between Sâr Dubnotal and these men, one of whom spoke with a heavy French accent, the other with an Irish lilt.

"But what about the dream?" the Frenchman said haltingly in English. He was thin, bearded, with a long face. He wore a cabby's hat atop his head, and sloppily put together evening wear. Yet, Becky had heard some gossip that he was actually from the wealthy Toulet family of Paris.

"I have written down my impressions," the Irishman said, producing a leaf of paper from inside his coat. He was handsome in a bookish way, but his disheveled hair added a distracted quality to his appearance that didn't seem appropriate in an academic — absent-minded or not.

As Sâr Dubnotal looked patronizingly at the paper, Toulet spoke again: "I, too, have shared this dream of Monsieur Yeats from across the channel. The *same recurring dream*, between two men who had never met until recently."

Sâr Dubnotal muttered aloud the lines as he cursorily read: "'*Widening gyres*' umm-hmm. '*The rough beast...hour come round at last...*'. Ah, I recognize the motif begun with the gyring falcons. Very nice."

"The dream began with me over ten years ago," Yeats said. "A figure of something half-man, half-beast. I thought of a sphinx..."

But the Great Psychagogue was no longer listening. He brusquely returned the paper to the Irishman. "I am sorry, Mr. Yeats, but the novelty of a sphinx sashaying about the deserts of Palestine must yield to a much more pressing affair of mine. But, please, if the Order of the Golden Dawn should ever need my assistance in the future, feel free to call on me again. Rudolph, before escorting these gentlemen out, make sure that they have my card."

Becky bristled at Sâr Dubnotal's approach, but her feelings were assuaged by the fact that a contingent of artists from the Victoria who were attending the soirée — and who were not part of the Psychagogue's usual crowd — had taken his cue and were also walking towards where she sat. Her father had been a painter, and though her childhood had been impoverished, it was the only time she had known a sense of security. This left her favorably disposed to men who wielded the brush.

Joining the group that was forming around her were the two men who had saved her from a head shaving: Villiers and Clarke, occult investigators who were compiling a mammoth repository of supernatural cases, originally begun by Clarke alone, entitled *Memoirs to Prove the Existence of the Devil*. Helen Vaughan, they had learned, was not the finished chapter in that book, as they had believed.

"Miss Sharp, if you have sufficiently recovered your wits after our unfortunate misunderstanding, we would like to question you about your relationship with Helen Vaughan," Sâr Dubnotal said. "All of these men with me — and little Jacques Courbé in the corner there — have seen their friends suffer catastrophe through their association with her. We have united in a single purpose: to purge this Earth of her vile stain — this time, forever."

"If that is the case, you will find a willing ally in me, gentlemen," Becky said. "Please. Be seated. All of you. I'd like to know the natures of all your grievances. Then I will tell you how my life was nearly destroyed by an ill-considered alliance with the witch."

"Introductions are in order, first," Sâr Dubnotal said. "You'll recall Messrs. Villiers and Clark…"

"Given the circumstances of our meeting," Becky said, looking *El Tebib* in the eye, "I dare say I would be hard pressed to have forgotten them."

Becky thought she could see a hint of a blush in the Psychagogue's face, but he did not design to acknowledge her veiled rebuff and continued the introductions.

"This gentleman," he continued, "is Mr. Aytown, whose own exhibit just closed at the Victoria. What was it called again, Mr. Aytown?"

"*False Impressions of a Hungarian Count*," Aytown said. Becky gave Aytown a slight smile and nod of her head.

"And this is Mr. Randolph, from America." Becky saw a man whose face shone with a mild fanaticism — but one of a benign, even *mirthful*, spirituality. This was no decadent *bon vivant* from the *fin de siècle*. She was intrigued.

Sâr Dubnotal, seeing her interest, seized the moment: "Mr. Randolph is conversant with the powers of good that radiate from the Empyrean void, though he and I conceive of these powers differently…"

The smiling Randolph beamed at her and said, "I see them as an electrical current…"

"…while *I* see them as currents in the fluid," Sâr Dubnotal said. "It is through the fluids that the parasitic larvae swarm, for corruption can only spread through that which is wholesome, fouling the fluids with their rot —"

"Sir, must I remind you that I am trying to eat while you prattle on about secretions and maggots?" interrupted Becky indignantly. "It's revolting!" She looked at the chicken breast she still held in her hands and set it down — loudly — on her plate. "You're about to put me off broiled chicken for life!"

The men about Sâr Dubnotal all squirmed uneasily — except for Randolph, who appeared amused.

For a moment, the mystic's lips pressed tightly, then he relaxed and continued. "An unfortunate aside. Forgive me, Mademoiselle. Your rebuff is an appreciated reminder to stay focused on the business at hand. If you are sufficiently recovered, I will continue:

"This New Englander is Richard Upton Pickman. His current showing at Mr. Serling's Night Gallery is entitled *Back Into the Fabulous Darkness.*"

Becky coldly regarded Pickman, his evening attire immaculate except for an asymmetrically gloved hand. "I loathe the dark," she pronounced curtly.

Sâr Dubnotal knitted his brow; he understood Becky's grudge against him, but wondered what she could possibly have against Pickman.

"The man beside Mr. Pickman," he continued, "is Monsieur Pierre du Prís — whose great-grandfather's canvases of graveyard tableaux were a source of inspiration to our Mr. Pickman. I trust, Messrs Pickman and du Prís, that what is on that draped canvas will not revolt the delicate Miss Sharp further?" Though addressing the men, Sâr Dubnotal looked Becky in the eye so that she wouldn't miss the caustic sparks that shone in his own.

"Indeed not, sir," du Prís said. "What is on that canvas represents a secret technique of great-grandfather's — you haven't visited what the locals call the Judge's House in Benchurch by any chance? Any of you? No? The eponymous judge was rendered by great-grandfather in the same manner as this painting. It is my great pleasure to share his advance on the *trompe l'oeil* with you all tonight."

"We will look forward to it," Sâr Dubnotal said and continued the introductions: "Also from New England, though by a different route than Pickman, is Mr. Tate."

Becky immediately liked the slim, handsome Tate. "And are you also showing at the Victoria, Mr. Tate?"

"I'm afraid not, Miss Sharp. I came here on a pilgrimage, you might say: a long delayed visit to pay my respects at the empty grave of my mentor, Basil Hallward."

"Now, as to these men's grievances concerning Helen Vaughan," Sâr Dubnotal continued, "they had a peer who, when barely more than a boy, fell into the salon which she presided over in the 1880s under the alias of Mrs. Belmont. His name was Aubrey Beardsley, and, like so many to fall under her sway, his life — while still a young one — was cut short."

Pickman spoke up: "Gentlemen, let us be careful to keep our heads lest our quest degenerate into a Salem-style witch hunt. I do want to remind you all that Beardsley's consumption may have been inchoate *before* he met Helen Vaughan."

"Then she sped it on," Aytown snapped. "Many with his affliction live far past 25 years. Are you defending her, Yankee?"

"My dear Pickman," Sâr Dubnotal said, raising his hand. "Villiers and Clarke have shown you their record of the trail of death she left in London. That her association with Beardsley was concurrent can leave no room for doubt."

"I've always suspected she had a hand in poor Basil's disappearance," Aytown said. "And Dorian's fate, too. That portrait could have only been painted under such a malign influence as hers."

"Apparently Lord Henry does not share that opinion," Pickman retorted. "He was intimate with both men, yet remained Helen Vaughan's friend until her demise."

Again, Sâr Dubnotal raised his hand commandingly and aborted Aytown's retort. "Mr. Pickman, need I remind you that Beardsley's death is not the only crime laid to Helen Vaughan's charge? Her maleficence is well documented in Clarke's book. Hers is an evil truly not of this Earth. My late associate Robert Matheson was a medical doctor of sober mind who described via sealed document — which I was instructed to burn or use upon my own discretion — Helen's true ungodly form revealed at the moment of expiration.

"I believe his discovery that she had somehow managed to reincorporate was responsible for the seizure that took his life three and a half years after her death, though, of course, this can never be proven.

"And you may add to all this what she did to poor Jacques over there."

Sâr caught the mischievous gleam in Becky's eyes.

"No, Miss Sharp," the Psychagogue added. "Before you ask, she did *not* shrink him.

"When he was with the circus, Jacques was in love with a perfectly proportioned midget ballerina named Minuette, who would pirouette on a specially prepared saddle atop a pony. Helen Vaughan saw her, proclaimed her adorable, and Minuette was accepted for the first time into the society of 'big people.' Helen would even buy matching outfits for the two of them and have her sit on her lap during her soirées. Minuette resented Jacques's warnings as an attempt to keep her within the fringe society of the circus freaks.

"Of course, by the time Helen was through with her, Minuette was destroyed. Brave Jacques stormed Helen's home in the midst of one of her decadent gatherings atop his previous Eustache, who, like the current one, could be most vicious when his master required it. Jacques himself was armed with a sword, and did not wield it in vain. What followed was…the epitome of 'too horrible to tell.' Let us leave it at that for the nonce.

"Now, Miss Sharp, you know all our grievances. If you will, please tell us yours."

"I shall gentlemen, but before I divulge my story, I think it expedient that we eliminate the traitor sitting here with us."

An almost audible muteness struck the men around the table. Their eyes darted reflexively from side to side despite the restraint they were exercising to not look from face to face.

Chapter Eleven: 1917 — What Lurked Within the Artists Gallery

Becky slammed one hand on the table and pointed with the other: "*J'accuse!* Pickman is Helen Vaughan's spy!"

"What? This is extraordinary!" a clearly stunned Pickman blurted out.

Only Aytown smiled at her revelation. Randolph appeared to be trying to keep an open mind while Tate, with a slight nodding of his head, seemed to already find her charge plausible. Only Pierre du Prís joined Pickman in protesting his innocence:

"Why — this is an outrage! You've never even met the man before tonight, have you?" du Prís said.

"I do not require a prior acquaintance," Becky said, looking Pickman in the eye. "Pickman knows I'm telling the truth, and if you wish to succeed in your quest to destroy Helen Vaughan, I suggest you see that he never leaves this room alive."

Pickman's face twisted with outrage and he stood to his feet, du Prís following his lead: "Clearly, I'm not safe in the same room as this woman! Don't anyone attempt to stop —"

Sâr Dubnotal, who had risen with Pickman, clamped his hand to his shoulder and exuded an inexorable pressure which returned the New Englander to his chair. The Psychagogue then relaxed his grip, and Pickman shrugged off his hand, looking up angrily at him.

"Never touch me again, sir!" he said.

"Believe me, Sâr, you will soon feel that once was enough," Becky said. "In fact, once you hear what I have to say, you'll want to make for the nearest W.C. and *wash* that hand."

"Why you revolting minx!" Pickman sprang across the table at Becky, hands spread and grasping toward her throat. Immediately, Aytown and Tate were on top of him.

Becky did not flinch but smiled, "Oh, dear, now you'll *all* want to make for the water closet. Queue starts on the right…"

They dragged Pickman back across the table, pulling with him the cloth that he clawed into and sending the dishes, cups and cutlery clanging to the floor.

"You're losing your touch, Sâr," Becky said gleefully. "I thought the first trick you magical chaps learned was pulling a table cloth free *without* dislodging the china."

Meanwhile, Naïni had bolted across the room and his strength decided the struggle. The Hindu slammed Pickman back into his chair and held him by his shoulders as the Psychagogue pointed at Becky:

"Woman, shut your mocking mouth — unless you're ready to tell us the basis of your accusation. As far as any of us still know, your 'child' is a fabrication. Perhaps it is you who are in league with Helen Vaughan. Do not make me regret having risen to your defense — if you have played me false…"

Du Prís, who had stood by during all this, helped straighten his friend's disheveled, evening clothes. The skirmish had, of course, captured the attention of the whole group. Eustache the hound growled in the corner and the hair on his back rose. Jacques snapped at him while grasping the back of his neck.

Sâr Dubnotal turned to the others who were moving tentatively from across the room toward the site of the altercation and commanded in a voice that none dared resist: "All of you, stay back. Return to enjoying your meal."

The Psychagogue then saw Rudolph, who had sent Yeats and Toulet on their way, standing in the doorway, eager to hear whatever his master's orders might be.

Sâr Dubnotal made a quick, slight shake of his head. "Rudolph, please close the door on the other side and lock it until you hear expressly from me to the contrary. Naïni, stand before the door on our side.

"Miss Sharp, as you have ruined my soirée, and, I am certain, reduced cook to tears, you had better have evidence to support your charges, or it will not go well with you."

"I think I know what you're capable of, Sâr," Becky said.

The Psychagogue expelled his breath from bloated cheeks. "Your evidence, Miss Sharp — *s'il vous plait*."

Becky sat back in her chair and dropped her hands into her lap, clasping them together and giving them all a demure look as she said, "Why, I don't exactly have it on my person…"

"Then why do you continue to look so revoltingly pleased with yourself?" Sâr Dubnotal thundered.

"It's on his!"

Now it was Becky's turn to rise suddenly from her chair and stretch across the table. She seized Pickman's gloved hand. He shouted indignantly at this new affront, grabbing at and then repeatedly and painfully striking Becky's hand with his other one.

But Becky refused to yield, continuing to wrench the glove from Pickman. Fortunately, Sâr Dubnotal once again came to her aid and grabbed Pickman's assaulting hand. A few more tugs and Becky pulled the glove free. She fell back into her chair and waved the glove over her head, shouting: "*Vive la France! Vive l'Empereur!*"

Pickman quickly clasped his hand over the other to cover an exposed claw, scaly as a rat's tail. Sâr Dubnotal grabbed the covering hand, but du Prís sprung to his friend's defense. The Psychagogue drew up and expanded his shoulders, sending the effete Frenchman falling backwards and tottering.

Then he returned to yanking Pickman's covering hand free, while speaking to du Prís behind him, "Do not attack me again, sir. Your actions make clear you have taken Pickman's part in this affair — pray, do not make your position even more fragile than it already is."

Du Prís stayed put, but struck out verbally: "You condemn him for a deformity he cannot help!"

"No," Tate said, looking down at the claw with his discerning blue eyes. "I was surprised to learn that Pickman was showing at the Victoria — or anywhere — since he vanished from the States without a trace a year ago. I do not know what his choice of subject has been since arriving here, but his paintings back in New England are full of rat-like, man-size creatures. A photograph taken from his studio the night he disappeared showed that he was working from models!"

"What? Impossible!" both Randolph and Aytown exclaimed.

"I tell you…*it was a photograph from life!*" Tate said, his teeth clinched. He then looked at Sâr Dubnotal. "A motif of his paintings was that of the Changeling. Ghoul spawns who become human cuckoos, while the ghouls take the human infants to raise as their own."

"Yes! Changelings! You're intimately familiar with the practice, eh, Pickman?" Becky said triumphantly. "Was that why you hit it off so well with Helen Vaughan, another Hell-spawn bastard like yourself who took *my* child for her own?"

Pickman remained silent, but kept his defiant expression, registering no remorse, though he no longer denied the accusations.

"You will, of course, tell Miss Sharp where we can find Helen Vaughan and her child," Sâr Dubnotal said, his tone making it clear that he was implacable in this regard.

A woman's shriek trilled through the room, and all attention immediately riveted on Gianetti Annunciata who stood, pointing at the draped painting.

Becky smiled at the defeated du Prís while pointing at the Psychagogue: "It would appear *his* medium doesn't care for *your* medium."

"There's blood seeping through the covering!" Annunciata shouted.

"Yes, but in the final analysis…" Becky said with an inquisitive cock of her head and a sideways stare at du Prís, "…is it *art*?"

"Will you ever stop your mocking mouth, woman?" Sâr Dubnotal said, as he made his way to the painting. "Must I remind you how grave is the situation for your own child?"

"You scarcely need to remind me of that, sir! My situation has been grave for two years! If I appear giddy — hysterically so — it's because, for the first time since she was taken from me, I have real hope that I might reclaim my daughter!"

Sâr Dubnotal now approached the veiled painting and carefully touched the red fluid on the canvas's drapery. Examining his wet fingertips to make certain that it wasn't merely wet oils, he then pronounced: "It *is* blood."

He pulled off the covering. On the canvas was a headsman, staring through the eye holes of his hood at the viewer as if he or she would be next. From the honed edge of his axe, the blood seeped.

Sâr Dubnotal indignantly turned on his heel to face Pickman and the blanching du Prís over whose now pale face a sickly glaze of perspiration glistened.

"Pickman!" du Prís shouted. "The painting has betrayed us!" In the next instant, he was bolting for the door, but the giant Hindu caught him. He beat and struck at him heedlessly — and futilely.

"Bring him here, Naïni!" Sâr Dubnotal ordered.

Du Prís's heels scraped the floor as the Hindu pushed the artist along, then planted him before the Great Psychagogue.

"Is *this* that advance on the *trompe l'oeil* you promised us this evening, Monsieur du Prís?" *El Tebib* demanded. "Or is it merely harbinger of something else to follow? Why were you so adamant about leaving the room? There is something more, is there not? A fate that you and Pickman have planned for all of us here, but which you do not wish to share?"

Du Prís slapped moist palms over his face, his nails clawing wretchedly into his flesh. "Yes!" he shouted. "Yes! I beg of you — it is not too late! The headsman has not yet come out of the painting! We can *all* still flee."

"But at least *someone* must die, yes? No matter where we scatter. Once the blood has begun to drip from his axe, I dare say the headsman cannot be turned back from the task at hand." Sâr Dubnotal surveyed the room: "You have all heard his confession. Will any of you dare come between me and the administration upon this person of the same sentence he would have dealt us all?"

Mutely, all shook their heads, though there was a sick horror in their eyes at the bleeding axe and the contemplation of what must now follow.

"Rudolph," Sâr Dubnotal shouted so that he would be heard through the door, "come to me. Naïni, quickly take Monsieur du Prís to the walk-in closet — no, the small room that connects with the W.C. I suspect that arrangement will facilitate leaving the facilities as clean as we found them when we remove hence. Ah, Rudolph, here you are. Take the canvas and go with Naïni. Lock in both artist and painting, Naïni. I suspect you will know when it's time to open the door again."

Du Prís sagged toward the floor. Naïni caught him in his arms. Rudolph came forward, balking at his first reach for the canvas. Then, grasping it by the edges, he walked briskly behind the Hindu, careful that the side with the image of the headsman was not facing him.

"Rudolph, lock the door on the other side on your way out. When you have finished assisting Naïni, return to the door and do not unlock it until you hear from me."

Now Sâr Dubnotal approached Pickman who glowered defiantly at him. The

Chapter Eleven: 1917 — What Lurked Within the Artists Gallery

Psychagogue, in turn, held Pickman in his own, commanding stare. Invisible to the others, inexorable currents of mesmerism from the Sâr were assaulting Pickman's psyche.

"I adjure, you, Pickman, to tell us where we will find Helen Vaughan. You *will* tell me. I sense your resistance, the awakening of defenses buried in your brain in so deep a strata of tissue that you yourself have forgotten that they sleep there. Slept to be awakened for just such a moment as this."

Becky noticed that the hair on Pickman's head was rising as though from a static charge. Then the cutlery began to tremble and Becky saw that his other hand — the "human" hand — was now drawing up into a claw with the same scaling beginning to manifest like a vile stigmata.

Pickman bellowed, leaping to his feet, and Sâr Dubnotal fell back, as Becky and everyone else retreated.

Pickman's body was warping, bursting the seams of his coat, sleeves and pants. His chest expanded, firing buttons from his shirt — and exposing a breast of scabrous flesh.

A snout thrust out from Pickman's face; his jaw seemed to have dislocated, and fangs jutted out from his lower gums and over his upper lip. His face and body had grown increasingly hirsute, sickly gray shoots spreading into tangled brambles of hair.

Now he stood completely revealed: Pickman — the Ghoul!

Eustache tore free from Jacques's grasp, leaving hair in his master's tiny clutching fingers. The dog hurled itself at the Ghoul, the weight of its body slamming into Pickman like a catapulted frozen side of beef. Yet the monstrosity did not even stagger, but grappled to keep off the fangs that frenziedly snipped at its throat.

The Ghoul sank its claws into the hound's sides, causing it to yelp in high pitches of pain, and cease its gnawing. Pickman raised Eustache over his head and hurled him at the crowd huddling on the far side of the room. They scattered as the hound flew towards them. But Eustache fell short, landing on his side in a slide. Still skidding, he righted himself, nails tapping a frantic staccato in an attempt to regain traction.

Jacques was already running toward the Ghoul, his short sword drawn. The rest of the group were surging against the door, shouting and beating on it. But Rudolph remained on the other side, holding the key, unyielding in his word to his master.

"Back, Jacques!" Sâr Dubnotal commanded, and the angered dwarf, while simmering with displeasure, obediently turned to see to his dog.

Only Becky and Annuciata had not run for the door — Annuciata lay in a fainted heap by du Prís's bare easel, and Becky had retreated to a corner, brandishing a steak knife.

"Pickman!" Sâr Dubnotal's voice resonated powerfully as he gestured at the hissing, screeching Ghoul. "Your true self is revealed. You can no longer remain here, for the light has revealed the darkness. Hear me, Pickman! Depart hence! Go to your own place! I bind you to the plane of Leng, into the region of unknown Kadath — there for expiation if it may be that something human remains within you!"

The Ghoul screeched in indignant agony at its humiliation, the screech rising into the unbearable pitch of nails dragging across slate as the room's lights began to drop. Pickman seemed to be drawing the darkness to him in a desperate attempt for succor. Up went a group cry from fear that they would be plunged into the darkness, locked in the room with that thing. But even more quickly than the lights had begun to dim, they rose — into a brighter splendor than they had cast over the chamber before.

And Pickman, the door still locked, was gone.

Sighs of relief were expelled over the room, ending in a moment of silence, pierced immediately by a shrill scream from the corner. Becky charged at Sâr Dubnotal with her knife, shouting:

"What have you done? You took him from me — the one man who could have told me where to find my child!"

She collided with the erect, unmoving mystic, knife raised. Sâr Dubnotal grabbed her thin, delicate wrist, easily disarming her and sending the knife clanking to the floor.

He now grasped both wrists together as Becky writhed in violent spasms: "You're as much a beast as that thing! You have just handed my child over to Helen Vaughan's corruption that will surely transform her into the same bitch of Hell as she is! This is on *your* head, Sâr Dubnotal! Do you hear me? I'll never forgive…"

"*Miss Sharp!*" Sâr Dubnotal's voice struck her like a slap. At once, she ceased her struggles and went limp, sobbing. She would have collapsed to the floor, but the Great Psychagogue caught her up and cradled her

"I did not mean to see it; I did not *mean* to see it. I had no choice…" she mumbled lowly over and over as though in a fever.

"Miss Sharp," the Psychagogue said gently. "I understand that I have given you little reason to trust me. But I do know that your burden is great, that you are in maternal agonies that I cannot begin to fathom. I am your friend, Miss Sharp, though I have not seemed like it. And apart from destroying Helen Vaughan, I wish nothing more than to reunite you with your child.

"But even I, the greatest of Psychagogues, cannot foresee all things. My desire to wrest the truth from Pickman, the unwise use of the fluids' currents as coercion, blew out what I thought were defenses, but were instead psychic barricades he

Chapter Eleven: 1917 — What Lurked Within the Artists Gallery

had set up to restrain the beast within. I could not open the door and unleash the Ghoul upon the city, which meant I was jeopardizing the lives of everyone in this room — including yours. If anyone was to be left to save your baby, Pickman had to be dispatched immediately. Your burden is already too great; I am so sorry for any additional grief I have caused you."

Becky raised her tear-streaked face up at this great man who cradled her, and for the first time, her expression softened as she looked at him.

"Now, dry your eyes," Sâr Dubnotal said as he gently sat her down next to the recovered Annunciata. Distraught as she was, Becky maintained enough of her wits to immediately slide down the couch away from her. "And when you have sufficiently regained your composure, and I have dismissed my extraneous guests, we who remain will hear the circumstances of your relationship with Helen Vaughan."

Chapter Twelve: 1917 —
The Testimony of Rebecca Sharp

"I suppose that when I take my dying breath, I will still be cursing the night I first laid eyes on Helen Vaughan. If only I had not walked into that tavern, choked with soldiers just about to head off to France. But foresight is a luxury those struggling to make it through the day can ill afford.

"I am not proud to say that I was there to barter my flesh with men who knew it may be their last night in their homeland forever. You must understand, gentlemen, how dire my circumstances were. I was with child; I dared not approach the father — and please do not ask why. Suffice it to say, the circumstances of our parting meant any future reconciliation quite out of the question.

"Nevertheless, I could not let our child die or be born sickly and weak for lack of nourishment. So I was in that tavern, surveying the room for the means to insure I would eat that night, and that was when my eyes were compelled to linger on Helen…

"No one *else* in the tavern saw it, or they most certainly would have immediately fled the establishment for France and the comparative safety of the trenches.

"At her shoulder was an impish little satyr, and it was revolting: the sallow skin of its man's torso with pink dugs stretching thin to the waist, the veins bulging on the purplish, pulsating sacks at the base of its horns, the jaundiced eyes that stared with utter contempt at the mass of humans about it, the nastily tangled fur of its legs….

"It was the same type of beast I saw at Pickman's elbow this evening. That was how I knew he was allied with Helen. And I reasoned his glove concealed that which, unlike that satyr, would otherwise be visible and which he did not wish to be seen.

"I can see the inevitable question in all your faces: 'how is it that you perceived something that we walked about — and that walked about us — and we could not?' I do not know for certain, gentlemen, but I strongly suspect that it has something to do with lingering effects from my pregnancy. Though I had seen such things before that night in the tavern, I had no such visions *before* I conceived.

"I'm certain it had nothing to do with the father. My body went through a preternatural change in its make-up — again, do not ask — some time before I met him."

She allowed herself a slight, wry smile. "Believe me: you would all be astonished by how my youthful beauty belies my true age.

"It would seem entirely logical, then, that the heightened state of a human body no longer merely 'a *little* lower than the angels' would have its own brand of prenatal quirks and unexpected side effects. Some women get flat feet; I saw monsters.

"I had not asked for this burden, but it was what caused me to linger my gaze longer than I should have on Helen Vaughan. To take note of a face that would have otherwise remained indistinct amidst the constant shifting of persons in the low lighting of the tavern.

"Well, I found my Jack for the evening, and we retired to the alley behind the tavern to transact business. Unfortunately, this solider was not so intoxicated that he disregarded my swollen abdomen which my clothing had so far concealed. With a look of shock and revulsion on his face, he began to beat me and did so until I lost consciousness.

"When I awoke, Helen Vaughan was over me, palpating my body — trying to ascertain that I was still alive, she claimed, though I'm sure now she was trying to take any money or valuables off my person. I have no doubt that she would have strangled me in my weakened state and then continued her pillaging, except that my eyes opened on her ring, and I blurted out in my confusion:

"The goat man on your ring — was it *he* at your shoulder?"

Her hands hovered over me. "You saw him?" she asked after a moment.

"In the tavern."

Her face froze in astonishment, and it was only when her hands dropped to my person and touched again my abdomen that her expression resolved into the sweetest, solicitous-of-my-health smile.

"My sister," she said.

"She gathered me up, took me to her own run-down lodgings, and nursed me back to health. During this time, she asked me repeatedly the identity of my baby's father, but I would not expose him to her so that she could blackmail him or charge him a ransom for our child. After a time, she mentioned it no more.

"I was not stupid, gentlemen. I knew she was trouble, but I had no other friend. I shudder now at how much like Helen my latest reversals had made me; I have never been a saint, but I had believed the love I had of one man, and the love I had for the one whose child I bore, had somehow redeemed me. Now, with no chance of recourse to either, I quickly warmed to Helen Vaughan's considerate ministrations.

"I found my bitterness and rage, tempered in a furnace of helplessness and despair, commensurate with what ever black, vile abscess festered inside her where a *human* heart would beat — at least to the point that when I was sufficiently recovered, we began to work as a team. Helen would seduce the soldiers into a private place and together we would rob them. I struck many of them over the head until they lost consciousness — repeatedly so, if need be — each time seeing the face of the soldier who had so beaten me.

"I am not proud of my behavior, gentlemen. But unless your life has ever ebbed into so dark a place that no beam of light can penetrate it, pray, *do not* judge me.

"With the money we had thus accumulated, Helen suggested since my delivery was now near, we remove to her home village of Caermaen. Though a scandal had caused her to flee from there — the cause, I suspected, of the nasty scar around her neck of which she would never speak — she assured me that many years had passed, and her appearance was much changed.

"Helen often took me walking along what had been her favorite childhood haunt — the Roman road. It was on such a promenade in the winter months that I went into labor. And it was Helen who served as midwife as the pains of labor came nigh to wrenching me out of this world. My agonies sent me teetering on the edge of it and the nightmare one that enveloped me.

"As I pushed, I saw on my breast a horned succubus, leering into my eyes. I could actually feel its weight on my chest, choking my breathing — that's how close I came to its hellish abode. As Helen tore my child from my body, I could see behind her, surrounding us, a crowd of horned, wretched, twisted things. I could make out every detail of their perverse anatomies: from the crusted matter caking the rims of their yellow eyes to the sickening pinkness of the dugs rowed over their foul abdomens. *And my child, not I, was the subject of their intent focus!*

"Like that of a crowing cock compelling what ghosts have walked the night back into purgatory, my child's first cry banished those monsters from the periphery of our world and returned them completely to their own sphere. A darkness that had hung over the whole dreadful proceedings suddenly passed, and I could feel a soothing sense of normalcy rush over me in the twitter of winter birds and the wind in the trees that surrounded us.

"Helen," I weakly croaked out, hearing my child's continuing cries, "I…want to see…my baby."

"But helpless on my back as an upside down tortoise, I could see only an empty sky, and now even the child's wailing had suddenly gone silent.

"My heart thudded mightily against my ribs as I tried to wrench myself up from the ground, but I was too weak after my ordeal.

"HELEN!" I shouted. "BRING ME MY BABY!"

Only then did she lean into my field of vision, but without my child. As she switched my papers with her own and slipped her ring on my finger, she said in mockingly sweet tones:

"Relax, Becky, darling. It's a girl."

And then I saw the large fragment of ancient Roman masonry rushing down upon me.

"You now understand, Sâr Dubnotal, the origins of that groove you found atop my head. My skull was sufficiently crushed, or you can be sure that Helen would not have left the job half-done. Nevertheless, I possessed a resilience she could not suspect, and I retained enough consciousness to hear that witch chanting to my child as she walked down the old Roman road:

> *Old King Cole was a merry old soul*
> *And a merry old soul was he;*
> *He called for his pipe, and he called for his bowl*
> *And he called for his fiddlers three.*

"And then the red mist that hung over my eyes darkened, and I knew no more.

"I know not how many days passed before I was found on that deserted road. Fortunately, no one checked my papers or recognized the ring until I was taken to a doctor, for Helen was not remembered fondly by the good people of Caermaen. I was told that as I laid unconscious in the hospital, I was saved from suffocation by pillow at the hands of some grieved parent whose child Helen had ruined years before.

"The village doctor, who had no love for Helen either, still insisted that any punitive action be delayed until my swollen features healed enough to see if they could be recognized. He realized I might be Helen's victim, that she could very well have switched our papers in hope that the locals would murder and bury me in an unmarked grave. They would thus serve their enemy's further purpose by erasing all evidence in the event of an investigation into *my* disappearance. I believe now there was a second reason Helen switched our papers: her fear that Villiers and Clarke might learn, as they indeed did, of her resurrection. I am certain this fear was why she chose the anonymity of a guttersnipe's existence for so long. Thus the need of a new identity — *my* identity — to move more freely about England and reunite her followers.

"Of course, when it became apparent that I was indeed yet another victim of Helen Vaughan, the locals took pity on me and nursed me, though all expected me to die. Even with my preternatural ability to regenerate, a year passed before I was able to leave Caermean in pursuit of my child. Yet another year went by before I again heard that cursed song from that upstairs window on Great Gualteney Street

"Once before, about six months after I left Caermean, I had a near reunion with my Annie and Helen. In one village, I learned of the arrival only a month before of a woman of an unsettling mien leading a toddler by the hand. Both were dressed in filthy and disheveled clothing. The authorities were so bold as to take the child from this unfit mother and place her in an orphanage five miles away.

"Naturally, I rushed to the site, and as night fell, I saw the glow of a conflagration on the horizon. I found the orphanage on fire. No children survived the night. They laid on the ground, burned black, some of them so much so that…" here Becky shuddered "…that their skins had split open in places."

"Dear Lord," Clarke said.

"I shall never forget," Becky said, "how the pain that would not release them to the relief of death twisted their little faces into the most ghastly of grimaces. It was as though their voices could not convey the depths of their pain, so the flesh itself was wailing.

"Each of their faces is so etched in my memory, gentlemen, because I did not know — *could* not know — which one of these wretched figures might be my child. I was forced to study each of the agonized little girls.

"How relieved I was to receive the news upon the breaking of day that Annie had been removed from the orphanage by Helen, and that the witch had set the blaze to conceal her latest abduction of my child by creating the impression she had been consumed in the flames. I had this account from one of the authorities who interrogated the orphanage handy man. Helen had seduced him into aiding her, but he swore on his death bed that he had no idea of her full plan until she put a knife in his back and began setting the fire. That the woman was Helen was clear from his description of the nasty groove around her neck.

"The Sâr, Clarke, and I are all very familiar with the events of this last episode in your story, Miss Sharp," Villiers said. "We three have been on Helen's trail since Sâr Dubnotal came to London with his letter from our late, esteemed associate Dr. Matheson. The Sâr wished to examine Helen's remains to add the description of such a creature to his repository of occult knowledge. It was then we discovered her body had vanished. Since only Clarke and I knew where she was buried, and the full range of her dark powers were unknown to us, it was all too possible that she had resurrected herself. Our subsequent investigation confirmed this horrible truth.

"That search led us, too, to that orphanage a few days after its burning, after reading in the papers that the villagers were certain it was the work of the "devil-woman" who sought revenge for the taking of her child. That Helen Vaughan had reproduced was perhaps more frightening to contemplate than her reincorporation.

"Miss Sharp," Villiers said, going on one knee so that he could look her in the eye as he warmly clasped her delicate hand between his two, "Helen Vaughan is the spawn of a human woman and an entity from that hellish dimension you glimpse

Chapter Twelve: 1917 — The Testimony of Rebecca Sharp

on occasion. After hearing your story, we are much relieved to learn that Providence has apparently rendered her sterile. When she saw you were pregnant, and that you could see the satyr — well, those were the circumstances of her own mother and father. When you steadfastly refused to divulge the paternity of your baby, it only confirmed what she already suspected: here was a child of a similarly abominable conception by the same sire, and — being of her own perverse lineage — her chance for a daughter."

"Clarke, if you would bring my valise…"

Once his partner had delivered it to him, Villiers opened it and took out a stick with a metal noose on one end. "We thought this sufficient to destroy her, and if Sâr Dubnotal had not arrived with Dr. Matheson's letter, requesting to see the remains of this foul creature, we would have never known she had resurrected. It appears you have paid the price for our folly."

"She suffered by this garrote?" Becky asked, sniffing.

"Much agony."

"*Bonne*," Becky said. "Please, might I hold on to it? It would be such a comfort."

An expression of both puzzlement and distaste immediately registered on Villier's face at her request. Still, he said, "Of course" folded her hands about the stick, and rose to his feet.

Sâr Dubnotal had listened intently to Becky's tale, and while Villiers talked, he had withdrawn into a deep state of meditation over her story. He suddenly snapped his fingers, as though to awaken himself from his own trance, turning the attention of all assembled upon him.

"Miss Sharp, do you still have Helen's ring on your person? Yes? If you would be so kind as to hand it to me. Ah — thank you."

Sâr Dubnotal held the ring out, pinched between thumb and forefinger, so that the satyr's head could be seen by all. "The nursery rhyme, Miss Sharp. Have you ever thought that it might have some special significance to Helen Vaughan?"

Becky slowly shook her head from side to side. "I must confess I have not."

Dubnotal now examined the inscription inside the ring band. "Here 'tis written, DEVOMNODENT-MAVORS CAMVLOS. The first part translates roughly "Nodens, the god" – of the abyss, in this case. That then is the identity of the satyr on this ring, though the name 'Pan' is by far more common. The second part of the inscription gives yet a third and fourth title: MAVORS CAMVLOS, or Mars-Camulos. Camulos was a Celtic god sometimes depicted satyr-like with the horns of a ram and who, through syncretism, became identified with their Roman conquerors' deity Mars.

"As to the significance of that tormenting nursery rhyme, Miss Sharp, it is a palimpsest through which we can still discern the pagan under-text: King 'Cole' *is* Camulos. We may *assume* that his pipe is for smoking, but the fact that he calls for three fiddlers indicates it was originally musical pipe*s* — *Pan* pipes.

"If this still seems mere speculation to any of you, let me add this to remove all doubt: the oldest city in England, built by the Romans, was named Camulodonum after Camulos. Today it still bears his name, though softened — just as in that nursery rhyme — to Colchester. It is inevitable that Helen will retreat to her father's house.

"Then, that is where my child —," Becky began, her voice choking on a sense of hope she wasn't sure she could trust.

Sâr Dubnotal reached down and firmly gripped her by her shoulders. "Be strong, Miss Sharp, for not all of what I'm about to say will be comforting: Helen *is* taking her to Colchester — to meet Camulos."

Chapter Thirteen: 1917 —
Out From the Abyss

"**B**ut do not despair," the Great Psychagogue said. "Helen Vaughan's arrogance and manipulative schemes have already given us the keys to her undoing.

"Villiers! Clarke!" he said. "Go immediately to the train depot, and obtain a list of every train station along the railways from Bath to Colchester. Have dispatched a telegraph to the stationmasters describing Helen Vaughan and ordering they place highly visible wanted posters for her, with your names prominently attached to each in large block letters.

"The dispatcher will be reluctant to do what you ask, of course. Therefore, take this signet ring of mine and have him describe it via wire to the county Somerset railway superior stationed at Cad Green. This man is in my debt for services rendered on his behalf in the Affair of the Leprous Bodhisattva."

"But…why would we want Helen to know we are on to her?" Clarke asked. "Even if we make it impossible for her to travel by train, and slow her progress…"

"Exactly, but my reason is twofold: you two are the only men Helen Vaughan fears, so she will take every precaution now that you are on her trail, most certainly including a disguise. You see, she does not have the option of turning back. I now recognize our earlier guest Yeats' poem about the return of a beast-man as the record of a prophetic — if distorted — dream. Based on his poem, I suspect *this* meeting of Helen with her father at Colchester will be a uniquely tangible one. Her cult, which is surely gathering there to join her for this event, will be alerted to expect her arrival incognito.

"Miss Sharp, I return Helen's ring to you. Keep it safe, for it, along with the papers she placed on your person, will aid in your passing yourself off as your enemy, thereby granting us ingress into this vile sabbat.

"Villiers and Clarke, little Jacques and his Eustache will go with you. Once that you see the telegram is dispatched properly, all of you will board the next train to Colchester. But first, make a second request of the Somerset railway superior. For my sake, ask if he will prepare an alternate schedule for all trains arriving at Colchester for the next forty-eight hours. It should place them two hours behind their actual arrival. *This* schedule is to be presented to any who might request it — except those whose duty is to see that the trains arrive safely. Helen's cult will be monitoring your pursuit, and this will grant us an element of surprise. Jacques — I suppose I need not remind you to bring your box? I thought not."

At that point, Naïni entered the room.

"Naïni — has du Prís received due recompense?"

"He has, master."

"Then justice has been served. Rudolph…Annuciata: normally I would dispense this detail to Naïni, but I have need of him elsewhere. To you, I'm afraid, falls the unpleasant task of disposing of du Prís's remains."

A stunned Rudolph opened his mouth but was mute, his face contorting with more and more revulsion as the exact nature of this grim detail settled in.

Annuciata, however, immediately found *her* voice: "Please master! Wouldn't I be more useful channeling his spirit – something more along my line?"

"If I may," Aytown injected. "One theory of Basil Hallwood's disappearance that we…," he nodded at Randolph and Tate, "…have investigated was that his murderer could have disposed of his body through dissection in a tub and then an application of acid."

"Yes," the Sâr replied. "That was exactly my idea in having du Prís taken to the room adjoining a water closet with bath. Messers. Aytown, Tate, and Randolph — though I'm sure you wish to personally take the battle to Vaughan, you would best serve all our interests here. But be assured, your friend Beardsley *shall* be avenged, and you all will be witness to it.

"Your investigation into Hallwood's disappearance has, no doubt, made you familiar with the milieu of such men who might discretely provide us with such items as we need in the matter of Monsieur du Prís. Will you be so good as to obtain them? And aid Rudolph in their administration? Poor Annuciata over there has actually managed to exceed her usual pallor — altogether, quite remarkable. Feel free to retire to your room, my dear Annuciata. And, for pity's sake — be careful of *which* WC you visit over the next forty-eight hours.

"In the meantime, Miss Sharp, Naïni, and I will board the earliest train to Colchester. Hopefully, the circulation of the wanted poster will force Helen off the railways sooner than later and allow us to arrive first, delaying her inevitable challenge of our ruse. This should give us plenty of time…," here, a smile parted the lips of the Great Psychagogue, a smile which, though slight, was weighted with foreboding, "…to do some damage of the irreparable sort."

The turbaned man who identified himself as Severus *El Tebid* and the cloaked and hooded woman calling herself Helen Vaughan strolled through the midsummer's eve twilight that had now enveloped Colchester. A giant draped under cape and cowl followed. Fresh dew shone on the grass, and the stars themselves seemed just minted. The night air was soft and all nature insouciant on the cusp of its dissolution.

"I still do not quite understand," the woman under the hood said, "why Helen has waited two years to deliver my baby to that thing she believes is Annie's father."

The three were passing an ancient oak which the locals had mentioned was 750 years old. At the sight of it, Severus *El Tebid* thought again of Yeats' poem that he had, on more than one occasion over the last 48 hours, regretted not committing completely to memory.

"It was not given to her to choose the moment of his coming," he said. "Take a lesson from the oak, Miss Sharp: should it be sawed off at the trunk, you would see concentric rings, one for each year of its 750 years of growth. The past, you see, is not simply done — it is yet present inside of that tree. Its cross section is both a chart of Time and a symbol of its cyclic nature.

"Camulos, I suspect, *was* here, in the deep time *before* men, but at some point was locked *out*. In the revolving of the ages, it seems there are certain junctures that could be favorable for his return. Among the natives in Africa there is a similar tradition of *L'mur-Kathulos*, while the South Seas Kanakas look to the gyring consolations as the harbinger of *Tulu*.

"Miss Sharp — are you trembling?"

"Just…the chill from the evening dew," she said and even her voice shivered. "Please, go on '*El Tebid*'…or should I say, 'doctor?'"

"According to Mr. Yeats, the last propitious moment for Camulos was approximately two thousand years ago. But at that point, Camulos was forced into slumber; the human race was granted an extension to allow for the grace of Christ to take global effect — which would have been sufficient to lock out Camulos forever. Well…to see what we did with that opportunity, I submit for your consideration 'the blood-dimmed tide' of 'the war to end all wars.'

"But I rather think this time around *we* are set against Camulos' coming as God's appointed conspirators. A motley lot to be sure, but then, so were Christ's first disciples."

"I suppose I fill the spot of the woman taken in adultery, then?" Becky asked, her smile sardonic beneath her hood.

El Tebid's cheeks burned under his beard. "It was perhaps…not so much an analogy as an *induction*, Miss Sharp."

"I understand all you have said so far, doctor — believe me, far more than you could ever suspect. But why are you certain that the cult of Helen Vaughan is gathering at the old castle?"

"Like a tree, a building may retain past time in its present: a phenomenon responsible for more than one haunting I have investigated. Now, that castle is built on the foundation of the burned temple of Claudius, erected contemporaneously with the rise of Christianity — which Yeats sets as the *terminus a quo* of the epoch which the arrival of his 'rough beast' will end. Within Colchester Castle, all time from the beginning of Christianity's spread throughout the world unto this very moment is present: as it contains the *terminus a quo*, it is the most apropos point for the inauguration of the *terminus ad quem*."

Now Severus *El Tebid* touched Becky's elbow while holding up his other hand at Naïni and nodded slightly at one of the Australian soldiers who currently filled Colchester Hospital. The trio stopped to watch the soldier angle up a telescope on its tripod. Nearby a large searchlight set on the ground.

Becky drew her hood down lower to veil her face as much as possible as *El Tebid* said, "Excuse me, sir. You seem to be surveying the constellations — may I ask you for what purpose?"

"I'm not stargazing, if that's what you mean," the soldier answered without looking at who addressed him, his face grimacing with the effort of keeping his eye properly attached to the viewfinder. "The first Zeppelins that bombed England last year chose a route in this vicinity for their return to Germany. Makes sense they might come *back* this way."

"I see. Goodnight, sir. And thank you for your efforts on all our behalves."

The soldier grunted something, still without looking at who addressed him, steadfastly intent on searching the skies.

Now they came at last to Colchester Castle. How Helen's cult had obtained the use of the facilities, *El Tebid* did not know, but he felt certain it had more to do with some mundane form of blackmail or coercion than any occult "hostile current."

Bearing electric torches, three muscular men in evening wear were quickly making their way across the lawn toward them. Naïni's cape rustled as he began to move it back to give his long, massive limbs freedom, but Severus *el Tebid* slightly raised one hand. "Not yet Naïni. Not until we see there is no other recourse."

Still, the cloaked giant had to do no more than stand there for the men to stop short of the trio. They were armed, and their hands were already at their holstered revolvers in case Naïni should begin to encroach upon them.

"Who are you?" the leader of the guards demanded.

Becky alone stepped forward. Her heart was racing, for if Helen had somehow managed to beat them here, things were about to get much more difficult.

She extended her hand from the long sleeve of her cloak, letting her wrist dip to display Helen's ring. "I am Helen Vaughan," she said. "Behold the ring that bears the visage of my great sire — god of the abyss, lord of fortresses. Surely you were told that the pursuit of my mortal enemies Villiers and Clarke necessitated I come in disguise? Was this identifying effect not described to you? Does anyone without my birthright *dare* wear it? Do any of *you* fools dare come between me and my father?"

The guards now were more cowed by Becky than Naïni. The leader took tentative steps toward her while the other two hung back. He did not dare touch her hand to lift it, but instead bent and held his electric torch near.

"My lady!" he gasped in awe and quickly stepped away. "I will run ahead to announce your arrival. My men will escort…"

"Fool! Do you not see that I *already* have an escort? And no one shall know I am here until *I* deign to reveal it. All of you return to patrolling the grounds."

"Well played, Miss Sharp," *El Tebid* said when the guards were out of earshot.

The threesome finished their approach without further impediment. Upon entering the main chamber of the castle, they found before them men and women from England's and France's highest societies, dressed as though they were attending the symphony.

"Dilettantes and elitists," Severus *el Tebid* said and sniffed contemptuously. "These fools all think they are attending nothing more than a glorified version of table rapping or *planchette*. They play with strange fire in the decadent idleness of the privileged, heedless of what they are about to unleash. '*Sur vous le Deluge.*'"

From behind Becky, a salutation delivered in an effete, urbane intonation: "Helen! Is it you? Here at last? It has been too long since 'Mrs. Belmont' held court over her infamous Ashley Street salon, eh?"

"Do not turn," *El Tebid* hissed under his breath.

The immaculately dressed man with his trimmed goatee the color of ash was now upon them. The whites of his eyes were shot through with tiny red tendrils, and the crevices of his crow's feet had reached his cheeks. Still, that this was once a devilishly handsome face was discernible under a now sallow complexion.

"Helen! Surely you have not forgotten your most devoted admirer, Harry? It's Lord Henry!" As a jaundiced hand reached for her shoulder to turn her, *El Tebid* imposed himself between Becky and the aristocrat.

Lord Henry withdrew his hand but did not step back. "Swarthy heathen! You dare come between me and a friend I thought I would never see again?"

"I dare nothing less! You, sir, certainly know of the trauma which she suffered and how she changed form into a writhing obscenity at the point of expiration. Perhaps you have not heard that, since her resurrection, she has not been able to completely assume full *human* form — and such human features as she retains have been misshapened. Even her vocal chords have thickened. She ventures out silent and hooded to spare herself the humiliation of the involuntary shock and revulsion that could not help but strike even the closest of friends."

Lord Henry's hooded pupils shifted from *El Tebid* to the giant who loomed protectively over the turbaned man. Still, he stood his ground. "Do you think me a fool? That I would just take a stranger's word?"

"*Harry*," Becky croaked as she turned and extended her arm, her hand thrusting from the sleeve of her cloak. Lord Henry gasped. "The ring!"

"Do you wish to examine it?" *El Tebid* said. "Helen told me beforehand to grant this dispensation only to her closest friends to assure them, under these extreme circumstances, that it is indeed her."

El Tebid reverently removed the ring from Becky's still extended hand, then placed it in Lord Henry's palm. As he held it close to his bloodshot eyes, Henry said, "This craftsmanship cannot be reproduced today — and there is the inscription of the names of her father. Only she and her nearest associates — of whom I am one — knew what was written on the inside of the band. And she wore it only on special occasions, keeping it at all other times in a place known only to her. It was not on her person when she died. We thought it either pilfered or its location lost with Helen."

He returned the ring to *El Tebid* who placed it back on Helen's finger. "My dear Helen," Lord Henry began, "I am so sorry for your misfortunes. Forgive me for adding to your distress. But we must announce your arrival!"

Severus held up his palm. "It is Helen's wish not to reveal herself until her father restores her former glory at his advent, and she takes her place at his left hand."

"Of course," Lord Henry said. "And please — you are?"

"Severus *El Tebid* — you may simply call me 'doctor.'"

"Quite. Please, Doctor Severus, accept my apology, sir. You and this" — he nodded at Naïni "— *giant* are her escorts, then? Ha! Few would be inclined to engage in fisticuffs with *this* bruiser, eh?"

"Villiers and Clarke would be most hesitant to attempt to murder her again with such a bodyguard, yes."

"Our spies have reported they are bearing down on us — in the company of a monstrous hound and its master, a most untoward dwarf I once had the displeasure of knowing. Although it was obviously something of a stretch for him, we of Helen's salon sought to school him extensively in the secret knowledge, but he could only see it as a short subject. When it became clear our investment in him was one of diminishing returns, he — and his flea bitten cur — were expelled from our company.

"No matter: they will all arrive too late. I assume, now that Helen is here, I may order those who have assembled in the Roman cellar to begin the summoning?"

"Immediately," *El Tebid* said.

"Sâr!" Becky said when Lord Henry was out of earshot. "What are you doing? Why are you hurrying this on with Helen and my child not yet arrived?"

"We would only revive his suspicions by not agreeing to what Helen Vaughan has expressly come to do. But be at ease, Becky, and let me concentrate. I have not before attempted hypnotism on quite this scale, but the wills of these people are as thin and pallid as their inbred blood."

El Tebid swept his gaze back and forth over the lengthy table where the idle rich had all gathered, until he made eye contact with a dandy. In an instant, the current of mesmeric magnetism rushed across the room, and the man was held by *El Tebid*'s will. After a pause, the man began arranging his dishes, cutlery, and other dining implements into diagonal lines, then did the same to the dinnerware of whom sat at his right and left. Baffled, they stared as he rose, compelled to carry on this task around the entire table, raising ires as more than once his leaning over his fellow diners put an elbow in someone's face.

El Tebid had now strolled across the room to the table. As the rest of the group looked up at him, he threw open wide the floodgates of his eyes and the rapacious force that swept out took them all.

In a moment it was over: his mission accomplished, the dandy returned to his chair, and all returned to their idle chatter, unmindful of 'the doctor' as he withdrew.

"What exactly did you do?" Becky asked.

El Tebid smiled and slightly raised his hand. "Watch," he said.

Becky noticed that as people tried to remove the dishes and other utensils back to their places in the wake of the dandy, they could not lift them despite what turned into strenuous efforts.

"Hypnotic suggestion," *El Tebid* explained. "Those diagonal lines form sigils wedged into Camulos' point of ingress. The sigils will snare him between our world and what lies behind it until his moment has passed, and he must return fully back into the abyss."

"But if someone you *didn't* hypnotized enters the room…?"

"Other than Helen and whoever accompanies her, no one else will. Lord Henry would not have begun the summoning unless the coven was complete. He was only awaiting Helen's arrival — which you were kind enough to supply. I dare say when the real Helen comes, she will not take time to count the silverware, and those who are with her will be too intent on their mistress to care how the table is prepared. As for Lord Henry, upon his return to the chamber, should he move toward the table, he can be persuaded to do otherwise easily enough."

"What the deuce does *that* mean?!"

They all startled at Lord Henry's exclamation, but he was still out of earshot of their lowered voices, his attention riveted on the action across the room.

When Henry had rejoined *El Tebid's* group, he asked, "What on earth did Monsieur N. think he was doing? Why, he has become as fantastical in his behavior as Doctor Johnson! I'll put an end to this before he further disrupts —"

"YOU WILL DO NO SUCH THING, LORD HENRY," *El Tebid* commanded and the force of his words struck Lord Henry stock-still.

"What the deuce?! Who…who are you? Who are you *really*?" Lord Henry said as his voice trailed into a whisper.

"The one who knows *all* that you have done in public and private over a lifetime that has lingered far too long in this world. I know by name those you have corrupted, and their loved ones to whom you have dealt a lifetime of woe with *no cause* but to satisfy your vanity and contempt.

"You who have sown the vile seed in the field of innocence, know that the reaping is at hand. 'The axe is already laid to the roots.' I will deal with you personally, Lord Henry. *Your* only choice is this: shall you suffer the fell stroke *now* or tomorrow…or the day after tomorrow? In a fortnight or next month? But be sure of this: *I shall not tarry!*"

Lord Henry's knees dipped and his face blanched. Even here, amidst the cult, he knew he was not safe.

"Retire to that corner where you will be under the watchful eye of my manservant. Speak to no one, nor move one muscle. Be as still as if…as if you are posing for a portrait. I trust I am clear. Naïni, if you will."

"You frighten me, Sâr Dubnotal," Becky said as Naïni escorted Henry. "And that is not an easy accomplishment."

He smiled down at her. "Rebecca Sharp, the downtrodden and innocent victim shall never have cause to fear me — only the guilty."

"That is most…comforting," Becky said as she withdrew her face even deeper into the folds of her hood.

"ALL RISE FOR THE ADVENT OF OUR LADY OF PANDEMONIUM!"

Four figures stood in the castle doorway which remained open, framing them against the night sky. The stars had gone out in the wake of Helen Vaughan, leaving behind the four a dark void that went on forever. The three men who had intercepted Becky, *El Tebid*, and Naïni made a guard about her. She stood hooded and cloaked, radiating a malicious self-possession. With a haughty toss of her head, her hood fell to her shoulders. Her hair was fire and her face a mask of porcelain most adamantine. And in her arms, she cradled a small child.

Sâr Dubnotal's hand was already reaching to restrain Becky. But he found Becky was the epitome of composure and stood as straight and regal as did Helen Vaughan. Only then did the Sâr think to look for Lord Henry, who, at the announcement of Helen's arrival, had stopped on his way to the corner. Now he was grinning triumphantly at Sâr Dubnotal as he brushed by Naïni and strode toward his new enemy.

But Sâr Dubnotal displayed no concern. It was clear he considered both Lord Henry and his moment of triumph beneath contempt. "Reduced to hiding behind a woman's skirts, Lord Henry?" he asked out of the corner of his mouth as the dissipated aristocrat stopped beside him.

Henry shot the doctor a sour look, then shouted, "Helen! I have found out three impostors among us! And this wench has gone so far as to dare impersonate *you*!"

He reached to pull away Becky's hood, but Naïni had followed and his hand shot out and enveloped Henry's frail one. He winced as he felt and heard something snap.

"*Manners*, Lord Henry," Sâr Dubnotal said, shaking a finger at him. Henry fell back, gingerly working the fingers of his injured hand while cradling it in the other.

And then, for the first time, Helen Vaughan spoke:

"All this is known to me."

"It would appear the guards have licked the red off Lord Henry's confection," Sâr Dubnotal murmured to Becky.

Helen put out her arm and flicked her wrist in an imperious gesture that ended with her forefinger pointing at Becky. "Let me see the face of she who has dared try to supplant the chosen daughter of Nodens, the handmaiden of chaos!"

All heads turned toward Becky as she calmly drew back her hood and smiled at the woman whose status as an enemy outstripped any adversary she had faced before.

Helen's eyes widened in reflex, and Becky was gratified to see 'the chosen daughter of Nodens' look at her with a disbelief that was almost awe. But she quickly turned her expression into one of a smiling, sinister dominance.

"I see you still have my ring," Helen said, slightly craning her head forward.

"I see you still have my child," Becky said, still smiling.

"Yes," Helen said, making a point to lower her head to the face of the child in her arms and smile as though she might coo. Then Helen looked up at Becky. "I am so happy that, in your final moments — and you may be sure you will most certainly be dead this time — you might see what good care I have taken of your baby. I hope, since your eyes shall close forever on this sight, it might keep your eternal rest peaceful."

Sâr Dubnotal remained silent. He was watching Becky for her reaction. Her shoulders had not slumped, nor had she ceased to smile. Her countenance showed no sign of defeat. Becky was up to something which she had not shared with him. Since Helen Vaughan was presently neither concerned with him nor Naïni, *El Tebid* bided his time.

"Until the opportune moment presents itself," thought the Great Psychagogue, "discretion dictates that I leave this one to the ladies."

"Now," Helen continued, "bring me my ring. While I hold your child, you will kneel before me and place it on my finger. Come, wench! And if you fail to keep your hands before you, you will be shot on the spot!"

Becky, serenely obedient, proceeded to do as told and soon stood before her archenemy. But she neither moved to kneel nor to remove the ring from her hand

"The ring!" Helen demanded.

Becky's gaze bore into Helen's eyes as she continued to remain still and silent.

"Do you want to die *now*, cow? No — you're too much of a survivor for that. What is wrong with you? *Say something!*"

"I'm going to kill you, Helen."

Helen's head jerked as though stunned by a slap, but immediately she turned this tremor into a spasm of a haughty laugh. "I do not die easily," she said.

"Why, Helen," Becky said with a guileless smile, "why ever would you think that I *want* it to be easy?"

Becky's right arm now dropped to her side — and from its sleeve slipped the end of the stick with the metal garrote which Becky had told Villiers she had returned to his valise. The necessary haste to carry out Sâr Dubnotal's orders had not allowed for reflection on Becky's earlier odd regard for that instrument of death until he, Clarke, Jacques, and Eustace were on their train to Colchester.

Upon sight of that metal noose, the imperious mask of Helen Vaughan cracked. She looked from the garrote into a face whose expression made clear that, despite her current unwinnable circumstances, nevertheless, Becky would, somehow, inevitably, mange to squeeze her throat by that noose until the wires touched.

Helen's hand went to the scar which the collar of her gown concealed. "Kill her!" she screamed at her guards. "Kill the bitch *now!*"

"I THINK *NOT!*"

Sâr Dubnotal's voice stunned the guards as though the mystic had hurled a thunderbolt across the room. In the next moment, they were again grabbing at their weapons. But the moment that Sâr Dubnoal had purchased was enough:

"I am going to kill you, Helen."

Chapter Thirteen: 1917 — Out From the Abyss

A large, airborne hound thrust through the still open door and struck full on the guard on Helen's left, sending him down before he could remove his gun. The dog's jaws clamped onto his throat. As their trajectory had carried them past the guard on Helen's right, the dwarf atop the hound had sliced the razor honed edge of his sword across the man's throat.

Helen, her features contorted by shock, fell back, shoving the remaining guard behind her off balance and out the door. He dropped backward onto the steps and the angle and impact of the fall broke his neck. For the first time, the child in Helen's arms began to cry.

Becky rushed forward, grabbing the staggered Helen by the upper arms. She wrenched her forward, so that, though cradled by her enemy, Becky felt for the first time her baby against her breast. "Let go of my child, bitch!" she snarled.

The jostled Helen cast a desperate glance over her shoulder toward the open doorway — only to see her archenemies Villiers and Clarke standing there shoulder to shoulder. Villiers held a revolver on her.

"You're not going anywhere, Helen," Clarke hissed. "Except when Villiers and I send you back to Hell."

Then all simultaneously heard for the first time a rumbling which, in all the excitement, had begun gathering itself below the threshold of their hearing. Now it seemed a sudden, apocalyptic blast that made the castle around them tremble.

Helen's chin rose as a look of smug satisfaction reappeared on her face. "You hear that, you fools? That is the footfall of Camulos! He has come at last!"

Though worry could be seen in the faces of her enemies, they did not retreat, and she could not pass through the door and the longed-for reunion with her father. Then, with a sneer, Helen threw the tiny Anne over Becky's head.

Wide-eyed, Becky immediately turned her head over her shoulder and Villiers instinctively lunged forward for assistance. This was the opening Helen needed. She bolted out the door. Clarke caught at her, and Helen raked her nails across his face.

Clarke fell back, cursing Helen, as she ran onto the castle lawn.

Becky watched as a squalling Annie landed, knocking her head against the leg of a chair in the process. Livid, Becky bit into her lower lip so that it bled.

"Oh, *that's* the limit!"

Becky shot out the door, Sâr Dubnotal's shouts to her drowned out by the rumbling that had descended upon them all — not that his commands would have been heeded. She hit the lawn in a run and found Helen standing there looking up, her mouth agape at what she saw:

Three zeppelins aloft over the castle grounds like airborne whales migrating through a starless sky. It was the pulse and throb from their engines that shook the castle.

Becky, however, remained heedless of what was above. While her enemy stood slack-jawed from the false note of her demonic father's arrival, Becky tackled her, the momentum behind her run yielding an impact that thrust the air from Helen's lungs.

Becky quickly turned Helen on her back and mounted her. As her knees bore into Helen's ribs, she brought the back of her hand like a cudgel to her enemy's mouth, bursting her lips. Helen winced as Becky again drew back her hand —

But the sudden flash of spotlights from the ground arrested her, their beams of brilliant white aimed at the zeppelins but revealing something *more*…

Glimpsed only in diagonal cross sections by the sweeping streaks of light angled into the sky, *Devomnodent-Mavors Camvlos*, the Great God Pan, loomed so large that his goat's head reached the altitude of the zeppelins; it seemed he might catch them on his giant horns and toss them out of the sky, or, by a few quick thrusts, burst them like a child's party balloons.

The sharp, frantic cries in German were faintly audible even over the oppressive droning of the zeppelins. The risk of switching on their floodlights to direct their fire meant losing what cover of darkness they retained. And their committed, slow drift combined with a limited ability to maneuver placed them, quite literally, on the horns of a dilemma.

A vicious metallic chattering heralded machine gun fire — their only defense — which followed wherever the beacons from the ground revealed the giant straddling Colchester with one hoof planted on the foothold of the castle. Ground fire followed — but no one could be certain if it was aimed at the Germans or Camulos.

Curiously, whatever parts of his massive anatomy which at any moment were outside the band width of each spotlight were simply *not there*, as though the beams rubbing over him in their passing erased what *was* seen as soon as it was revealed. There was complete lack of presence in their wake until the lights swept over in cross sections again.

It was said that the world would dissolve with the weight of Camulos' glory as he placed his hooves upon it, but it was *he*, rather, who was rendered ethereal —

— for the diagonal bars Sâr Dubnotal had lodged against the door to the abyss had held!

Helen was forced to glimpse her father's near advent upside down as she lay flat on her back under Becky. "He's not coming through!" she wailed.

"Allow me to offer my condolences," Becky said and brought down a rock she'd found within reach upon Helen's mouth, smashing her front teeth.

"Sauce for the goose, eh, Helen?" Becky said with a smile. She tossed the stone aside and clamped Helen's mouth closed, angling her head back. "Swallow, Helen! I want those teeth lodged in your throat!"

But Helen fought. In her paroxysms, her esophagus swelled and rippled like an engorged boa constrictor.

"Choke!" Becky ordered, digging her knees into Helen's ribs. "Very well, then," she said, withdrawing the garrote from her sleeve, "…this has proven fairly effective before."

Despite her distress, Helen's bulging eyes immediately took note of the garrote, and Becky was rewarded by the sheer fear in her adversary's eyes. But before she could get the noose over the still convulsing Helen's head, Naïni's powerful arms locked around her and yanked her up.

"What are you doing?! Let me go you fool — are you trying to *save her* now?"

"Miss Sharp!" Sâr Dubnotal's thunder clap of a voice caused her to immediately cease her struggling. She saw now that along with the Sâr and Naïni, Clarke, Villiers, Jacques and a growling Eustace had also arrived. The latter two were guarding Helen, who was on her knees, spewing out teeth.

"Why did you stop me?" Becky wailed bitterly.

"Miss Sharp, you must remember you are not the only one Helen Vaughan has sinned against. Others have suffered grievously as well…would you rob them of their share of vengeance?"

And then, for the first time, Becky noticed Annie was cradled by the Great Psychagogue.

"Annie…," her voice trailed off softly. She slipped free of Naïni as he relaxed his grip, and, for the first time, Becky took her daughter into her arms.

"I have examined her," *El Tebid*, the doctor, said, "but only cursorily so due to the circumstances. I will be much more thorough later. But she seems perfectly sound physically. In fact, she is developed beyond a child of two. It seems little Annie at an early age will blossom into young womanhood, where I suspect she shall remain for an indeterminate period of time. All due, no doubt, to her mother's own preternatural defiance of the normal aging process.

"Now, my friends, the zeppelins have gone, and Camulos, his moment now passed, has vanished in their wake. It would appear Pan has been replaced by an upstart, particularly twentieth-century kind of evil. In any event, while there is still general confusion, let us remove hence, before the interference of the authorities somehow grants Helen Vaughan a succor she must assuredly does *not* deserve."

Chapter Fourteen: 1917 —
The Judgement of Sâr Dubnotal

Helen Vaughan was transported by surreptitious route to a concealed estate Sâr Dubnotal maintained at Cornwall, his base for whenever his battle against the principalities of darkness brought him to England. It was here, surrounded by those whose friends had been destroyed by Helen Vaughan, that the Great Psychagogue pronounced her sentence.

He sat upon a raised judgment seat, Helen Vaughan bound before him. Standing and watching were her accusers: Becky with Annie in her arms, Clarke, Villiers, Jacques with Eustace — and his little box of tremors — and Aytown, Tate, and Randolph. Seated to the side were Ruldolph, Annuciata, Naïni, and three detectives on permanent retainer to Sâr Dubnotal. These three had managed to obtain a list of the names of the children who had perished from Helen's act of arson. At the end of the voicing of the charges against her by those present, each detective, by turn, read aloud the names of fifty silent orphans.

"Helen Vaughan," Sâr Dubnotal said when they were finished, "you have inflicted anguish not only on your victims — whose sufferings were blessedly cut short when death removed them from your hands — but also their survivors, who will endure a deep and abiding anguish for the remainder of their lives. Were we to execute you now, they would still not be free of you. If the end of their suffering will not come quickly, then neither shall yours, Helen Vaughan.

"Therefore, it is my decree that you will fulfill your boast to not die easily. Jacques, come forward. And Naïni, if you will now perform what I instructed you to do earlier."

The dwarf commanded Eustace to stay, then approached the throne, bearing the thumping box before him. He stood before Helen and flashed a nasty smile up at her. Naïni knelt between Helen and Jacques as the dwarf removed the box's lid.

Up jumped two small, rubicund objects which Naïni's great hands snatched out of the air like grizzly paws catching fish leaping from a rapids. Naïni rose and turned. At the sight of what the Hindu now held, Helen Vaughan's eyes widened and her face paled.

"I believe you recognize these shoes, Helen," Sâr Dubnotal said coldly.

Thrusting to be free of Naïni's hands were tiny red ballet slippers — and within them, tiny white feet. Holding one shoe in the pit of his arm, Naïni's fingers dislodged its mate's foot, which hit the floor and skipped frenziedly over the room. The other

Chapter Fourteen: 1917 — The Judgement of Sâr Dubnotal

foot soon followed.

"Open the door, Rudolph," Sâr Dubnotal commanded. "Allow them the dignity of at least attempting to rejoin their mistress's other remains before the residual enchantment fades and they begin to decompose.

Rudolph did as told, and the feet that had been throwing themselves against every wall in their imbecilic dance immediately ran out.

"*Au revoir, mes enfants,*" Jacques said, as his tiny hand rose to a salute, wiping away a single tear in the passing.

The red shoes, now free of the tiny feet, seemed to have grown in Naïni's hands. And Helen Vaughan contemplated them in horror.

"Ah," said Sâr Dubnotal. "I see you *also* recall that whosoever wears these ballet slippers cannot stop dancing until another removes them. Did you think Jacques would not tell me how Minuette's tiny heart failed after you placed them on her feet? How your laughter mingled with that of your guests while she begged *you* — her most cherished friend — for help? And how, for the amusement of subsequent salons, you would open the trunk in which you kept her corpse and send it prancing even in the advanced stages of decomposition? And that it was only Jacques' sword that released Minuette from this continued indignity, this…*violation*…to her person.

"In the hour you purposed to commit this abominable atrocity, it was *you* who decreed your own sentence. These shoes will drive you ever on like a fury, Helen, until your heart stops from exertion. Of course, *your* heart will beat far longer than Minuette's little one did under the same duress — but it's all a matter of proportion, wouldn't you say?

Now Sâr Dubnotal said to Rudolph: "Bring the saddle, reigns, harness and bit."

"What…for?" Helen whispered.

"Why, Helen — did you actually think we would just set you loose?" Sâr Dubnotal said. "To be rescued by the first fool whom you would most assuredly murder at the earliest opportune moment and then begin a new reign of terror — the focus of which would, no doubt, be innocent Annie there?

"It is my sentence, then, that while propelled by the red shoes, you be repeatedly ridden 'round the coasts of Britain — from the drowned lands of Lyonesse to the regions of the Hebrides and back again — until you expire.

"Oh, saddle me up!" Becky said and would have passed Annie into poor Villiers' arms right then, except he was so stunned by such an instantaneous shedding of maternal instinct that his hands were rendered torpid.

"Miss Sharp!" Sâr Dubnotal said. "You have already enjoyed the privilege of crushing the face of the woman who crushed yours and taking back the child she claimed as her own. You must see to Annie and leave to others the administration of justice for Helen's sins that are not against you. Do I have to ask you which is more important?"

Becky gathered Annie back to her and tucked her head in token abashment, yet her hooded eyes could not conceal the gall of resentment therein.

"I already have riders stationed along the shores of this isle." the Sâr said, as his gaze bore down on Helen like the most pitiless sun. "You will be ridden until death, at which point, the shoes will be removed, and you will be dismembered, your body burned, and your ashes scattered into the ocean.

"Ah, here is Rudolph. You will now be shod and saddled, and then you will be ridden to the first station by Naïni…"

Helen's mouth dropped. "That *giant*? Atop *me*? How can you expect me to go even five feet under the Hindu without being crushed?!"

"Helen, the sentence of the red shoes punishes you only for what you did to Minuette. But the children of the orphanage yet cry out as well for justice from the ground. The children for whom a single comforting touch against their blistered skin was rendered into a hornet's sting. Do you dare say you deserve one less such touch of encouragement?

"Therefore, when you fall, you will receive a goad until you rise — one for each child who died in the orphanage to which you set fire. No more; no less."

Helen's jaw dropped. "But there were a hundred and fifty children in that orphanage! Your sentence is too cruel, Sâr Dubnotal!"

"HELEN VAUGHAN!" Sâr Dubnotal's voice roared down upon her so that she dipped at the knees and clasped her hands over her head. "You who never showed mercy to your victims, who mocked them in their agonies that were the fruit of your corruption…you dare accuse *me* of cruelty? Beware lest 'having whipped you with whips, I whip you next with *scorpions*.'

"Yet this mercy I will grant you. If, while you might still rise, you choose to end your torment, whether it be two feet from where you now stand or twenty miles, you have but to lie there, endure how many of the goads might remain, and then you will be immediately beheaded. Upon my word, Helen, you shall have no more or no less of the goads than what your transgression has decreed. Afterwards you will have but to say 'enough.' Unless your heart bursts first, you, Helen, shall decide the length of your agony; a dignity you never allowed *any* of *your* victims."

"But what…what do you mean by 'goads'?" Helen asked, her voice small and trembling.

"Jacques?" Sâr Dubnotal said and turned his head toward the little man.

Jacques again grinned toothily up at Helen as he reached into his pocket and produced a leather pouch from which he took two mean-looking, barbed objects.

"From my experience," said the dwarf, "nothing will drive the Devil out of this woman like a fine set of spurs."

Chapter Fifteen: 1925 —
S. Latitude 47° 9', W. Longitude 126° 43'

**From Becky Sharp's Journal:
March 23, 1925**

I am alone at sea, and despite having lived years on the ocean, I am not a self-sufficient sailor; therefore, where this boat will come ashore is uncertain. Behind me now is the stretch of ocean floor recently raised to the surface. That ancient ocean's bottom, flecked with rotting fish, swells into a mountain; hovering upon its peak, the Nephilim proportioned sanctuary whose slime slick walls cloister Armageddon.

The first rumbles of the apocalypse to come were manifested, not on that nightmarish landscape risen up from eons past, but in an upper class bistro by the Seine.

I was having coffee with a couple of men who belonged to that peculiar Lost Generation living in the wake of the Great War. One of them was an American veteran.

"I did not take you for a Bible thumper, Jacob. But, really, all but citing me chapter and verse . . ." I shook my bobbed locks, took a drink, and agitatedly twirled the beads that lay straight over my breasts, uncomfortably flattened in the fashion of the day. I longed for my old corsetry, despite its reputation. They were *comfortable* for a woman of my frame.

"I was just responding to what you said . . ." Jacob began.

"All I *said* — wistfully — was it would be marvelous if the movable feast we're enjoying might go on forever."

"And *I* said, 'Only the *earth* abides forever.' Just as the ancient Hebrew who wrote *Ecclesiastes* observed long ago."

"Well, then, you're *both* killjoys, you *and* your Jewish friend! Charles, what *are* you scribbling at so intently over there?"

My other companion, Charles, was a poet of the Modernist school.

"Hmm? Oh . . . trying to translate into verse a dream I've had the past two nights. It's of a . . . temple, I guess . . ."

He leaned back in his chair and rubbed his eyes.

"I'm grappling with adapting Cubism into stanza form, to suggest other kinds of perspectives, to convey the temple's geometry. The architecture is eldritch."

"Really, Charles . . . I need a dictionary handy whenever I talk with you," I said.

I would have thought no more of his artistic aspirations, except for the unexpected sequel that night. I was the mistress of Michigan steel industry scion Rodney Gelbourne. Rodney fancied himself a painter and had come to Paris to join an artists' colony in the Latin Quarter.

In the middle of the night, I awoke to find Rodney sitting up in bed beside me, sketching feverishly. I stretched, running a hand through my mussed hair, and said, "I hope, *mon amour*, that you are not drawing me sleeping. That would be *très* unchivalrous of you."

"Don't worry, Becca. You are *la femme de mes rêves*, not my nightmares, and that's what I'm drawing here."

"Nightmare?"

"This is the third night I've had it. Of some inhuman edifice. A . . . temple, perhaps?"

"Inhuman . . . temple?" I asked.

"Something *like* a temple, but trying to get it on paper is difficult — I can't seem to wrap my mind around its angles to wrest it into the two dimensions of a sheet of paper. Truth to tell, I don't think *five* would be enough."

"Did Charles talk to you about his poem?"

"What poem?"

I snatched his sketch pad from him, causing the pencil to stray.

"Hey! Easy, bird!"

"Impossible!" I gasped — but not at the dream temple itself. In Rodney's drawing, the edifice's massive door was open, revealing a large, winged gargoyle with an octopus' tentacle-fringed body as a head.

Rodney had never seen the Tulu fetish, which I kept with its staff in a certain safety deposit box at the *Banque des Champs d'Elysse*.

I could sleep no more that night, and rose early in the morning to go to the *Bibliotheque de Paris* to check the papers for some hint of any event in the world that might also be the harbinger of Great Tulu. Rodney and Charles both had their first nightmares of the alien temple three nights before. I checked the papers according to that time frame, and discovered seismic activity was felt on that date in New Zealand.

New Zealand! Noot had prophesied Tulu would come from the waters at the bottom of the world! Further, according to the *Sydney Herald*, following the tremors, Kanakas of the South Seas had been driven into bloody, orgiastic rites to welcome the return of a long slumbering ocean god!

I insisted to Rodney that we journey down below immediately. He looked at me incredulously. "Are you nuts, bird? No white person would be safe to venture among those blood thirsty savages!"

"You mean no white *livered* person!" I drug heavily on my cigarette, then expelled my contempt in a jet of smoke. "Look, if you're too afraid of wrinkling your Arrow Collar, there are plenty of others who'd be glad to take me, for all I've got to offer."

I am not proud that I used sexual jealousy to provoke Rodney to agree. But I had to act immediately, and I couldn't explain to him why. He would have thought me mad — until he saw the nightmare image from his drawing loom before him in waking life.

I secretly collected the Tulu totem from my safety deposit box, and we traveled by whatever were the fastest means available: plane, train, or ship. First to Italy, then over the Mediterranean; across the Arab nations, then India, Thailand, and Indonesia. Our course was uncomfortable and often dangerous, but timing was essential. Finally, we hopped over the continent of Australia.

I thought, then, of my old friend the Magus. This continent down under had been the land of the Great Race, but in the far distant past. No doubt, Yithian agents had kept tabs on me — at a distance — over the last eighty-five years. But even here, at the consummation of their scheme, they could not be seen to interfere. I was on my own.

Rodney and I set sail from Melbourne to New Zealand — I having learned from the papers the latitude and longitude from which the tremor had radiated.

On the second day at sea, we received the rather awful consolation that we were headed in the right direction when our nautical path crossed that of the *Alert* — a ship manned by Kanakas, the natives responsible for the reported carnage.

"Becca, get below," Rodney said with a steely resolve I had never heard in his voice before. "Maybe they haven't seen you yet," but his tone told me it was unlikely. If we had a spy glass, no doubt they did as well.

"Rodney, they will search the ship anyway. There's nowhere for me to go. Let me take one of the guns and —"

"I said, get below, Rebecca," he repeated. "You don't realize the things they'll do to you! It makes no difference if you're a woman. Or a man."

I had not taken three steps when I hesitated and looked back. His back to me was held rigidly straight, his hands on his rifle shaking. My mouth worked mutely for long moments —

Then I headed for the hold, not to hide but to fetch, perhaps, our salvation: the Tulu caduceus. I had just reached it when a single shot rang out, followed by no others. I tucked the fetish under one arm, and ran topside.

I was shocked to see the *Alert* was still a good pace away. A warning shot from Rodney? No! Rodney lay on his back, the rifle's barrel still in his mouth, his brains and hair smearing the wall behind him.

I winced and shut my eyes against the sight, then I turned my head, so that when I opened my eyes again, my view was out to sea.

The Kanakas were coming closer. And I remembered I had not been left defenseless against this day. Or so I had been told. Since that fleeting moment on the deck of the slave ship, there had been barely an inkling of the power of the flame of Kor said to reside in my body. But should I attempt to strike down the Kanakas and succeed, would there then be measure enough of the power remaining to deal effectively with Tulu?

So, what I did instead was brandish the Tulu idol high on the pole, so that the dark men might see and think that I was one of their own cult.

It caused not a little stir among those Kanakas. They boarded the ship, taking hold of my idol, though they did not molest me. They conferred among themselves and escorted me to their own ship. I was taken into a cabin which sported a carved stone version of Tulu's image in a now defiled Catholic reliquary. There I was left alone but locked in.

My greatest concern at the moment was my separation from my caduceus. But I could do nothing but wait and rest for whatever ordeal was ahead.

I knew, of course, that it was naïve to assume that I was safe. My fate might yet prove to be a harsh one. And if my mission was forcibly aborted now, what of the world?

Not that I gave a fig for the faceless, bleating masses that compose the human race. They are all making the inevitable progression into the abyss any way, and, if I was shortly to die myself at the Kanakas' hands, what did I care if they arrived at the pit sooner than later? Yes, and not only they of *this* world, but all dwellers in the infinitely stratified reality that is the multiverse. No one in it touched me personally.

Except . . .

Except for three.

Nathaniel could still be out there, outside time, though that would not put him outside of Tulu's reach. And there was the father of my child and the girl herself.

Lord, could my little Annie shriek! She certainly inherited her prodigious vocal endowments from her Papa. How I wish he might have known her, but I feared for my own life should he be made aware of the circumstances of her conception. I dare say he would not have proven sympathetic to my tale of loneliness in the African wilderness.

Nor would it matter that my regard for him was genuine. I took him against his will; that's all he would see. I and my child would not be welcome in his home. My Annie would have been his bastard, and if he had to choose between the babe he had no memory of conceiving and his precious wife, well, that would have been no choice at all, would it?

So instead of remaining in Africa, I returned to the States for my confinement. Unfortunately, I was not to be delivered in the customary nine months. No, the flame of Kor had endowed me with a gestation span that would give an elephant pause.

Beyond that, I stayed with Annie until she was weaned, but then what was I to do? I could not be encumbered with a child clutching at my skirt when called to face Tulu. Besides, my maternal instincts were never sterling in the best of circumstances.

So, I arranged for her adoption by a farm family in the Midwest. When I could, under the guise of an anonymous "uncle," I sent money to her. I thought to do well by her when I became Rodney's mistress, but those checks were returned, the envelopes unopened.

She would be in her mid-twenties now. Her whole life ahead of her.

I actually managed to fall asleep, but was suddenly roused rudely to consciousness from a commotion topside: the sound of gunfire, men's screams, the pounding of footsteps on the deck.

Then there was silence above. Whether I was in the hands of new captors or still those of the old, I could not know, nor which to wish for. So, I chewed my lower lip and waited. After a while there were voices — English speaking voices — along the corridor. I took a chance:

"Help me! Please! I'm the prisoner of these savages!"

There was a muffled exchange, footsteps heading toward the door, and then I saw its lever-like-handle turn, and a grizzly, sun burned, blond mariner burst into the room. His bright blue eyes started at the sight of me, and he cried out over his shoulder in a thick Norwegian accent:

"Ja! A white woman! Down here!"

I was taken onto the deck. Alongside the Kanakas' ship, which my rescuers had boarded, was their own now-sinking schooner, ravaged by the Kanakas' artillery. The last of the bodies of the Kanakas were being thrown unceremoniously over the side. I noticed three respectfully covered corpses on the deck and was informed they included the captain and the first mate.

The man who discovered me, Second Mate Johansen, was now in command. He explained that the Kanakas' ship — the *Alert* — had intercepted his own ship's path and ordered it back — back from *what* he had no idea since there was nothing for miles except open sea. However, he would now find out what the Kanakas had guarded so jealously that they took the lives of three good men.

The next day, we found a mountain the ocean floor had belched up, and a temple-like building upon its crown. It was, indeed, the edifice that poor Rodney had sketched from his dreams. However, I found it hard to continue gazing at it, its angles seemingly demanding other dimensions — to which human eyes and minds were not privy — to make sense of the architecture.

Second mate Johansen took five other men to explore. I, of course, was to remain behind in the safety of the captured boat with Henshey, an Australian who seemed relieved not to have to move any closer to that awful masonry.

I learned from Henshey that certain occult effects of the heathen were stored in the hold, and there, I was sure, was where Noot's caduceus had ended up. I managed to slip away from my guardian to reclaim it, for I dared not openly express familiarity with the idol, lest my rescuers think me also a worshipper of Tulu.

The hold, thankfully, was unlocked, but it was not easy to locate the caduceus. It lay somewhere in a pile of other Tulu fetishes which the Kanakas had brought. I began sorting frantically through the heap of idols, wondering how long I had until Tulu himself emerged.

Apparently, the footfalls of Johansen's crew upon the temple's Cyclopean doorsteps served to summon the creature. Above me, from the direction of the risen mountain's top, I heard a gigantic groaning, what would be the massive door to the temple opening . . .

It was the sound of the world ending.

Frantically, I plucked up and thrust aside the icons that were not my own. I began to despair that I had fatally erred, and my caduceus was not in this hold, not on this ship at all! Perhaps it had gone overboard in the fight between the Kanakas and Johansen's men —

And then my hands were grasping Noot's familiar craft work. I turned, ready to rush top side, only to see Henshey standing in the doorway. He regarded me with slack jaw, his eyes starting.

"You . . . you're one of . . . them," he choked out.

"No. No I am not," I said trying to keep my voice calm. "If you'll only hear me out —"

"No! You won't bewitch me — you're summoning that . . . thing!" He nodded toward the Tulu icon on the end of the staff I held.

I realized that Henshey must have witnessed the opening of the temple door and the Terror it revealed. His eyes darted wildly about, his mind trying to come to terms with having registered things which should not be —

And then his eyes locked again on my caduceus —

"— I won't let you!" he screamed and in the next instant, he was leaping toward me. I thrust forward the staff I held in clinched fists to block his assault. He grabbed hold of it with both hands and began trying to wrench it from my grasp, but my grip and resolve remained firm.

Then he took a change of tact. Still holding on to the staff, he now bore down on me with his superior strength, and soon I was on my back, desperately pushing the staff upward, for he was pressing it down on my throat.

I could not breathe, and I knew I had failed at the hands of a fool, when I had survived all else, perils of distance and time ...

And then lightening flashed in the room, and I was rising, choking, but breathing again. A shrill, womanly scream emanated from across the room, and I saw Henshey, his body now steaming, clawing at his eyes.

Had *I* done that to him? Had the force that I carried within me manifested at last — erupted instinctively in my struggle for life? The realization that it *had* settled inexorably upon me.

Meanwhile, Henshey darted blindly about the room, finally finding the open door and bolting topside. I never saw him again. Whether he remained on board when I was left behind, or fell over the side and drowned, I do not know, nor do I particularly care.

I followed in his wake to the deck.

It was then that I saw what had driven him mad with fear. I was stricken stock-still in the face of the incarnate Madness, whose lumbering bulk of massive green sludge slid down the stairway of the mountain-top edifice. Its head was indeed that of the giant squid, just as rendered on my caduceus.

The staff — I tightened my grasp on the one thing I needed to stop great Tulu's progress.

Two sailors — one of them second mate Johansen — were scrambling over the side of the ship and onto the deck. Johansen shouted, beckoning me back wildly. Before he recognized what I held in my hands, I turned my back to him, blocking sight of the Tulu totem pole, and scurried away.

While seeking a vantage point from which to strike at my terrible adversary, I saw its rolling, gelatinous mass slide into the surf, its horrible eyes focus in our direction. Leathery wings stretched out as though it might take flight, and its talons opened —

It was coming after the ship. Coming to me.

I readied myself before the approaching monster. When I struck down Henshey, it had been in panic. What was coming now, I realized, would involve control on my part. I could not simply fire wide and often, hoping to strike home.

Then the boat surged under me. For a moment, I feared Johansen was doing the sensible thing and fleeing. Then I realized, amazed, that the Norwegian was propelling us *at* Tulu — with apparent intent of ramming the beast!

I focused, not on the creature that the ship was hurling me toward, but on its idol that I held before me, grasping the staff on which the graven image was perched with both hands. I felt the power humming inside me as I willed it to a peak, hoping I yet had sufficient reserves from which to draw.

Then I found a center, a peace, as an old, familiar ecstasy flushed through my body —

— as the ship collided hard into the monster's very teeth, its bulbous head almost mounting the entire height of the bow —

— and the ancient power of life rumbled out of my hands and up into the idol atop the staff. It glowed with a ruby force that erupted from the idol's maw and into the actual giant head on which it had been modeled.

And Great Tulu shrieked, a sound like metal being rent by hurricane winds. My power and the ship together lanced the gargantuan pustule that was his body, and his ponderous, protoplasmic girth exploded in a miasma of green stinging acid. I, in the midst of it all, burned. I opened my mouth to scream — and the wretched smell of Tulu's ruptured body flooded my sinuses.

I stopped my nose and mouth and ran blind — I dared not open my eyes to the atomized acid that stung my exposed flesh. Over the side of the ship I threw myself, hoping for the relieving salve of water. But I struck the surface hard, and, stunned, sank like the proverbial stone.

Could I have died there at the ocean's bottom? I do not know. Perhaps it was the force within me that carried me aloft again. All I know was when I surfaced, the *Alert* was steaming away from me toward the horizon. And Great Tulu?

The writhing Abomination flowed up its temple's steps, its churning mass resembling from the distance a herd of Gadarene swine running in reverse, fleeing up *from* the sea instead of *into* it.

Then the temple swallowed its god, and the great door slammed shut. Great Tulu was indisposed. But for how long?

I dragged myself ashore. My skin was blistered from the acidic rain that had engulfed me from Tulu's rent body, but at least I was no longer burning.

The *Alert* long gone, I was effectively marooned with that monstrosity. What would I do should it come forth again? My staff and icon had gone over the ship's side with me; Queequeg's fetish had at last rejoined its former owner at the bottom of the sea. Which meant I lacked the means to intensify the power within me — assuming any remained. I felt *spent* on every level, in fact, and sank thankfully into unconsciousness. Should Tulu come again, I could not begin to withstand him. If he found me slumbering, my death would be painless at least.

I awoke, though, after all. There was still no sign of Tulu. I was astonished, instead, to see my and Rodney's yacht off shore. Some of the Kanakas who had Shanghaied us had taken possession of it and had returned to the house of their

"I focused, not on the creature that the ship was hurling me toward, but on its idol that I held before me..."

Chapter Fifteen: 1925 — S. Latitude 47° 9', W. Longitude 126° 43'

god.

I was not inclined to enquire what their intentions toward me might be. After my rest, the power within me felt renewed, at least lethal enough for humans, and I struck them all dead in an instant.

There were still provisions inside the yacht. And my boudoir vanity glass which confirmed a pocked face. But I already seem to be healing, thanks to that strange force inside me. And for that, I am grateful.

Now that I had a means of escape, I was loath to hesitate any longer. I decided I had already done more than my share for humanity. Should it be threatened a second time, let the rest fend for themselves — and me. I've already given up at least three life times, when many would not give even one.

So I am free now. The 20th century before me, the past to my back . . . literally so, in the form of that inhuman edifice on its primordial ocean floor. I am aware that past may yet rise again to meet me at some future date. *Could* there be occasion for the world to hear of me again?

Only on my own terms. Not those of the Great Race of Yith. And, make no mistake, with the power within me, my beauty returned, and my full wits about me, there *will* be terms. But I promise you, world, they will be far kinder than that Thing's from the risen ocean bed. You may yet be compelled to own me as queen, but my seduction is sweet, and I can be a kind mistress.

Or so I have been often told.

Afterword

She and Me

by MICAH S. HARRIS

I first met Becky Sharp in my local Barnes and Noble back in the 1990s. I was, of course, surprised to encounter her. But there she was, the nineteenth-century villainess, still well and active in the late twentieth century.

It said so, right there on the page.

That is, the page of the collection of short stories I was perusing at the time. It would turn out to be a seminal moment in my own history of creativity, so it's a bit frustrating, and odd, that I have long forgotten the name of the story, the author, and the title of her collection.

What I do remember is that the story featured William Makepeace Thackeray's anti-heroine moving among, perhaps, the upper crust of Manhattan – and wearing fur among this group she is well aware includes card carrying PETA members.

Audacious? Outrageous? Impertinent? Completely unacceptable? She couldn't care less.

The author knew her subject.

So, while it's hard to remember the exact sequence for certain, I'm sure that story was what interested me in the character of Becky Sharp, which probably led me to attend one of Dickens' scholar Elliot Engel's always excellent literary lectures, this one on Dickens' rival William Makepeace Thackeray, and my finally reading Thackeray's 1848 classic, *Vanity Fair*.

Oddly enough, what I *do* recall is that 1) I was reading *Vanity Fair* concurrently with that cult novel about a family of sideshow freaks, *Geek Love* (make of that what you will); 2) I was reading it during a family trip to Disney World.

Hercules was the studio's current animated feature then, and the subject of a parade where the majorettes had batons shaped like Zeus' lightning bolts, so that makes this the summer of 1997. *The Eldritch New Adventures of Becky Sharp* would not be published until over a decade later in 2008…slow growing literary fruit, indeed.

But already the seeds were planted. I now knew the original novel, and the idea of Becky Sharp alive in the present day from that short story collection led me to endow her with preternatural longevity via the mystic flame of Kor (from H. Rider Haggard's 1887 novel

She: A History of Adventure).

Before all *this*, however, in the late 1980s, I had gotten into science-fiction author Philip Jose Farmer's Wold Newton Family, which he lays out in theory in his meta-fictional biographies *Tarzan Alive* (1972) and *Doc Savage: His Apocalyptic Life* (1973). Later, he used the concept to connect both thinly concealed and authorized versions of others' fictional characters and concepts.

My actual introduction to the "mash-up" genre in fiction, and still one of the top three I've read – and I've read a lot of them – was Gene Wolfe's wonderful "The Island of Doctor Death and Other Stories."[1] However, Farmer was the first author I read who not only connected such seemingly disparate characters as Tarzan and Sherlock Holmes, but also brought them together to share adventures.

Then, in the early 2000s, I remembered that meeting with Becky Sharp in the previous decade. She was still alive. Or she *could* be, if Haggard's flame of Kor was still spouting in fictional Kor. And, being fiction, it hadn't gone anywhere in the century-plus since Haggard had conceived it for *She*…

And because I like to write what I like to read…

Out came my own crossover novella, *The Eldritch New Adventures of Becky Sharp*.

Yes, *novella*. The original version, the one I submitted for magazine publication, was much shorter. I sent it out to a now defunct but gorgeous periodical of the day, *Realms of Fantasy*. I remember getting a personal letter back lauding my writing…did I mention it was a rejection letter?

(This was something of a pattern with me. Regarding a different story I once sent out, I received another letter telling me how good a writer I was, how I was going to make it…and then a loud silence that added the unspoken postscript: "just don't expect us to be publishing anything by you." Thank you, guys, for all that encouragement to a young writer. I think.)

So, I expanded *The Eldritch New Adventures of Becky Sharp* and sent it out as a novel to Jean-Marc Lofficier at Black Coat Press. Although Jean-Marc also rejected *The Eldritch New Adventures of Becky Sharp*, he kindly followed up with an offer to contribute a story to his on-going annual anthology *Tales of the Shadowmen*. Ah, but it was nice to be wanted!

So, I wrote a new Becky story which I then inserted into the novel as chapter three, "The Ape Gigans." I also continued to publish with the affable and brilliant Mr. Lofficier's *Shadowmen* series, including two new Becky stories.

---

1 For the record, the other two are Farmer's "After King Kong Fell" and John Kessel's "Pride and Prometheus." Along with Wolfe's "The Island of Doctor Death and Other Stories," these are the three instances I know of where the crossover genre rises to literary heights. Perhaps not coincidentally, they are three unusual approaches to the mash-up concept.

The first was "The Scorpion and the Fox" which I was flattered to do with fellow *Shadowmen* writer Matthew (*The Vampire Count of Monte Cristo*) Baugh, an always enjoyable raconteur. The second was the two-part novella *Slouching Toward Camulodunum*, the latter reprinted here as chapters ten-fourteen in the expanded vision of this 2020 edition.

I always found it gratifying that people who enjoyed my take on Thackeray's anti-heroine tended to be intellectual, and often creative people themselves. I've mentioned Matt Baugh already, who has contributed to the chronicles of the classic popular culture characters The Avenger and The Phantom. He suggested our teaming up Becky with an obscure Russian hero Matt had discovered, "Rakhmetov."

Then Mark Schultz, award-winning artist, writer/artist of the *Xenozoic Tales* graphic novel saga, writer of the *Prince Valiant* comic strip, and former Superman writer, had the idea that I pitch Becky against the otherworldly wickedness of Helen Vaughan of Arthur Machen's cosmic horror classic *The Great God Pan*.

More recently, short story writer and 18thWall Publications publisher James Bojaciuk wrote the insightful essay on my novel, debuting as the special introduction for this edition, which reveals the heretofore unexpected (and I'm talking about to me!) Cthulhu / Becky Sharp connection.

Writer and publisher of Wild Hunt Press Chris Nigro invited me to contribute a Becky Sharp story to his Dorian Gray anthology (the first dedicated to further adventures of the character in his over-a-century existence). "Portrait of a Lady" presents an alternate version of Becky's life than the one chronicled here, one where she toppled She-Who-Must-Be-Obeyed from her rule and is the governor of the British Colony of Kor. It is the latest Becky adventure and is still available on Amazon in *Dorian Gray: Darker Shades*.

So, there you have, in brief, the story behind the publication history of my version of Becky Sharp and her career as an agent of Lovecraft's Great Race of Yith, culminating in this 2020 Visionary anniversary edition.

As for future adventures…I've had different ideas over the years: to see Becky in a mini-skirt hanging out on Carnaby Street with the British Invasion bands in the 1960s; to have her reconnect with her child's father while a giant ape is running amok through New York City; to send her to a Mars that it is a hybrid of popular culture representations…

She's still out there, living in Bath, North Carolina, with a former pirate -slash-clergyman, not far from where I live, last I heard. So, who knows? I might run into her at the local Barnes and Noble again at any time. And once we catch up, there would certainly be stories to tell.

"Frontal Development"
The Making of the Cover of *The Eldritch New Adventures of Becky Sharp*

by MICAH S. HARRIS

These head shots trace the development of Becky's cover girl looks by artist Loston Wallace. While Loston may think of an actor or actress as a basic starting point for a character design, he doesn't use models. Instead, he employs an understanding of how human anatomy works and how human facial features and expressions array to convey personality, attractiveness, etc. and creates out of his imagination.

Dated February 2008, this unfinished conceptual sketch is probably Loston's first take on Becky. Right from the get-go, he has already begun to capture the proper characterization in a combination of visual contrasts:

Note how the high cheekbones convey elegance, refinement, and a sense of propriety, and the full lips, perfect teeth, and large eyes, beauty. Now observe how the eyelids hood the eyes as though to conceal, and how that one eyebrow is arched... and we can begin to perceive her thoughts. This lovely woman is up to no good — proceed with extreme caution, men!

Loston's first full rendering of Becky's facial identity. Rejected as the definitive portrait, because here she appears completely sinister, the expression was perfect for this special edition, twelve years later, to represent the moment when Becky is about to turn the tables on Helen Vaughan.

Loston altered the hair, added the appropriate costuming for the scene, and voila! Compare with the revised version in Chapter Thirteen.

The full lips and high cheekbones and all that they imply are back in the final cover version of Becky's face. However, now the face is fuller, conveying youthful innocence while the free-flowing long hair gives her a sense of abandon. This combination makes her seem the perfect male-fantasy concoction…

…but, again, those hooded eyes suggest she is really an artful schemer who knows exactly what she's got and will use it to manipulate you — gleefully. The arched eyebrows signify a sense of triumph, a secure knowledge that you are hers already, even if you haven't realized it yet.

Now, at last, the proper, devil-may-care, blithesome spirit of our adventuress is completely there on the page to be enjoyed by all her admirers…poor, lost souls that they are!

All art for this essay © 2020 Loston Wallace

Biographical Note

MICAH S. HARRIS really wishes that, if Stanley Kubrick were going to adapt only one William Makepeace Thackeray novel, it had *not* been *Barry Lyndon*. Nevertheless, if you are reading this note after the foregoing novel, he hopes to have disabused you of the idea that *Vanity Fair* was originally a magazine name thought up by a bunch of Madison Avenue fashion plates.[1]

No one will ever accuse Micah Harris of being a fashion plate . . . though it is rumored that, as a courier for the syndicate, he once led the gendarmes on a merry chase through the garment and textile district of New York City.[2]

He is a former instructor in the North Carolina Community College System. On a particularly good day, he got to teach British Literature and Introduction to Film.

He is the author, with artist Michael Gaydos of Marvel Comics *Jessica Jones*, of the Image graphic novel *Heaven's War*, a historical fantasy pitting Christian fantasy authors Charles Williams, C.S. Lewis, and J.R.R. Tolkien against occultist Aleister Crowley.

His *Ravenwood, the Stepson of Mystery: Return of the Dugpa* for Airship 27 Productions won the 2016 PulpArk award for best novel.

He has contributed novellas and short stories to Black Coat Press' annual anthology series *Tales of the Shadowmen*, Airship 27's *Ghost Boy* and *Jim Anthony, Super Detective*, 18thWall Productions' *The Chromatic Court* and Wild Hunt Press' *Dorian Gray: Darker Shades* (in which we learn what happened when Becky Sharp met Mr. Gray and other assorted literary and pop culture immortals).

Readers interested in the fate of Becky Sharp's infant daughter after she grew up should read both Micah's novel

Ravenwood, Stepson of Mystery: Return of the Dugpa and his novella "On the Periphery of Legend" in *Jim Anthony, Super Detective: The Hunters*, preferably in that order.

Micah's latest novel is *Portrait of a Snow Queen (Being a Memoir of My Not-So Fairy Tale Romance)*, an epic fantasy romance that chronicles the coming of age of a princess who is possessed by the Snow Queen and fated to rule her kingdom with a strong hand and icy heart.

You can learn more about Micah by visiting his website at minorprofitpress.com. While there, please sign up for his newsletter, *The Books of Micah*.

And if you enjoyed *The Eldritch New Adventures of Becky Sharp*, please consider leaving a review on Amazon! A good number of reviews are essential to a book's success, and even less than five stars is desirable! You would be helping out tremendously by writing just a sentence or two…and Becky will love you to pieces for it!

---

[1] Though to be fair, Thackeray cribbed it from John Bunyan. See *Pilgrim's Progress* — ed.

[2] See all Jerry Lewis episodes of *Wiseguy* — ed.

If You Enjoyed
The Eldritch New Adventures of Becky Sharp
Please Consider Leaving a Review on Amazon!

AND

Visit **www.minorprofitpress.com**, the official web site of author Micah S. Harris, for news, blog and free fiction. While there, please be certain to sign up for my newsletter "The Books of Micah!"

NEW FROM MINOR PROFIT PRESS AND AUTHOR MICAH S. HARRIS!

THE WITCHES OF WINTER TRILOGY: BOOK ONE

PORTRAIT OF A SNOW QUEEN

BEING A MEMOIR OF MY (NOT SO) FAIRY TALE ROMANCE

MICAH S. HARRIS

"Amidst humorous events and witty banter... Micah Harris has created a perfect romance that can never be, yet the plot hints at hope.... (T)he reader will crave more time with the princess and her tutor."
— Ankita Shukla
Reedsy Discovery

"Epic Fantasy at its best!"
— Dr. Arthur Sippo
Art's Reviews Podcast

"...(R)eminded me of grand storytelling of the past."
— Sheila Staley
Book Blogger,
Because I Said So

"...For a fantasy, it has a lot of comedy..."
— John G. Pierce
No Evil Shall Escape the Light (An Alpha-Omega zine)

"I loved the banter between the characters in the book."
— Donna Feyen
Book Blogger, *More Than A Review*

"After a certain scene, I was intrigued and rushed to finish this. I had to know what was going to happen!"
— Carole Rae
Book Blogger,
Carole Rae's Random Ramblings

The Epic Fantasy Romance of a Princess Possessed by the Snow Queen and Fated to Rule Her Kingdom with a Strong Hand and Icy Heart.

COVER ART BY AARON LOPRESTI (*WONDER WOMAN*)

AVAILABLE NOW
In Print and on Kindle at **amazon.com**

Visit the Snow Queen at **aarastad.com**   Visit author Micah S. Harris at **minorprofitpress.com**

Made in the USA
Columbia, SC
26 November 2024